"You're Mel?" Cole checked his mom's note again for the correct name.

"Yes. Mel McNeil." The woman's smile broadened. "Mel is short for Melissa."

"Oh. I..." When he'd been asked to talk to Mel, he'd pictured a younger version of another Mel, the grizzled Texas cowboy who'd taken Cole under his wing when Cole was new to the rodeo circuit. He tried to rearrange his expression as thoughts of gray-haired fatherly cowboys fled. "Beth said you might help us out."

"If you're still looking for volunteers, sure, I can help." Mel handed him the dog's leash.

"We are." Cole cleared his throat.

Mel was attractive in a wholesome, girl-next-door way. Although he sure appreciated her features and easy kindness, he'd always steered clear of any woman who'd want to settle down—and deserve things he couldn't give her. So, why was his tongue tied in knots like a thirteen-year-old boy asking a girl for a first date?

Dear Reader,

A Family for the Rodeo Cowboy is my second story for Harlequin Heartwarming and The Montana Carters miniseries. Welcome back to High Valley, Montana, the Tall Grass Ranch and the Carter family. If you haven't read the first book, *Montana Reunion*, both stand alone so you'll soon feel at home.

In *A Family for the Rodeo Cowboy*, injury forces rodeo star Cole Carter into retirement. But who is Cole if he's not a rodeo cowboy? With help from animal physical therapist Mel McNeil and her adorable daughter, maybe Cole's retirement isn't an end but instead a chance for a new beginning.

Along with heartwarming happily-ever-after romance, I also love writing about family relationships, friendships, animal characters and small-town life. *A Family for the Rodeo Cowboy* has all these and more. And as an only child, I've often wondered what it would be like to belong to a big family. In the Carters I've created one I'd like to be part of, and I hope you feel the same.

I'm happy to hear from readers so contact me through my website jengilroy.com where you'll also find my social media links, blog and newsletter subscriptions.

Happy reading,

Jen Gilroy

HEARTWARMING

A Family for the Rodeo Cowboy

—

Jen Gilroy

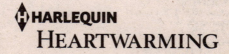

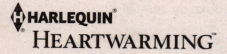

HARLEQUIN®

HEARTWARMING™

PLEASE RECYCLE
THIS PRODUCT IS RECYCLABLE

Recycling programs
for this product may
not exist in your area.

ISBN-13: 978-1-335-58495-3

A Family for the Rodeo Cowboy

Copyright © 2023 by Jen Gilroy

For questions and comments about the quality of this book, please contact us at CustomerService@Harlequin.com.

Harlequin Enterprises ULC
22 Adelaide St. West, 41st Floor
Toronto, Ontario M5H 4E3, Canada
www.Harlequin.com

Printed in U.S.A.

Jen Gilroy writes sweet romance and uplifting women's fiction—warm, feel-good stories to bring readers' hearts home. A Romance Writers of America Golden Heart® Award finalist and short-listed for the Romantic Novelists' Association Joan Hessayon Award, she lives in small-town Ontario, Canada, with her husband, teenage daughter and floppy-eared rescue hound. She loves reading, ice cream, ballet and paddling her purple kayak. Visit her at jengilroy.com.

Books by Jen Gilroy

Harlequin Heartwarming

Montana Reunion

Visit the Author Profile page
at Harlequin.com for more titles.

For my parents, in loving memory.

With thanks for my western Canadian childhood and the Montana vacations that shaped me as well as the fictional world of this book.

I love and miss you both, always.

CHAPTER ONE

As Cole Carter shut the pickup truck's door, his nine-month-old beagle pup stuck his nose out the half-open rear window and whined in protest.

"Sorry, Blue." Cole reached inside and rubbed the dog's silky brown ears. "You can't come with me this time, but I won't be long." He drew in a breath of crisp May air. Once again, the seasons had turned, and it was springtime in Montana and for him too. A new start after a long, dark winter.

He stuffed his keys into the front pocket of his faded jeans and set his cowboy hat more firmly on his head. Then he moved around the truck with the Tall Grass Ranch logo on both doors toward a red-brick building at the far end of the block.

With the Memorial Day weekend coming up, High Valley's wide main street was busy. On the warmest day of the year so far, diners enjoyed the Bluebunch Café's outdoor patio. Across the street, the owner of the Medicine Wheel Craft Center had strung a banner across her front window advertising a local art fair.

"Afternoon." He nodded at several women gathered in a knot outside the bank who went to the same church as his family.

As the women greeted him in return, he was conscious of the muted buzz of conversation that followed in his wake.

Waiting for a truck to pass before crossing the street at the corner, he imagined a variation on the theme he'd heard since second grade when, joking with another boy, he'd knocked over the advent wreath with its lit candles and accidentally set the church's Christmas tree on fire. His dad, the minister and a bunch of others had put the fire out but from then on and until he'd left to ride rodeo, here in High Valley the name *Cole Carter* had been synonymous with *trouble*.

He straightened his shoulders and crossed the street. He couldn't keep regretting and thinking about what might have been—or imagine what people were saying about him either. He wasn't the first guy who'd had to retire from rodeo earlier than planned, and now was his chance to make something of himself beyond a rodeo arena.

And despite everybody knowing your business and having an opinion on it, Cole had to focus on the good parts of once again living in the same place where he'd grown up. In this small Montana town in foothill country, where the Rocky Mountains nestled along the western horizon, he had family, friends and community. Although a lot of them had witnessed his mistakes, today was the first step in proving to himself, his family and the town that he could change and be a different man in this next part of his life.

As he continued along the street until he reached Healing Paws Animal Rehabilitation Center, for the second time today he noted the business name in black swirling script on the front window. Over a hundred years ago, in the town's early days, it had been a newspaper office. He pushed open the glass door in the center of the building, a bell jingled overhead and Carla, a girl he'd gone to school with, looked up from behind a desk.

"Hey, Cole. You must be here to pick up

Jess. I heard you dropped her off when I was at lunch." Carla smiled as she moved around the desk, her heavily pregnant stomach coming ahead of her in a scrub top patterned with yellow and green dogs against a blue background.

"That's right." His boot heels clacked on the white tile floor in a sunny waiting room with pale yellow walls hung with framed paintings of animals. "I also want to see Mel McNeil about the cowboy challenge we're running out at the ranch in August." A one-day public event his older brother Zach and sister-in-law Beth had come up with to raise the ranch's profile and, through sponsorship, entry and admission fees, support the local animal rescue. "Beth said Mel might be interested in helping us out." Although Cole was supposed to be in charge, everything Cole knew about event organizing could be summarized in one word. Nothing. He had a sneaking suspicion Beth and Zach had given him this job to make him feel useful and needed.

"Sure. Your mom already paid online, so I'll go get Jess and grab Mel too. The cowboy challenge will be a fun day out for the whole family." Carla patted her belly. "This little one will be here by then."

"Super. The more the better." He'd forgotten how many kids Carla and her husband had, but, like most people he'd gone to high school with, this new baby must be number three or four.

Cole had left High Valley because he wanted a different life. But even though he was no longer a rodeo cowboy, he still wasn't one to settle and have a family. As Carla went into the employees-only area at the rear of the clinic, he put a hand to the pocket of his flannel shirt and rummaged for the handwritten list his mom had given him.

"Drop off and collect Jess from her treatment." Before today, Cole had never heard of a dog having physical therapy or massage, but Healing Paws had opened a few months ago and was associated with the veterinary clinic that treated all the Carter family's animals. "Talk to Mel McNeil, who's new in town, about the cowboy challenge. Buy nails at the hardware store. See the farrier and—"

"Here's your daddy. Are you going to tell him what a good girl you've been?" The voice was light, feminine and cheery. The kind of person who saw a glass as half-full, no matter how dire the circumstances.

"She's not… I'm not…" As the sable-and-white collie skidded across the floor, barking a greeting, Cole bent to pat her. "Hey, girl."

Jess bounced around his legs with remarkable energy for an almost eleven-year-old dog who'd recently had surgery. More often than not, Jess slept the day away, following the sunshine from room to room in the spacious ranch house where Cole had grown up and, after his father's death, his mom lived alone.

"Thanks for taking care of Jess." He tried not to wince as he straightened and the muscles in his lower back spasmed. His back, and most other parts of him, had never been the same since that accident at a rodeo in Arizona. Although not the one that had ended his career, it had likely helped shorten it, and at thirty-five, he sometimes felt like a much older man.

"My pleasure." The woman who'd brought Jess out smiled. Around Cole's age, and with hazel eyes behind green-framed glasses, she had a round face and friendly smile. "Jess is a wonderful dog. Along with a gentle exercise program, these massage and physiotherapy treatments are helping her regain a lot of mobility." The woman's curly brown hair had reddish tints and was pulled back into a high ponytail that swayed as she talked. "One of my colleagues usually sees Jess, so this is the first time I've worked with her. Your wife, Beth, gave us all the information for Jess's chart, though."

"That would have been my mom, Joy. Beth is married to my older brother, Zach. I'm Cole Carter. I'm not married."

"Oh." A faint flush crept across the woman's cheeks. "I'm sorry. There must have been a mix-up." She darted a glance at Carla, who was behind the desk again and tapping on a computer. "Carla said you wanted to see me about a riding event raising money for an animal rescue?" Freckles dotted the bridge of her nose. And when she ran a hand through the fringe of hair covering her forehead, Cole glimpsed a small daisy tattoo inside her right wrist.

"You're Mel McNeil?" Cole checked his mom's list again.

"Yes." The woman's smile broadened. "Mel is short for Melissa."

"Oh. I…" When Beth had asked him to talk to Mel, he'd pictured him as a younger version of another Mel he knew, the grizzled Texas cowboy who'd taken Cole under his wing when Cole was new to the rodeo circuit. Friend, mentor and, after Cole's dad passed, surrogate father, that Mel, Manuel Garcia, had helped shape Cole's career and had been an anchor in his restless life. His death last year had left Cole even more adrift.

He tried to rearrange his expression as thoughts of gray-haired fatherly cowboys fled. "Beth said you might help us out." On both the rodeo circuit and in his family, Cole was the joker and good-time guy. He was never ill at ease with people. Yet, and even if he hadn't started off on the wrong foot by assuming she'd be a man, something about this Mel made him uncharacteristically awkward.

"If you're still looking for volunteers, sure I can help." Mel handed him the dog's leash, and Cole wrapped it around one hand as Jess sat between them.

"We are." Cole cleared his throat.

Mel was attractive in a wholesome, girl-next-door way. Although he had nothing against that kind of woman, he'd never gone for one because she was the type who'd want to settle down—and ask for things he couldn't give her. So, why was his tongue tied in knots like a thirteen-year-old boy asking a girl for a first date?

"I haven't lived here long. I met Beth last week when we were both waiting to pick up an order at the Bluebunch Café. She introduced herself and said volunteering would be a good way for me to meet people. She didn't give me any details, though." Mel studied Cole, her expression curious, before she bent to give Jess a treat from the pocket of her pink scrubs. "What can I do to help?"

Cole had only returned to town ten days earlier. That explained why he'd never heard of Mel until Beth mentioned her, one of five or six other volunteers she'd already approached.

"I'm supposed to organize the event, but Beth and Zach already have a lot of people handling things like ticket sales, participation entry fees, company sponsorships, advertising and refreshments." Was it because they didn't trust him to do the job? He swallowed. "However, there's always room for more volunteers either to help with planning or on the day. Do you know about horses?"

"Does *she* know about horses?" Carla's laugh rang out in tandem with the phone. "Mel competed nationally in show jumping."

"Wow. Good for you." He tripped over the words. "But this is a Western event and—"

"It's fine," Mel interjected and took a step back. "I understand. My background is in English riding. Western riding is a different sport. I'm sure there's someone else who can help. I'll ask around and we can put a notice here in the clinic too. If you—"

"No, wait." Cole took a step forward. "Sorry. I didn't mean you couldn't contribute. I'd welcome your help.

"English riding *is* different, sure, but now there's Western dressage as well." Cole couldn't go back to the ranch without having gotten Mel to help. Beth had asked him to do one simple thing. If he didn't do it, he'd show, once again, that, although he was a rodeo champ, outside the arena he usually fell short. He couldn't fail at this job before he'd even started. "If you helped at the event, maybe we could learn from each other. Bridge the gap between English and Western riding."

"Sure, I guess." Mel's smile was tentative. "But I don't have a horse. I sold mine almost seven years ago." She fiddled with the hem of her pink scrub top. Her fingernails were short and unpainted, and her hands looked both gentle and capable. "I haven't ridden since then either, but I..." She glanced at the sixty-something couple and their black poodle who'd come into the clinic after Cole. "I should—"

"I'm sorry. I caught you in the middle of a busy day. Why don't you come out to the ranch so we can talk more? I can show you around the stables, and you can meet the horses and get a sense of our operation and the kind of event we're planning. You don't need a horse of your own to volunteer."

Asking her to the ranch was the only thing he could think of. Besides, that way nobody would see them together and think it was a date.

"That sounds good." Mel's smile broadened, and Cole's tight breath eased. He liked how her smile began in her hazel eyes and moved to her mouth, like the sun coming out after rain. "I also know where the Tall Grass Ranch is. I was out that way yesterday treating one of your neighbor's horses and saw the sign from the highway."

"Is tonight around six good for you?" The sooner Cole could show Beth and Zach he'd made progress, the better.

"Sure." An expression he couldn't read flitted across Mel's face, dimming the sunshine before she bent to pat Jess again.

"See you then." Cole tipped his hat, nodded to Mel, Carla and the couple with the dog and moved with Jess back toward the clinic's door.

Cole Carter is sure the odd one out in that family. It's a shame he can't be more like his brothers. They're such good boys, but that one? His middle name is trouble.

The words he'd heard a gossipy neighbor say at a long-ago town picnic echoed in his head. At ten, that was the last time Cole cried, hiding in the trees that edged the town park until his dad had come looking for him.

Although the woman had soon moved away, Cole had never tried to prove her wrong.

And as the years passed, her words had become a self-fulfilling prophecy. Now, though, he was determined to change. He'd done what Beth asked, so why did he still feel off-balance, as if he might have made yet another mistake?

"YOU CAN HAVE dessert when we get home." Mel glanced at the clock on her car's dashboard. It was already ten past six. She'd be at least fifteen minutes late for this meeting, but since she didn't have Cole's number, she couldn't stop and text him.

"You said I could have ice cream." From the rear where she was strapped into her booster seat, six-year-old Skylar's voice rose in a whine.

"If you hadn't taken so long to eat your supper and those apple slices, you'd have had plenty of time for ice cream." Mel made her voice even.

On either side of the two-lane highway, rolling fields stretched as far as she could see. In the distance, the snow-covered Rocky Mountains poked out of a blue-, gold- and pink-tinted sky. This part of Montana looked a lot like the Alberta foothills in Canada, where she'd spent the first eight years of her life. But even though the landscape looked familiar, it was also strange. Or maybe it was because *she* was different. The girl who'd traded her larger and heavier Western saddle for an English one and made herself become someone else, until she'd lost sight of who that girl had been and what she wanted.

"It's still not fair. If we'd stayed home, I'd be eating ice cream right now." Skylar kicked her feet against the rear of the front passenger seat.

"You know the rules about kicking and talking back. Besides, I already told you I have a meeting, and you can't stay home by yourself." Mel looked for the Tall Grass Ranch sign on the right-hand side of the highway.

The Carter family owned one of the biggest and oldest ranches in this part of Montana. Before today Mel had only met Beth who'd joined the family by marriage. However, after Cole left the clinic today, Carla had told her about the rest of the Carters, who were active and well-respected in the community.

"I'm bored." Skylar let out a huff.

When Mel glanced in the rearview mirror, her daughter's mouth was in a pout.

"Why don't you read that book you got from the school library? It's about a horse and soon you'll see real horses." Although Mel hadn't asked if she could bring Skylar to tonight's meeting, Cole came from a big family. Hopefully, he'd understand because, as a single mom with no family nearby, she didn't have anyone to help out.

"Can we get a horse?" Skylar grabbed the book from the bag Mel had packed before they left home. Things to keep her daughter occupied while she talked to Cole.

"Not right now. Horses cost lots of money." Mel signaled to turn into the driveway where a sign with "Welcome to the Tall Grass Ranch" extended from wooden poles on either side of pastureland.

Skylar leaned forward and rummaged in the bag again.

"No juice box in the car, remember?" Dust from the winding gravel driveway rose in clouds around the vehicle. It had been a dry spring, and if it was a dry summer too… Mel made herself push away the thought of what could happen with a drought year. She hadn't lived on a ranch since early childhood. Together with a passion for healing and good animal welfare, she'd become a physical therapist and specialized in animal rehabilitation for stability. She didn't have to worry about the weather or any of the other uncertainties that came along with ranching. After some tough years, the toughest when Skylar was a baby, her life was finally in a good and secure place.

"Look." Skylar squealed. "It's a barn like this picture in my book." She waved the story in Mel's direction.

"It is." Mel drove by the barn and past a gracious house with a wraparound porch painted a soft gray with white trim. Then, following Carla's instructions, she hung a right along a smaller driveway that led to another barn several hundred yards behind the house. Two horse trailers with the Tall Grass Ranch logo sat outside. Beyond them was a fenced pasture with a large water trough in the middle, suitable for several horses.

Mel parked beside the pasture, turned off the vehicle and got out to help Skylar get unbuckled. "Watch where you walk." She held

out her hand, but Skylar ignored it, instead
jumping from her seat.

"Why?" Skylar glanced at the ground and
at her new purple running shoes.

"Horses and cattle come through here.
Unlike people, they don't have a separate
bathroom." She pointed to a patch of fresh
manure near the fence.

"Yuck." Skylar wrinkled her button nose
and jumped back.

"Hey, Mel." Cole came around the far corner of the barn, leading a beautiful blood
bay gelding. The early evening sun gleamed
off the horse's polished reddish-brown coat
and black mane and tail. Cole still wore the
jeans, boots and hat he'd had on earlier, but
his blue button-down Western shirt was
topped with a black jacket, half undone.

"Hi. Sorry I'm late." She drew in a breath.
Apart from being of a similar height, around
five feet ten or eleven, with dark blond hair
and easy charm, Cole wasn't anything like
Skylar's birth father. Cole was a Western
rider too. A man Stephen would have looked
down on in principle. "Gorgeous horse." The
kind of horse that before the accident she'd

ridden with ease, never thinking about the risks.

"Is he a cowboy, Mommy?" Skylar's clear treble piped up as she hopped from one foot to the other beside Mel. "Like in the rodeo? My teacher's brother is in the rodeo. She showed us pictures."

"I used to be a rodeo cowboy. Now I'm retired." Cole stopped the horse several feet away from them. "Meet Bandit. He's the horse I rode on the circuit. Since a big part of me will always be a cowboy, that's why we're having a cowboy challenge here at the ranch. It's a Saturday charity event in August to raise money for the county animal rescue. Zach and Beth hope it will also showcase what we do at the ranch. We've started offering public horse boarding and there's some cattle and agricultural initiatives we're excited about."

"A cowboy challenge?" Mel's stomach flipped.

Beth had talked about trail riding but because they'd been busy at the clinic, Mel hadn't asked Cole any questions. She could have managed trail riding. But a cowboy challenge was a lot more active—and potentially dangerous.

"Don't let the name put you off. The event is for cowgirls *and* cowboys and there are separate divisions for each. There'll be things for kids and families too."

"It's not that." Mel paused. It was more than seven years since she'd been thrown off her horse midjump and had hurtled through the air at speed. Although it wasn't the horse's fault, she hadn't ridden since. But besides facing her own fear of being around horses, she wanted Skylar to be part of this community and make friends. It was too late in the school year for Mel to volunteer with the PTA or anything else that would help Skylar feel at home. The cowboy challenge was likely her only option. "Okay, I'll do it." She forced a smile.

"Great." Cole grinned and his glance shifted from Skylar back to Mel and then to Skylar again. "I'm Cole. Who are you?"

"Skylar Mary Margaret McNeil." Her daughter stepped closer to the horse. "He's really big."

"Bandit is way too big for you, honey." Mel put a hand on Skylar's shoulder and gave it a gentle squeeze. "I'm going to help Cole with something that will be fun for everyone in High Valley."

"Can I pat Bandit? Please, Mommy?"

"If you and your mom are okay with me lifting you up." Cole turned to Mel. "Bandit's big but he's well-trained. Skylar will be fine giving him a scratch behind his ears."

"I guess so."

"Yay." Skylar bounced toward Cole and, chattering about the horse, she held out her arms so he could pick her up.

When they'd met at the café, Beth had been so friendly that Mel had let down her guard. She wouldn't make that mistake again.

"See what I'm doing?" Skylar giggled as she rubbed the horse behind one ear. "His hair tickles my fingers. Do you think Bandit likes me?"

"He sure does," Cole said.

"I like him too."

"We have lots of other horses. If you and your mom want to come inside the barn with me, you can meet them."

Mel studied Skylar's excited face as Cole held her and she patted the horse, who stood quietly, its dark eyes solemn. Things had started with Stephen because of a horse too and that whirlwind relationship had almost destroyed Mel. She was finally ready to be around horses again. But, for Skylar's sake, as well as her own, she wouldn't let herself get close to any other man who, even superficially, reminded her of her ex-husband. One who, if she wasn't careful, and thanks to a flutter of attraction when Cole had said he wasn't married, could not only break her heart but her daughter's too.

CHAPTER TWO

Cole led Bandit into the barn as Mel and Skylar followed. All he had to do was introduce Mel to the horses and tell her more about the event. Given her horrified expression when he said it was a cowboy challenge, he was surprised she'd agreed to help out and wasn't already heading back to town.

Since coming home to the Tall Grass Ranch to stay, the horse barn had been Cole's domain. From cleaning out stalls to organizing tack and feeding, grooming and exercising the horses, he did most of the work alone, and he liked it that way. Sheltered by the barn's familiar sturdy wooden walls and high-beamed ceiling, he found comfort here. Working with the horses suited him because they didn't need to be impressed. And for the first time in his life, he didn't have to pretend to be someone he wasn't.

"You've got a beautiful barn. How many

horses do you keep?" As they reached the barn's wide central aisle, Mel broke the awkward silence. The tightness in her voice was at odds with her bright smile. It was almost as if she was forcing herself to be here. She liked and understood horses. That was evident from how she'd assessed Bandit and made eye contact with him. Why was she edgy?

"We have twenty horses of our own and we're currently boarding ten others." Offering horse boarding was one way they were diversifying the ranch's income. "Hey, girl." He patted Daisy-May's head as the placid Appaloosa nickered in the stall next to Bandit's.

"That's a lot of work." Mel patted Daisy-May too, and the horse leaned over the half-open stall door to greet her.

"It keeps me out of trouble." He made himself give a carefree laugh.

"Don't you have help?" Mel didn't laugh. Instead, she rubbed Daisy-May's neck, and the horse gave her an equine version of a pleased smile.

Cole opened Bandit's stall and led him inside to get settled for the night. "I ask one of

the ranch hands to pitch in if I need them."
Although he hadn't so far. It wasn't as if Cole
had anything else to do. Besides, the hard,
physical work tired him out and kept him
from brooding.

"Look, Mom. There's a cat." After talking
a mile a minute outside, Skylar, a cute-as-a-
button little girl with blond hair in pigtails,
had been quiet since they'd come into the
barn. However, now her blue eyes were once
again wide with excitement as she pointed to
one of the barn cats. It was black with four
white paws and a white chest and looked
like someone wearing a tuxedo.

"That's Mr. Wiggins. My sister named
him. Mrs. Wiggins is somewhere around
too." Like his dog, Blue, whom he'd left
with his mom while he did chores, the cats
calmed Cole. They accepted him as he was
and didn't ask questions he couldn't answer,
including what he planned to do with the
rest of his life.

"Can I go pet Mr. Wiggins before I meet
the other horses?" As Skylar hopped from
foot to foot, lights on her sneakers flashed.

Mel glanced at Cole and, when he nodded, she turned back to her daughter. "Yes, but remember to be gentle."

"I will."

After Skylar dashed to the far end of the barn, Mel leaned against the bottom half of Bandit's stall. "Skylar's never been in a barn or around animals before. We moved here from San Francisco when I got the job at the clinic. I'm on my own with her, and although she was fine with you, she can be shy around new people."

"Living in this area, she'll soon get used to animals. As for people? There's nothing wrong with holding back." Cole had been shy as a kid too but had masked it with bravado until the mask had become a habit. "I expect Skylar will come around with others in her own time."

Cole brushed Bandit, the familiar gesture soothing.

He was supposed to be talking to Mel about the cowboy challenge, but she still looked as if she was poised to run. From her tight-lipped smile, the worry in her eyes and stiff body language, there were a lot of things Mel wasn't telling him, but it wasn't any of his business either.

He bent to check Bandit's bedding. As he straightened, he winced. His back always hurt more in the evening after a day's work.

"You might want to get that checked out." Mel moved away as he left Bandit's stall.

"What do you mean?" He latched the stall door.

"Your back. At the clinic, it looked like it was giving you trouble and now again here. I hope picking Skylar up to pat Bandit wasn't too much. How you move suggests you might have chronic back pain." Mel gave him a rueful smile. "I'm a physical therapist and, although I work with animals now, I treated people first."

"It's nothing. I toss hay bales heavier than that little girl." He tried to joke but the words died in his throat.

Mel was looking at him in genuine concern. Not because she was family. Not because she was one of the rodeo corporate sponsors he'd let down when he got hurt. And not with the pity he saw on the faces of the other cowboys. Even though Mel didn't know him, she cared and wanted to help.

"If it's ever not nothing, there are several excellent physical therapy clinics in town. Your doctor can refer you." Mel patted Daisy-May again. "There's usually something that can be done to help with pain. Even if it doesn't go away, it can still be better."

Physical pain, perhaps. But the pain in Cole's heart caused by losing his job, his way of life and hopes for the future? That kind was a phantom pain no physical therapist could help with. "Thanks. I'll think about it." He brushed chaff off his jeans.

"I know what I'm talking about." Mel hesitated. "Not only as a health care professional but as a person. I haven't ridden for a long time because I had a freak accident attempting a jump." She crossed her arms in front of her chest. "The horse got spooked and…well… You can probably guess the rest. I was thrown and hit the ground headfirst. I was lucky not to be left paralyzed. I had a bunch of broken bones and banged up my right knee but, all things considered, that's pretty minor. I lost my competitive equestrian career, though. It took me a long time to come to terms with that."

"You…" Cole stopped.

Mel was a stranger, but maybe that was

the best reason of all to talk to her. Out of everyone, she might understand.

"I had an accident too. A lot of accidents, but the last one was the worst. That's why I can't ride rodeo anymore." And when he'd lost rodeo, he'd lost his sense of self and place in the world.

"That's rough. I'm sorry." Mel touched his arm, the brief gesture comforting. "Have you talked to anyone? A professional?"

"You mean a counselor?" All winter, both in the hospital and once he'd been discharged, Cole had tried to figure out where he belonged. In the end, he'd come back to the ranch because it was home, but now he had to figure out a role for himself here. One that was meaningful and not a make-work project devised by family in an attempt to try to help him feel better.

"After my accident, I saw a counselor for a year. She helped me a lot."

"I tried, but it didn't work out." Or maybe he hadn't given the counselor—or himself— a fair chance. Cole gathered several empty buckets and stacked them by the barn wall.

"You should try again. Because the first counselor wasn't a good fit doesn't mean another one wouldn't be." Mel grabbed a dustpan and broom and swept stray straw.

Maybe like in dating. Some people had to kiss a bunch of frogs before they found their prince—or princess. Although Cole had dated a lot, he'd only found who he thought was the right woman once. Except, she'd decided he wasn't the right man so maybe he was destined to be alone. However, each time he looked at Zach and Beth, he got a hollow feeling in his chest. Not jealousy, because he was happy for them, but an ache like the loss of something he'd never had.

"I guess I could ask for another referral. There are three others in the practice." That's what his mom had said, but she was training to be a counselor. Yet, although Cole didn't want to examine why, the advice meant more coming from Mel.

"It's hard, but if you find the right person, counseling will be worth it." Mel patted his arm again as she propped the broom and dustpan beside the buckets. "So, about this cowboy challenge." Her smile faltered. "Do you want to have activities for adults and children?"

"That's what Zach and Beth had in mind.

I'd thought of an obstacle course for kids to take their ponies around and maybe mini roping. Trail riding for adults and teens who want to take part in a fun competition and work on horsemanship skills. Then for the true cowboys and cowgirls, a cutting competition."

"Is cutting a timed event where riders and horses separate one or more cows from the herd?" Mel's expression was thoughtful as if she was remembering something far back in her mind.

"Yeah, you got it. It's a Western show event. There's a bunch of others too." He rubbed Daisy-May's neck how she liked it. "My dad used to enter this girl in the ranch riding class at local events. She won ribbons too. She's versatile, has a good attitude, picks up patterns quickly and is consistent. Exactly the kind of horse you need for ranch work."

Mel nodded as if she understood. For someone who'd trained in English riding, she had more understanding of Western events than he expected. She knew her way around a barn and seemed comfortable in a ranch environment. She was kind and caring. Pretty too, in a sweet and understated way. To become a physical therapist, she also had to be smart. But, along with all those things, and although he could let himself be attracted to her, she was a single mom who, from the sounds of it, and like him, had baggage of her own.

"Come see the cats, Mommy." Skylar's voice echoed.

"Sure, sweetie."

As Mel turned away, Cole glanced at Skylar, who ran along one of the barn's side aisles tossing a small red ball for Mr. Wiggins and the other cats.

"You too, Cole." Skylar waved. "I've made up a game and you and Mommy can play with me."

"My daughter can be very insistent." As she spoke in an undertone, Mel gave him an apologetic smile. "It's okay if you still have chores. We've taken up a lot of your time already."

"Bandit's settled and the other chores can wait." It had been too long since Cole had had fun. "What's this game about?" he called to Skylar.

As she explained the "rules," he nodded

but they were soon forgotten as he and Mel pretended to chase Skylar while she laughed and evaded them.

"Got you so you're it." Mel touched Skylar's shoulder. "Now you have to tag us but I need a minute." As Skylar made another circuit of the barn, Mel stopped to catch her breath. "Those cats had the right idea." Mel pointed to Mr. Wiggins and the rest, who now sat on the edge of the hayloft looking down at them.

"They did." Cole leaned against an empty stall and chuckled. "Skylar's great but she's wearing me out."

"Thanks for playing with her." Mel sobered. "With the move and a new school, she needs to find a little fun."

"It's fine." But despite the fun, he had to watch himself.

Although an impromptu game was harmless enough, before he got involved with any woman, let alone her kid, Cole had to figure out his own life. He also had to become the kind of man who'd be worthy of a woman like Mel. One who needed roots, stability and a man she could count on—not only for herself but for Skylar too.

JOY CARTER PLUMPED the throw pillows on the family room sofa and folded the crocheted blanket to drape over the back. Through the half-open window at the rear of the spacious ranch house, cattle lowed and several horses whinnied. The air was scented with the sweetness of spring earth. May was her favorite month, and this spring she had extra reason to be grateful.

After a beautiful Valentine's Day wedding, her son Zach had settled into married life with Beth and their adopted daughter, Ellie. And Cole had come home safe after what would be his last rodeo. She hadn't wanted him to return to the circuit last winter, but he was a grown man so she wouldn't stop him. But five weeks later, he'd had an accident that could have killed him.

Joy pressed a hand to her chest as if she could physically push the memories down. She'd already buried her husband, oldest son and a daughter-in-law. How could she have coped with losing Cole as well? Fortunately, she hadn't had to. Her fingers trembled as she smoothed the cream-colored blanket. She'd made it, in a tree of life pattern, last winter when Cole was in the hospital. Crocheting had kept her mind and hands occupied during those anxious days and the pattern celebrated her family and their roots. But now Cole was home and he was well— at least, his body was. The emotional and mental healing would happen in time.

"You all set for the first meeting of the Sunflower Sisterhood?" Beth's voice came from the kitchen before she joined Joy in the family room. "I'm here early in case you need help. I brought oatmeal cookies—" she gestured to a tin before she set it on the buffet table "—and a new friend. You remember me mentioning Mel McNeil?"

"Of course. The new animal physical therapist at Healing Paws." Joy moved away from the sofa and smiled in welcome as another woman entered the room with Beth. "I'm happy to meet you in person."

As Beth introduced them, Mel offered a tentative smile in return. "It's nice to meet you too but I hope I'm not intruding tonight."

"Of course not. You're most welcome. We all want you to feel settled here." Of medium height, Mel wore a denim skirt with a mint-green knit top and her reddish-brown hair was in a twist at the back of her head. She had an interesting face and a kind one too. When Joy had asked Cole about Mel after he'd picked up Jess, he'd been uncharacteristically vague. And although Zach had mentioned Mel had come to the ranch to talk about the cowboy challenge, Joy had been at her book club meeting so missed her.

"We left Mel's daughter, Skylar, in the horse barn with Ellie, Zach and Cole. Skylar wanted to see Ellie's horse." Beth hugged Joy. "The girls will join us later when the others get here."

After returning Beth's hug, Joy gestured for Mel to sit on the sofa. "Several of my friends are bringing their daughters or granddaughters. I made cupcakes for them to decorate."

"Skylar will love that. She misses baking and cake decorating with my mom. My family's in California." Mel dug in a tote bag and produced a bottle of wine. "Beth said I didn't need to bring anything, but I didn't want to come empty-handed. It will be nice to meet other women here." She sat on the edge of the sofa, where Joy had indicated.

Joy took the wine and thanked Mel. "I vacationed in California once. I planned to go back but then..." Joy stopped and searched for a change of subject. California was beautiful, but she thought about Dennis and that wonderful second honeymoon trip whenever anybody mentioned the state. "As Beth has likely told you, we're pretty friendly here, but you must miss your family. How old is Skylar?"

"Six, seven in September."

"Near my granddaughter Paisley's age. I'll ask Paisley to look out for Skylar at school."

"That would be great. We do miss family but I love my new job."

"We love Healing Paws too. After you treated Jess, she's been almost puppy-like."

At the sound of her name, the collie came into the family room from where she'd been napping in her bed in the adjacent den Joy used as a home office.

"Jess is a wonderful dog." Mel bent to pat Jess, and the dog wagged her tail.

"My husband gave Jess to me for my birthday, and I've had her since she was a few months old. I got this fellow last year." She indicated the beagle puppy who'd followed Jess in pursuit of a squeaky green chew toy. "He's Gus and the other one—" she gestured to the second and bigger beagle "—is Cole's dog, Blue. They're from the same litter."

Although Gus kept Joy busy and made her smile, no other dog could mean the same to her as Jess did. She suppressed a sigh. Dennis would want her to go on with her life, which was what she was trying to do. But his death had left a huge hole that a puppy, her children, college classes, her book club or any of the other activities she was involved in could ever fill.

"What's the Sunflower Sisterhood all about?" Mel rubbed Jess's ears, and the dog wriggled in pleasure.

"I didn't explain because I wanted Mel to hear about it from you first." At Joy's nod, Beth arranged serving and dessert plates on the buffet table.

"It's something new so this is only our first official meeting." Joy put the wine aside to open later and reached for the stack of sunflower-patterned napkins she'd sewn from leftover quilt fabric. "Sunflowers are such happy flowers, aren't they? Friendly too. I've been thinking about organizing some kind of women's group for a while now and 'sunflowers' seemed to fit with 'sisterhood.' Most of us are involved in the town's first sunflower festival later this summer so it works that way too."

"I've always liked sunflowers," Mel said. "It's neat how they turn in a group to follow the sun."

Joy folded napkins and smiled at Mel. "Truth be told, they're my favorite flower. I even had them in my wedding bouquet. Each summer, my husband, and now my sons, grow a field of sunflowers for me. No matter what else is going on in my life, looking at that field gives me hope. So along with thinking about a women's group, when I thought of sunflowers I thought of trying to do something practical to give hope to others who need it."

Beth nodded. "Joy and I talked about how small kindnesses can mean a lot so the Sunflower Sisterhood came from there. Get women of different ages together to support each other and our community. We're all so busy if we didn't set a meeting time nothing would happen."

Mel looked between them. "It sounds like

a good idea, but how can I help? I'm so new here I hardly know anyone."

"You can help the most because you *are* new." Joy held Mel's hazel gaze.

Mel had pretty eyes, but there was a wariness in them, even when she smiled.

"Except for Beth, we all know each other and this area far too well. We need new perspectives." *If you speak with confidence, people will think you are confident.* She'd learned that maxim in one of the college courses she'd taken last winter and had to do a class presentation.

"I guess I could contribute in some way." Mel's tense expression eased.

"Wonderful."

Mel looked like she needed a motherly hug, but Joy didn't know her well enough to give her one.

"The other women will be here soon. We can—"

"Mom? Is Mel with you?" Cole's voice rang out. "Skylar's had a bit of an accident and she—"

Mel jumped to her feet and darted across the family room, the dogs and Joy following. "Is she hurt?"

"No, she's okay." Cole stood outside the family room in the tiled hall. A blond girl who must be Skylar had her arms around his neck and water dripped from her sodden jeans and pink T-shirt. "One of the barn cats fell into a water trough. Skylar climbed on a hay bale to try to rescue the cat and she fell in too. I pulled her out before her head went under."

"I'm okay, Mommy." Skylar gave Mel a broad grin. "The cat is too. It was Mr. Wiggins. Remember him? Cole rescued me and his brother got the cat. There wasn't much water, and I can swim."

"Oh, honey. You've only just started swimming lessons. You can float with your water wings, but that's about it. Come here, sweetheart." Mel held out her arms, and Cole lifted Skylar into Mel's embrace. "We talked about how to be safe in a barn and on a ranch. Did you forget?"

"I guess." Cuddled into the curve of Mel's shoulder, Skylar reached for Cole's hand and wrapped her small fingers around his. "Ellie and me were laughing at Mr. Wiggins trying to climb the barn wall and he fell. He could have drowned."

"That cat has more than nine lives." Cole's voice was husky and, as he looked at Skylar, and then at his hand in hers, there was a tenderness in his face Joy had never seen.

"I forgot to bring a change of clothes." In Mel's tone, worry mixed with frustration. "We'd better go home and—"

"No need. My granddaughter is only a bit bigger than Skylar. I keep extra clothes for Paisley upstairs, and I'm sure something of hers will fit."

"Thank you." Mel glanced between Cole and Joy as Beth greeted Zach and Ellie, who'd joined them. "Thank you both. If anything had happened to her…" She stopped and her mouth trembled. "Skylar has always been adventurous."

Like Cole. Of all Joy's children, he'd been the risk-taker. It wasn't surprising he'd ridden rodeo, but underneath his daredevil antics and jokes was a sensitive man. A vulnerable one too, although he rarely showed that side of himself.

"I raised five children and one or more of them was always having some kind of mishap. There's no harm done, and Skylar can soon get cleaned up. There's a utility sink and bathroom off the kitchen. Cole can show you where while I find some dry clothes. I'll get a blouse and leggings for you too and pop your clothes in the dryer." Joy indicated the wet patches on Mel's top and skirt. "We're about the same size so mine should do until you can change back into your own things."

Since Cole had had more "mishaps" than the rest of Joy's family combined, it made sense that maybe he remembered more of them too. She studied his bent head and flushed cheeks. Was he still focused on how he'd acted up as a kid?

"And then can I go to the barn with Cole again?" Skylar's voice was hopeful. "He said I could help feed Princess. She's so pretty. She's brown with a white star on her head."

"If your mom says it's okay, sure." Cole continued to stare at his boots.

"You can go back to the barn as long as you promise you'll do exactly what you're told. No more climbing on hay bales or anything else." Still carrying Skylar, Mel followed Cole to the kitchen.

Although Joy had helped bring Zach and Beth together, she'd promised herself and them too she was done trying to play match-maker in her children's lives. But what if she could help Cole find happiness with the right woman's love? He needed to build a new life after rodeo, and Mel was new in town. Maybe she was looking to do the same. They were already working together on the trail-riding course, one of the activities for the cowboy challenge event. It wasn't interfering to give them a nudge.

"Mom?" Zach joined her. "You have that look again."

"What look?" Joy gave a light laugh. "I was only thinking how nice it is to have another young girl in the house. With school and all her other activities, Paisley isn't here as much as she once was. I loved having Beth and Ellie stay with me before your wedding, and I miss Ellie especially. Since Molly's got her nursing job and will only be home for a week this summer, I miss her too. Skylar looks like Molly at that age, don't you think?"

"The same hair color, sure." Zach gave her a one-armed hug. "Molly is excited about living and working in Atlanta, and you see

Ellie almost every day when she comes to ride Princess."

"I know." Joy pasted a smile on her face. She wanted Molly to have her own life, but this was the first summer since she'd left for college that her daughter wouldn't spend at home. And while it was right that Zach, Beth and Ellie make their own family, when Beth and Ellie were here, the big ranch house had been less empty. "It's fine. I have lots to keep me busy." But was Joy filling her life with activities to avoid being alone?

"I'm proud of you, Mom. With your college classes, book and quilting clubs and now this Sunflower Sisterhood idea, you're moving forward and making a good life for yourself. Dad would be proud of you too." Zach squeezed Joy's shoulder. "But remember, Cole has to find his own way like I did."

"Of course. I told you I was done meddling." And at the time Joy had meant it. "Everyone will be here soon and—"

The front doorbell sounded.

"Have a good evening." Zach gave Joy's shoulder a final pat before rejoining Beth and Ellie in the kitchen, taking the dogs with him.

But what if as part of finding his way, Cole

also found something he never expected? Something Joy had never expected for her restless son either.

She left the family room to greet her friends, Cole still on her mind. The Sunflower Sisterhood was about women helping each other, along with family and community. So maybe Joy could help Cole and perhaps Mel and Skylar too.

CHAPTER THREE

MEL ATE THE last delicious forkful of lemon cheesecake, set her dessert plate aside and refolded the sunflower napkin. Except for Beth, she'd only met this small group of women tonight, but thanks to their warm welcome, she felt surprisingly relaxed and comfortable with them.

Joy sat on the sofa and explained the idea behind the Sunflower Sisterhood. She must only be in her late fifties or early sixties, but Beth had said Joy had been widowed a few years earlier. In her simple blue linen dress and with her ash-blond hair in a sleek bob, she was both understated and elegant. Yet, from the conversation tonight, it was clear Joy worked as hard on the ranch as the rest of her family.

Rosa Cardinal, a local artist and silversmith, sat at Joy's right and had talked about the Medicine Wheel Craft Center she owned in High Valley. She described her efforts to reach out to women returning to the workforce and looking for part-time employment. "Even if I can only hire two women, it's still a helping hand and way of giving back."

Kristi Russo, owner of the Bluebunch Café, who sat across from Mel, nodded. "Exactly. I'll never forget everyone who helped me when I started my business and was trying to get back on my feet after my divorce. Now it's my turn to support others who may be where I was."

Lauren, a former Paralympic equestrian athlete who ran a stud farm with her husband, a Carter cousin, and Diana Fitzgerald, a nearby rancher, offered to help as well. And then there was Kate Cheng, the special education teacher at Skylar's school. She'd suggested organizing volunteer opportunities for children and youth with disabilities.

"What about a few placements at Healing Paws? Many of my students love animals and if they could help at the clinic, they'd get practical experience before they're old enough for paid work." Behind her glasses, Kate's expression was earnest. "My daughter's almost fourteen and, apart from a few babysitting jobs and the time we'll spend at camp, she'll be at a loose end this summer. The early teenage years are hard for many kids."

"I'll talk to my colleagues and see what we might be able to offer." Mel was too new at the clinic to promise anything on her own, but surely her boss would agree to take part in some way. "Your daughter is Ellie's friend, right?"

"Yes, Lily." Kate beamed. "She's the dark-haired girl across from Skylar." She gestured toward the kitchen, where Mel's daughter was decorating cupcakes with Ellie and several other girls.

"Even if we can't set up something formally at the clinic, I'd like to help." Mel glanced at the group in the kitchen, separated from the family room by a soaring archway and fieldstone fireplace. Lily rolled her wheelchair around the farmhouse table to help Skylar use an icing spatula. Beth had told Mel she and Ellie had met Kate and Lily at Camp Crocus Hill, the summer camp the Carter family ran for children and youth with disabilities and their families. "The cowboy challenge will have children's activities. I'll talk to Cole and see what we can do." Mel put Kate's number into her phone. She'd added more new contacts tonight than she had in months.

"I understand how meeting lots of new people at once can be overwhelming." At Mel's other side, Beth spoke in a low voice. "I've lived here less than six months so, in groups, I still find it hard to remember everyone's names. We're all glad you're here, though."

"Me too." When Mel couldn't compete and she and Stephen had separated, most of the friends Mel had had in the equestrian world had drifted away. And between Skylar, school and work, Mel had only had time for her family and casual acquaintances. Although she'd forced herself to come to tonight's get-together, she was glad she had. When she was younger, she'd made friends easily. She needed to rediscover that girl. Friendship was an important part of life, and tonight had reminded her how much she missed it.

"I'm also glad you're helping Cole with the cowboy challenge. Zach and I want it to be a success, but we've never tried anything like it." Beth's expression was worried. "Cole isn't one to ask for help, and I don't want him to feel I'm checking up on him, but having you on board eases my mind."

Mel didn't like to ask for help either, but there were times when you needed to. "Cole's fantastic with horses."

He was what Mel would call a "true horse person." Someone who cared for and respected horses, understood them and put their needs first. The kind of person she used to be.

"Oh, he is." Beth laughed. "My husband, Zach, says Cole's better with horses than people. It's…" Beth stopped and glanced at the other women, but everyone was also talking in small groups. "Cole had several rodeo accidents in quick succession and, after the last one that ended his career, he changed. He used to be so outgoing and such a joker. You know the expression 'life of the party'?"

Mel nodded.

"That was Cole before he got hurt. Now, it's as if he's gone somewhere inside himself where none of us can reach him. Not even Zach, and they used to be close. I hoped working on the cowboy challenge would help Cole, but I'm concerned that it's too much of a reminder of what he lost."

"Or maybe it'll help him find something new." Like Mel should talk. Until now, she'd avoided everything to do with horses and horse people because of that same reminder.

"I hope you're right." Beth's expression was worried. "From what Zach says, all Cole ever wanted to do is ride rodeo. When he lost that, he lost his job, his friends and, except for his family, his whole life."

But he didn't lose horses or his love of working with them. Something Mel had tried to convince herself she could live without. "Maybe he needs to focus on what he can still do with horses instead of what he's lost."

Beth looked around the circle of women and nodded to Kate, who'd joined Joy and Rosa on the sofa. "When Kate and I first met, she said something similar, except she was talking about her daughter and my Ellie and living with disabilities."

"Kate's right. No matter what, you have to keep going. Focus on new or other strengths." If Mel didn't face her fears, she'd never move forward. For Skylar's sake, as well as her own, she had to do that work, no matter how hard.

Her heart constricted. A few weeks before her ninth birthday, she'd lost her dad and soon thereafter the ranch that had been the biggest and most important part of her childhood world. Although Mel loved her stepfather, and, with his support and encouragement, had concentrated on an English riding career, she'd always felt there was something missing. Something essential to who she was. And because Skylar's dad hadn't stepped up, Mel had parented for two, never letting herself think about what she needed for herself.

A small smile tilted one side of Beth's mouth. "Since Cole won't listen to anyone else, not even Joy, maybe he'll listen to you."

"No promises." Mel made herself smile back. She'd become a physical therapist because she wanted to help people and now animals heal. But had she focused on healing others because she was afraid to heal herself?

Nobody knew her here, so she had a chance for a fresh start. Working with Cole was only one part of the cowboy challenge. She had to think of the big picture and what the event could give her. Friends, community and a whole new life. Not least, one where she could reconnect with horses and the ranch life she hadn't let herself think about, let alone miss.

COLE STOOD APART from the group of parents by the corral fence and pulled his cowboy hat farther over his forehead. If his brother Bryce hadn't had to coach his son's soccer team, Cole wouldn't be here. However, as a single parent, Bryce couldn't be in two places at once, so Cole had offered to pick up his niece Paisley from her friend's birthday party.

In hillier country northwest of High Valley, the Squirrel Tail Ranch was a small spread, less than a quarter the size of the Carter family's operation. When the new owners, a widower and his son from Wyoming, had taken over eighteen months ago, they'd sold most of the cattle and rented out all the land but the pastures near the ranch house. As a result, Squirrel Tail was now more hobby farm than ranch, offering luxury bed-and-breakfast accommodation alongside events like weddings and children's birthday parties.

Cole stared at a pony dressed as a unicorn led by a teenage girl in riding clothes. A group of excited girls followed, Paisley included, and she stopped by Cole on the other side of the fence.

"You okay, kiddo?" He took the riding helmet she held out.

Seven-year-old Paisley rolled her eyes. "I hoped we'd have a barrel racing lesson, but it's only dumb games and grooming and tacking up ponies. I do that at home."

"You just turned seven. You still need to work on horsemanship skills, but when you're ready, I'll give you barrel racing lessons. You need the right horse too." Cole held back a laugh. Paisley was a lot like he'd been at that age. "Not all kids live on a ranch either. Since it's your friend's party, the most important thing is she has fun, right?"

"I guess so. At least the birthday cake was good. I also got two scoops of ice cream because another girl didn't want hers." Paisley's expression was resigned. "Ava's not really my friend, though. A few girls she invited got sick and couldn't come so she had to make up the numbers at the last minute. That's what I heard her mom say. Even the new girl, Skylar, got invited. See?" Paisley pointed to the group around the pony at the far side of the corral.

Mel's daughter stood apart, with her arms crossed in front of her chest, looking everywhere but at the others. Cole didn't know much about kids, but even he could see Skylar didn't look happy.

"She's all by herself. Why don't you go talk to her?"

"She's probably on her own because she thinks a pony dressed as a unicorn is dumb too." Paisley let out a heavy sigh. "But yeah, maybe she needs a friend. Grandma asked me to look out for her too."

As Paisley clumped across the corral, her sneakers kicking up dust, Cole exhaled. He knew what it was like to not feel you belonged, and, whether you were a kid or an adult, it was hard. He didn't belong here either. He wasn't a parent, but it was more than that. Apart from when he'd been injured, he'd spent his adult life moving from rodeo to rodeo and town to town for most of the year. These people were settled in their lives and families like he'd never been. A way he never thought he could be.

"Thank you."

He turned at Mel's voice. She wore black leggings, a sweater the same vibrant green as the new spring pasture grass, and she sounded out of breath.

"For what?"

"Asking Paisley to check in with Skylar." Mel shoved her tote bag higher up on one shoulder. "Skylar didn't want to come to this party, but I thought it would help her make friends. It's hard to join a new school, especially partway through the year. I wanted to be here for the party, but I got called in to work." She gestured to the Healing Paws lanyard around her neck, glanced at the other parents and lowered her voice. "If I'd known it was this kind of party and Skylar might feel left out, I'd have taken her to work with me. My boss is okay with her staying in the break room to color or watch a movie on my tablet."

To Cole that didn't sound like much fun either. "I don't know what kind of birthday parties kids have these days."

"All different kinds, but I could never afford this type of party for Skylar." Mel gestured to the unicorn pony as the teenager led it around the corral again. This time, a girl in a glittery pink T-shirt with "Birthday Girl" in white lettering across the front sat in the saddle. "You know Skylar's not used to horses either."

"When Skylar was in the barn with Zach and me the other night, she said she wanted to take riding lessons. If it works for you, she could start this summer at our ranch. We offer children's beginner classes as part of our summer camp activities."

"Ever since she visited your ranch, all Skylar's talked about is horses." Mel tucked a stray curl of hair behind one ear. "I shouldn't be surprised. I was crazy about horses as a girl and her dad, well... I guess horses are in her blood."

"You don't want her to be interested in horses?" If so, Cole understood. Horses were an expensive hobby. From what Mel had said about the party, and since she was a single parent, money must be tight.

"Not really." Mel fiddled with her hair again. "Part of it's the cost. Not only the horse but board, feed, veterinary care and everything else. If Skylar ever wanted to compete, those costs would only go up. But it's more than that. If she wanted to do another sport that cost a lot of money, I'd find a way." She dug one of her sneakers in the sand by the fence. "I haven't ridden in seven years. I used to be the girl who'd never met a horse she didn't want to ride. I'm finally okay being around horses, but I still can't bring myself to ride one. Or watch Skylar ride one either."

Cole's stomach knotted. "Was it your accident that changed things?" Despite all his rodeo injuries, he'd never been afraid to get back on a horse again. But deep inside, in a part of himself he'd never before acknowledged, maybe he'd had that last accident because he'd lost his nerve. He'd hesitated and, a split second later, everything—his career, his identity and the only way of life he knew—had all been wiped out. Not his life, though. He still had that and, as his mom kept pointing out, it was up to him to make the most of it.

"The accident and then Skylar." Mel leaned on the top fence rail and rested her chin in her hands. "Although I didn't know it at the time, I was pregnant with her when the horse threw me. I could have lost Skylar, but I didn't. I can't lose her now."

Cole wasn't a psychologist. His formal education had ended with high school, but it seemed Mel might be associating her fear of losing Skylar before with her fear of horse riding now.

"Whenever I see people riding, I remember the accident and I..." Mel's voice cracked. "It's not logical, but one of the reasons I volunteered to help with a riding event is because I need to face my fear and get back on a horse again."

And Cole had taken on the cowboy challenge because he needed to figure out his life and face the reality of not going back to rodeo. "What can I do to help?" Maybe by helping Mel, he'd find a way out of his own mess.

"Not let me back out?" Mel's laugh was forced. "Along with conquering my own fear, I need to let Skylar be her own person and not hold her back. If it wasn't horses, she'd likely choose something else risky. For all she can be quiet, she's also one of those kids that the bigger the adrenaline rush, the better. In California, I enrolled her in gymnastics. She was determined to do back flips off the sofa so I wanted her to learn how to do them safely on a mat."

"That explains it." Cole shook his head. "Before Skylar climbed onto that hay bale and fell into the water trough, I stopped her jumping from the hayloft ladder."

Mel shuddered.

"I won't let you back out of the event but…" He glanced across the corral to where Paisley talked to Skylar. "Only if you don't let me back out either?" He wasn't used to letting himself be vulnerable, but something about Mel made him open up in ways he never did.

"I won't." She touched his hand on the top rail of the fence before linking her little finger with his. "Promise."

"I promise too." The childhood gesture made him smile, even as Mel's brief touch sparked a tingle of awareness. "As for Skylar and horses, and you facing your fear, what do you say to getting Skylar involved in the kids' part of the event, along with Paisley? My niece likes an adrenaline rush too, but if she and Skylar work together, we can keep an eye on them and make sure they take any risks safely."

"That's a terrific idea." Gratitude shone in Mel's eyes behind her glasses, today a cute pair with dark-red frames. "Thank you."

"You're welcome, but you should thank my mom instead." Cole cleared his throat. He wasn't used to anyone, let alone a woman, looking at him with such genuine warmth and respect. Admiration, yes, especially when he was riding rodeo, but Mel's response to something that didn't have anything to do with what Cole did in an arena was new. "My mom is the one who thought Paisley should be involved in the event and my brother, Paisley's dad, agreed."

"But you thought of Skylar." Mel's voice hitched.

"Anybody would do the same." Cole's face heated. "Skylar's a wonderful girl."

"She is, but I'm her mom so I'd say that, wouldn't I?" Mel laughed and waved to Skylar as the party began to break up.

"Of course." He smiled at Paisley and Skylar, who joined him and Mel at the fence, exclaiming over the contents of their party goodie bags, but it quickly faded.

Mel was wonderful too. She was smart, attractive, kind and a great mother—a woman any man would be lucky to have in his life. However, from the little Cole knew of her, and, apart from friendship, neither of them was ready for a relationship. He couldn't let himself be drawn to Mel more than he already was.

CHAPTER FOUR

THREE DAYS LATER, Mel checked the time on her phone, said goodbye to Carla behind the clinic's reception desk and pushed open the door to go out onto High Valley Avenue, the small town's main street. Since Beth was picking up Skylar from school along with Ellie, Mel had time to grab a coffee and snack from the Bluebunch Café before meeting Cole at the ranch. She'd texted him her work schedule and they'd arranged to get together several times in the next few weeks to plan cowboy challenge activities. First was mapping out the route for the trail ride and obstacle courses for the adult and children's events and brainstorming what those obstacles should be—everything from standard barrels to more complex water and rail features.

As she walked along the street, passing a florist where Memorial Day decorations were being replaced by red, white and blue for July Fourth, she shaded her eyes against the bright afternoon sun. After a late-May snowstorm, it seemed like Mother Nature had skipped over spring and headed straight into summer. It was the kind of weather she remembered from her Alberta childhood but had almost forgotten during those years in California.

The sunshine warmed her shoulders through her light sweatshirt as she waited for traffic to clear before crossing the street. One of the many things she liked about living in a small town like High Valley was she could walk to work, Skylar's school and wherever else she needed to go. Today, she'd pick her car up at home and drive to the ranch.

"Mel?"

With one foot off the high curb, she stopped and turned around. Cole waved at her from in front of a building around the corner from the bank. "Hi." She waved back and waited as he walked toward her. Even if he hadn't been wearing a cowboy hat, along with boots, jeans and a blue-and-white-checked Western snap shirt, his loping walk spoke to a man who'd spent most of his life on horseback. "I wasn't expecting to see you until later at the ranch."

"I hadn't planned to be in town this afternoon but..." He stopped in front of her, touched the brim of his hat and glanced back at the building he'd come out of. The entrance was shaded by a green awning and the sign by the door indicated it held office suites. Mel hadn't lived in High Valley long enough to be familiar with all the local businesses. And apart from Ruby's Place, a restaurant farther down the street owned by one of the women who'd been at the Sunflower Sisterhood meeting, she hadn't even explored most the streets leading off of High Valley Avenue.

"Forget it. None of my business." Mel stepped back from the curb to give space to a woman near her age pushing a double stroller with two toddlers who, apart from their pink cowboy hats, wore outfits that were miniature versions of Cole's. "I'll see you later and—"

"Wait. If you have a minute, I wanted to thank you." He touched his hat brim again, this time to hold it on his head as a gust of wind buffeted them.

"Thank me for what?" Mel stepped into the shadow of the bank building. It was quieter on this side street and they were sheltered by the building too.

"What you said about talking to my doctor about physical therapy." Cole glanced from side to side but since they were away from the bustling main street, nobody was in earshot. "And a counselor." He met Mel's gaze. "You were right. I need to get more help. My doctor had a cancellation today so I got those referrals. I have to build a new life and I need help to do that."

"Good for you." Mel studied Cole's face, only a curve of his clean-shaven cheek visible beneath his hat. "For me, taking that first step to recognize I needed help and ask for it was the hardest."

"Really?" He kept his gaze on her, and Mel drew in a breath at the raw pain in his dark blue eyes.

"Sure." She made herself sound more confident than she felt. Everything about building a new life was hard but you didn't have to do it alone. What did it say about her, though, that she still hadn't gotten back on a horse? She'd also spent the last week avoiding Skylar's questions about why she'd stopped riding, and why she hadn't decided whether to let her daughter start lessons either. If she wanted Skylar to be brave, independent and resilient, Mel had to model that behavior herself. "Your physical therapist and counselor can support you in doing the work to build that new life."

"After your accident, did you... It must get easier with time?"

"In some ways." She stared along the street toward the distant mountains, the snow-tipped peaks blending with the blue haze of sky. "It took a long while for me to accept I couldn't compete again but having Skylar helped." She'd focused on her daughter to ignore the problems in her marriage too. "It was a few years before I could be around horses, but both my counselor and physical therapist helped me move beyond that and set new goals."

"Is that why you became a physical therapist yourself?"

"Yes." Almost without noticing, Mel and Cole had crossed the street and were meandering toward the Bluebunch Café in the middle of the next block. "For me, and whether working with animals or people, my job in health care is a way of giving back. For whatever reason, I got a second chance at life and I want to make the most of it."

"My mom told me that's what I need to do." Cole's grin was sheepish. He moved to Mel's side as a boy on a skateboard careened out of a sporting goods store. A woman followed and called to him to not use the board on the sidewalk.

"I like your mom, but I'm not sure I like being compared to her." Mel smiled back. Although she hardly knew him, there was something about Cole that put her at ease. She could also tease him in a way she'd never done with her ex-husband.

"Sorry, I didn't mean…" Cole's cheeks pinkened. "What I should have said is that idea means more coming from you because you've gone through something similar."

Mel sobered. "I know and I appreciate that. If you want, and if you ever need to talk to someone else, I hope you feel you can talk to me." In this new part of her life, she was making all kinds of friends. Maybe Cole could be one of them.

"Thanks, I do." His voice was gruff.

Mel hesitated as they stopped near the café by a board advertising local blueberry ice cream. *New life. New goals.* She thought of Skylar. "You might be able to help me too."

"Oh?" Cole's expression was puzzled.

Mel took a deep breath. "I want to try riding a horse again. For Skylar's sake, I have to face my fear and I wondered..." She worried her lower lip. "Could you help me with that? I trust you." Especially when it came to his knowledge and skill with horses. "From what I've seen of your work in the horse barn, and also what Beth has said about you, if anybody can help me get back on a horse, it's probably you."

"I'm honored." Cole extended his hand and Mel took it. "We can go as slow as you need. Baby steps." A smile glimmered. "Or hooves."

"Thank you." Cole's hand in Mel's was warm as they shook to seal the deal. His hand was also calloused and a pale white scar bisected his knuckles. It was a working man's hand with a firm clasp. And it belonged to a man who wouldn't hurt anyone in his care, horse or human.

Mel stared at their joined hands and her stomach tingled in an almost-forgotten way. Then she pulled her hand away. "I planned to get a coffee and snack at the café before heading out to the ranch. Beth picked up Skylar from school." Her words came out in a nervous rush.

"Why don't we get that coffee and snack together? I can drive you out to the ranch. I'm looking forward to showing you the route I picked out for the children's trail ride. I want to get your opinion on it along with some of the ideas I've had for the obstacle courses. Afterward, my mom could likely drive you and Skylar back to town. Her quilting group is meeting at Ruby's Place for dinner at five. There's no sense using your vehicle if you don't have to." Cole's tone was hesitant as if he expected Mel to say no. "My mom has a booster seat in her car for Paisley, which Skylar could use."

"Sounds good." Although Mel's new job had given her both stability and a regular full-time paycheck, she was still getting back on her feet financially. Gas was expensive and she didn't walk everywhere she could only because of exercise.

Cole held the café door open for Mel and turned to greet Kristi, the Bluebunch's owner, who was writing desserts of the day on a chalkboard by the display counter.

"Hey stranger." Kristi gave him an exuberant hug. Her long brown ponytail bounced under a baker's net, and her jeans and T-shirt were covered by a red apron trimmed with white piping. "I've missed you in the café, and when I was out at the ranch for the Sunflower Sisterhood meeting, your mom said you were working in the barn. Not avoiding me, are you?"

Cole hugged Kristi back. "Of course not, but you know me. Footloose and fancy-free." He laughed and moved away but not before giving her a teasing smile and pat on the arm.

"Aren't you in High Valley to stay this time?" Kristi swatted his arm.

"Who knows." Cole laughed again. "But

I'll always come back for your coffee and huckleberry pie."

"Don't let your mom hear you say that." Kristi darted a glance at Mel and rolled her eyes.

"Never." Cole made a zipping gesture across his mouth and grinned.

"Joy Carter makes the best pies in town." Kristi turned to Mel. "I'm an amateur compared to her."

Mel inhaled the nutty scent of fresh ground coffee and stared at the mouthwatering array of baked goods in a glass display case. What was with that flicker of what might be jealousy? Cole's manner with Kristi was easy, like she was a sister or cousin. He wouldn't act like that if they'd ever dated, would he?

It was none of Mel's business. She mentally shook herself. And besides, even if there had once been something important between Cole and the pretty café owner, it wasn't relevant. Mel didn't want to date Cole. Although she was finally in a place to consider dating again, and despite that unexpected tingle of attraction whenever they were together, "footloose and fancy-free" Cole was the last man she'd choose.

He might no longer be riding rodeo, but he was still the walking, talking embodiment of instability.

She shivered as Cole continued to joke with Kristi. Mel would never risk her heart on a man like Cole again, or let herself care about someone whose family owned a ranch either. She ordered a Bluebunch blend latte and fudge brownie bar and followed Cole across the busy café to the table Kristi indicated.

Almost thirty years later, losing her childhood ranch still cut deep. Not only the house and rolling fields that had belonged to her family back to her dad's grandparents' time, but gentle Clover too, the pony her parents had given her for Christmas six months before her dad died.

She could still picture the red "Foreclosure" notice nailed to the pasture fence as her mom had driven them along the dust-choked driveway for the last time. While her two younger sisters had cried most of the way to the city, Mel had stared stony-faced out the passenger-side window at the drought-stricken fields. If she'd let herself cry, she might never have stopped. But she remembered exactly how she'd felt and despite only being nine, she'd vowed to never put herself in a position to feel that way again.

COLE LED PRINCESS, a brown horse with a white star on her forehead, and the calmest mount at the Tall Grass Ranch, out of the barn to where Mel waited. She sat atop the rail fence talking to Bandit. After he'd opened up to Mel, they'd talked about ordinary things at the café and during the drive back to the ranch—favorite movies, music, Skylar and Mel's new job. Once they'd arrived here, and after Mel had greeted Skylar, who was helping Cole's mom and thirteen-year-old Ellie with a sewing project, Mel had been all business.

They'd walked the route for the children's trail ride along a grassy path edging nearby fields. They'd also made a good start on the children's obstacle course, ready for Skylar and Paisley to add their ideas another day. Thanks to Mel, cowboy challenge activities had begun to take shape. "What do you think about those white-striped barrels?

Are they too far apart?" He gestured to the three they'd set up in a circle near the fence.

"Maybe." Mel looked where he pointed. "But the kids will be on ponies so maybe not. I'll add it to the list to ask Paisley to test. You were riding Bandit, and as well as being trained for rodeo, he's like a giant in a doll's house on this course. Even the more difficult obstacles like that jumble of logs are easy for him."

Bandit nickered in welcome as Cole neared the fence with Princess. "You're a smart guy, aren't you?" He rubbed the big horse's black-tipped ears before turning back to Mel. "That idea for a curtain made out of strips of tarp and hung between two poles is genius."

Either Mel already knew something about Western riding or she'd done her homework.

From her perch on the fence, Mel gave him a . small half-smile. "My mom is the original DIY expert. Everything in her house gets reused and I learned from her."

How are you and Bandit getting on?" He glanced from his horse to Mel.

"Okay." Mel's voice was hesitant and she gripped the fence rail. "Bandit's fine. It's me."

"Baby steps, remember?" Cole moved be-

tween Princess and Bandit, and Bandit nuz-
zled his jacket pocket looking for one of the
apples Cole usually kept there. "You don't
have to ride or do anything else that makes
you feel uncomfortable. Not today or any
other day." He could give himself the same
advice, but if he didn't slip out of his comfort zone, he'd stay stuck. Forever the guy
who'd once been a rodeo cowboy as if that
was his only identity.

"I know." Mel rubbed the daisy tattoo on
the inside of her wrist. "But if I don't at least
try to get on the back of a horse today, when
will I?" She leaned closer to Princess and
patted the mare's forehead. "At least there's
nobody else around. If I chicken out, we're
the only ones who'll know."

"Princess won't let anything bad happen
to you." Cole ran a hand along the horse's
neck, and Princess turned her head to gaze
at him as if she understood what he'd said.
"Most of our new riders at Camp Crocus
Hill start with Princess. She has a sixth
sense for when people need a bit of extra
support."

"Horses are smarter than some people."

Mel clambered off the fence and stood beside Princess. "They don't judge either."

"No, they sure don't." That's why Cole was more comfortable around horses these days. "Ellie began riding Princess and although she now has a horse of her own, Ellie still takes Princess out. She says Princess knows all her secrets."

"I had a pony when I was younger than Ellie. Her name was Clover." Mel fingered Princess's saddle horn. "She knew all my secrets too." Her voice was wistful.

Like Bandit knew Cole's secrets. He glanced at the other horse now grazing nearby.

"As long as you're not in the bone orchard, you gotta keep on going, boy. You're brave, I know you are."

The words of that other Mel echoed in Cole's ears. The old cowboy had been around a lot of rodeos and his friend was right. Cole wasn't in the cemetery and he wasn't a coward either. Maybe this new Mel was here to get Cole in gear just as his mentor would have.

"What do you say? Want to try getting on her?" Cole held Princess's lead rope and made his voice sound encouraging. "You'll be used to a lighter English saddle. Smaller too. This Western saddle is designed to be more comfortable when you're riding for hours over rough ground."

Mel moved to Princess's side and shifted from one foot to the other. Then she gathered up the reins in her left hand and grabbed a handful of the hair in Princess's mane before moving to stand near the horse's forelegs.

"That's right. Now turn the stirrup."

"I got it." Mel's expression was determination personified.

Cole nodded and took a step back. She was a pro. Although Mel had asked for his help, she was doing fine. Unlike a less experienced rider, and despite her fear, she was showing Princess who was in charge.

Mel put her left foot in the stirrup and grabbed the saddle horn. Still holding the horse's mane, she pushed herself straight up, hesitated for a brief instant and then swung her right leg over Princess to lower herself into the saddle, her right foot now in the right stirrup.

"I did it." A smile spread across her face

as she held Princess steady, and the horse bobbed her head and blinked.

"You sure did." Also unlike an inexperienced rider, Mel held Princess in check, waiting until the horse was calm before giving any signal to move forward. Cole patted Princess's neck. "Now you're up there, what do you say to a slow walk around the paddock. We'll avoid the obstacles."

Mel glanced at the ground and back at Cole. "I think I could handle that."

"Good." He gathered up Princess's lead rope and the horse took a few steps forward, her hooves dainty on the green spring grass. "Seems like you might have ridden Western before."

Mel nodded as she gripped both the reins and saddle horn, her face white beneath the riding helmet she'd borrowed from the stash they kept in the tack room. "My parents had a ranch in Canada. Alberta. But my dad died suddenly and…" She stopped and glanced at the distant blur of the horizon. "My mom, younger sisters and I moved to Calgary and a few years later my mom remarried. My stepfather has a horse farm in California near San Francisco. At first, it was a weekend place but now he and my mom have retired there. That's where I got into English riding."

"Different from a ranch." For Cole's family, ranching was a way of life, but a weekend horse farm sounded more like an expensive hobby.

"A lot." Mel's voice was strained. "My stepdad is great. I miss him and my mom a lot, and my sisters who live in California too, but I need to be independent. Do you—"

As they neared the corner of the paddock by the horse barn, Blue darted out of the barn to bark a greeting. Mel gasped and squeaked in fright.

"It's okay." Cole patted the dog as Princess eyed the beagle. "Princess and Blue are good friends. Not much spooks either one of them."

"Oh." Mel let out a shaky breath.

"You're doing great." Cole's chest tightened.

"Even if I'm terrified?"

"Especially because you're scared. True bravery is facing your fears." He swallowed the lump in his throat. He needed to follow her example. If his rodeo days were truly done, now that he'd seen his doctor, he had to act on those referrals to the counselor and physical therapist he'd stuffed into his pocket. He also had to think seriously about what he wanted to do with his life from here on.

If Mel could get back in the saddle, he had to do things that were hard for him.

"I want to go again."

Cole glanced at Mel as he led Princess back toward the fence where they'd started. The breeze lifted her reddish-brown hair below her helmet, and behind her glasses her hazel eyes, a mix of green with brown like the dark green of her top, sparkled.

"You got it."

The two of them had helped each other today. Perhaps they could keep on helping each other too—in life as well as in the cowboy challenge. Apart from his family, all of Cole's friends were in the rodeo world. What would his life be like if he had a friend closer to home? A friend like Mel with whom he could be himself?

CHAPTER FIVE

"FROM WHAT COLE told me, the two of you are making great progress on the cowboy challenge event." On the first Saturday afternoon in June, Beth patted earth around the sunflower seeds she was planting in Mel's small garden. With Skylar's help, Mel had dug the garden in the backyard of the cozy remodeled bungalow she'd rented on a tree-lined street several blocks from downtown High Valley.

"It's more Cole than me." Mel scattered the last of the cucumber seeds an inch deep in the bed next to the sunflowers. "I helped him plan and map out the trail-riding and obstacle courses, but Cole's building most of the obstacles. He's also organizing horse-drawn wagon rides and the cutting competition."

"Don't be so modest." Beth grinned, sat back on her heels and brushed dirt off her gardening gloves. "From what I heard you're the one who came up with the idea for those wagon rides and a lot of the obstacles too. And who suggested fixing up the original cookhouse so visitors can see how cowboys cooked and ate together a long time ago?"

"Me." Mel grinned back and viewed her new garden with pride. Along with cucumbers and sunflowers, they'd planted peas, squash, corn, potatoes and tomatoes. "To be honest I'm glad we're here gardening while the guys are cleaning and painting that cookhouse."

Beth got to her feet as Joy came around the side of Mel's house from filling a watering can at the outdoor faucet. "It's good for Zach, Cole and Bryce to spend time together on something other than ranch work, and Joy and I needed 'girl' time."

"We did." Joy came across the grass to join them. "Your house is so cute, Mel. I've always liked white clapboard and those blue shutters and flower boxes on the front windows are adorable. This garden looks great too."

"My mom loves to garden and she taught me, but until now I've lived in apartments so had balcony containers." Mel took the watering can and moistened the soil. "When my landlord, Shane, said he was fine with me digging up this patch of grass to make a small garden I was thrilled."

"Shane's just joined my pickleball club. He was talking to a bunch of us after last week's lesson and mentioned how grateful he is to have such a good tenant." Joy plucked a stray leaf out of the sunflower patch. "This garden will be fun for Skylar too."

"Pretty much everything here is fun for her." Mel glanced at Joy and then Beth. "It's great to see her so happy and a lot of that is because of you two, along with Ellie and Paisley. Before, Skylar would likely have wanted to stay home with me this afternoon but she couldn't wait to go bowling with Ellie and Paisley."

"You look as if you're happy here too." Joy gathered up the empty seed packets, several garden forks and put them in the red wheelbarrow Mel had bought at a neighbor's garage sale.

"I am. It's good to be working on the event with Cole, and I love riding Princess." And with Cole's support and gentle Princess, Mel had begun to reclaim what had once been an important part of her life.

"Good for you." Joy's smile was motherly. "The whole town's talking about the cowboy challenge and how you and Cole are getting everyone involved. From Rosa's craft sessions to Kristi baking corn bread and biscuits in the cookhouse, and Rosa's hubby and his dad sharing traditional stories as part of the teepee display, the event's become so much more than cowboys and cowgirls. That's because of you." She eyed Mel from behind the wheelbarrow. "Own it."

"Okay." Mel's face heated. She needed to take credit for her achievements. For too long, she'd stayed in the shadows because her ex had occupied the limelight as if it was his right. She stood and stretched. The knee she'd hurt in the accident still bothered her when she knelt or sat too long. "It's teamwork but thanks for reminding me I'm part of that team."

"Sometimes I need that reminder too. It's kind of what the Sunflower Sisterhood is all about." Joy pushed the wheelbarrow toward the small shed at the end of the yard and

Mel and Beth followed her. "Unlike Beth and Rosa, I've never been in business. Apart from a high school job in a grocery store, I've only ever worked on the ranch. Now I'm a widow long before I expected, it's as if the biggest part of me is missing." Her expression clouded. "I'm still figuring out how to be more independent."

"You're doing a fantastic job." Beth gave her mother-in-law a firm hug. "Before moving here and marrying Zach, I'd only ever worked for big corporations. Having my own financial consulting business is new too. Rosa's one of my role models. She started Medicine Wheel Crafters from her kitchen table and now she's running her own gallery and selling to other galleries and collectors around the world."

As Mel helped Beth and Joy organize the tools in the shed, her heart swelled. The job offer at Healing Paws had been too good to pass up. She'd also been determined to be independent and not rely on her family so much. But when she'd moved from California and left her mom, stepdad and two younger sisters behind, she'd also felt alone.

Isolated. But now, she had new friends to go along with her new life.

"Sorry, what did you say?" She closed the shed door and turned to Joy.

"Before we pick up the girls from bowling, we have a present for you." Joy's blue eyes twinkled. "And Rosa's here to deliver it." She waved at the other woman who walked toward them along the path at the side of Mel's house.

"A present?" Mel's mouth dropped open. "It's not my birthday or any other special day."

"Some days you have to look harder, but most are special in one way or another. Let's go over to the patio." Joy walked back across the lawn to the small patio outside Mel's back door, where Rosa joined them. Four blue-and-white-striped canvas chairs sat around a glass table shaded by a matching blue-and-white umbrella. Mel had bought the set at the same garage sale as the wheelbarrow from a couple who were downsizing.

"I'd have been here earlier to help with the garden but I was short-staffed at the gallery. Here." Rosa handed a green paper gift bag tied with raffia ribbon to Mel. "It's a welcome-to-town present from all three of us."

Mel sat in a chair between Rosa and Joy with Beth across from her, untied the ribbon, pulled out cream tissue paper and unfolded it. "A dream catcher." A white hoop encircled an intricate center web dotted with gleaming green beads. Wispy white feathers hung from the bottom of the rim. "It's beautiful. A work of art." The backs of her eyes burned.

"I made it especially for you." Rosa pointed to the beads. "The green represents growth and moving forward. The white is for healing and a fresh start, while the feathers are a reminder of the power of intuition."

"Rosa gave Ellie a dream catcher for her birthday last year, and she also made a large one for Zach and me to mark our wedding." Beth touched one of the feathers.

"And Rosa gave me one soon after I lost my Dennis." Joy's voice quavered.

"I learned how to make dream catchers from my mother, who learned how to make them from her mother. Like all my crafts, dream catchers come from my heart. However, when I make one with a particular person in mind, it comes with a bit of extra love." Rosa paused. "It also comes with a wish from all of us that from now on you have more good dreams than bad."

Mel nodded as emotion clogged her throat. None of these women knew about any of the events, large or small, that had made her who she was and led her here. Yet, with this gift, they'd grasped the most important part of her and why she was in High Valley. They'd offered her their friendship too, along with unconditional caring and support.

"I don't know what to say." She swallowed hard.

"You don't need to say anything." On Mel's left, Joy squeezed Mel's hand.

With her free hand, Mel stroked one of the dream catcher's wispy feathers.

Healing. Intuition. Moving forward. A fresh start.

What would happen if Mel not only trusted herself but let herself trust other people again too?

For years, she'd focused on surviving. Now it was time to instead focus on living.

"Why do I have to lead Luna in a walk around the barrels?" Paisley stood at her pony's head and eyed Cole. "Why can't I ride her and run around them instead?"

"Because neither Luna nor you are barrel racing. It's an obstacle course. Besides, you need to teach Luna the pattern first." While he'd thought it would be a great idea to get Paisley and Skylar involved in helping with the cowboy challenge, now Cole wasn't so sure. When he wasn't keeping an eye on Skylar, who darted here, there and everywhere, he was answering his niece's endless stream of questions.

"It's boring." Paisley stuck out her bottom lip.

Skylar looked up at Cole, her blue eyes wide. "When can I ride Luna?"

"When your mom says so." Cole wiped a hand across his hot face. Looking after a couple of kids was harder than rounding up cattle or cutting hay. How had his folks managed with five children?

"I started riding Luna when I was three." Paisley's expression was smug.

"Only with me, your dad or Zach watching you and because it kept you out of trouble." Cole nodded at Skylar. "Most kids start around the age of six."

"I'm almost seven." Skylar nodded back.

"I'm still bored." Paisley led Luna around the barrels, following the pattern Cole had cut out of yellow construction paper and placed on the ground, weighted with stones.

"Out of boredom comes creativity." Mel joined them and gave Cole a brief smile over Skylar's head.

"My dad says stuff like that too." Paisley made an annoyed face. "Usually when he won't let me watch TV or use his tablet."

"Kids should spend a good chunk of time outside instead of in front of a screen." Cole took another piece of construction paper and gave it to Skylar. "Want to help by making more arrows? You and Paisley can use them for a new pattern around the poles and barrels. The marker and scissors are in that blue plastic storage box by the fence."

"Sure." Skylar grinned, and Cole's stomach twisted as she jogged off toward the fence. The only time he'd thought he might like a family one day, his ex-girlfriend, Ashley, had broken things off and said he wasn't husband or dad material. So he'd set that dream aside and tried to pretend it'd never existed.

"Thanks for watching Skylar while I took that call." Mel tucked her phone into the back pocket of her jeans.

"Everything all right?" In faded denim overalls, a white T-shirt and boots, with her hair pulled back in a messy ponytail, Mel looked like any other ranch worker. She wasn't, though. Cole's heartbeat kicked up a notch as the warm breeze feathered the loose hair at her temples, and she raised a hand to tighten her thick brown ponytail.

"Yes, it's fine." She took her glasses from the bib pocket of her overalls and slid them onto her nose. "The call was from a client. Mrs. Shevchenko's dog had surgery last week and I saw Pixie for her first physical therapy appointment on Friday. Mrs. Shevchenko needed some advice." Mel shaded her eyes against the sun. More freckles dotted her nose and face like tiny kisses.

"You're on call on a Sunday afternoon?"

"Not officially, but Mrs. Shevchenko was worried about Pixie so I gave her my cell number. She's a widow and all alone. Pixie is her family." Mel gathered up the pages Cole had printed out with more ideas for the obstacle course and put them back in a plastic folder.

"Nina Shevchenko is great. She and her husband owned a convenience store in town. When I was little, she gave me chocolate-covered raisins when I came in with my mom. She hired me to work Fridays after school and Saturdays as soon as I was old enough." Apart from his parents, kindly Mrs. Shevchenko had been one of the few adults in Cole's life who'd seen something more in him beyond the troublemaker he pretended to be.

"When I told Mrs. Shevchenko I was here at the ranch, she asked about you." Mel patted Princess, who'd ambled across the pasture to greet her. "Now you're back in town, I'm sure she'd like it if you dropped by."

Like his mom and Mel, Mrs. Shevchenko would see through any bravado. "Maybe we could drop by and visit her together?" Cole picked up the lasso he'd used to show Skylar and Paisley how to rope the wooden rocking horse that doubled for a steer he'd set up beyond the barrels. If Mel came with him, he could avoid talking about himself.

"Sure. I planned to drop by her house

after work on Thursday this week anyway." Mel studied Cole as he fiddled with the rope. "I got the impression she cares a lot about you. Why do you want to avoid her?"

"I'm not." With a flick of his wrist, Cole let the lasso fly and it landed by a fence post.

"Really?" Mel grinned. "If you're not avoiding Mrs. Shevchenko, I'm not avoiding riding any other horse but Princess anywhere except around this small pasture. I'm also not avoiding letting Skylar ride Paisley's pony even though Luna is the calmest, gentlest pony anywhere." She gestured to where Skylar stood cutting out pieces of yellow construction paper by the fence as Paisley led the sturdy brown-and-white pony in a figure-eight pattern around the barrels.

"I guess." Cole stared at his boots and hoped the brim of his hat hid his face.

"So?" Mel moved closer and put a finger under his chin, making him look at her. "I'm tired of avoiding because I'm scared. What about you?"

Her face was so close Cole could see the gold and green flecks in her hazel eyes. And behind her cute glasses, the expression in those eyes wasn't judging or accusatory.

Rather, it was compassionate, as if she understood him deep in his soul. "Maybe I'm avoiding but it's not because I'm scared."

"I don't believe you." Mel glanced at Skylar and Paisley again. "I'm a mom. It gives me a special lie-detecting ability. I believe you can do the work to change your life. Have you followed up on the physical therapist and counselor referrals to make those appointments?"

"No, but I'm planning to." He tried to sound firm. Mel's gentle teasing made him want to be the man she believed he could be.

"I don't doubt that." She gave him a mock glare and tweaked his chin again.

Cole sobered as his face warmed and he adjusted his hat. Even though he'd only known Mel a few weeks, he had feelings for her. They weren't maternal, sisterly or even solely friendly. They were the kind of feelings that could grow into something special and loving. "Okay. You're right. I'll call the physical therapy clinic and counselor's office as soon as they open tomorrow morning and make those appointments."

"Good." Mel took a step back as if she'd only realized how close together they stood.

"I have tomorrow off work. Since Princess will be needed for riding lessons, could I take Daisy-May out in the morning on that trail along the creek? I remember it from when we walked the first part of the children's trail ride. It's a level, easy path and not too far from the barn."

"You don't need to go on your own. I'll come with you." At the ranch house, the dinner bell rang from the porch, the clang echoing through the pasture.

"I'm sure you're busy." Mel stuck one hand in the side pocket of her overallss and took out her keys. "I should get going. Your mom invited Skylar and me to stay for supper but—"

"Please stay. I want you to." With his free hand, the one not still holding the rope, Cole touched Mel's bare arm. Like her face, her arm was dotted with pale freckles too, and her skin was soft and warm. "I also want to go riding with you. I'll ask one of the ranch hands to cover for me for a few hours tomorrow morning."

"Really?" Mel stared at Cole's hand on her arm and her expression held both vulnerability and caution.

"Really." He slid his hand along her arm to cover her hand. "I like spending time with you. We're friends."

"Me too. And yes, friends." Her hand quivered in his before she took it away. "I need to help Skylar get cleaned up for supper."

"Of course." Cole fumbled with the lasso rope again.

Friendship was precious. Mel was too. He couldn't risk her friendship by asking for— or expecting—anything more.

CHAPTER SIX

THE GRASSY TRAIL led beyond the pasture by the horse barn in a gentle slope toward the creek. Meandering through the middle of the Tall Grass Ranch, Cole had told Mel the creek had its origins in a glacial river high in the distant Rocky Mountains. Here, though, it was placid, its pale blue water still in the June morning. Insects skimmed across the water, and a light wind rustled the prairie grasses that lined the high banks where daisies and pink wild roses bloomed.

"The creek doesn't have a name?" Mel reined Daisy-May, the good-natured Appaloosa, to a halt on a level area by a sandy bank.

"Maybe on a map somewhere but not as far as I ever heard." Riding Bandit, Cole stopped beside her. The powerful horse snorted and pawed the ground. "This is where my brothers and I used to fish. Swim, too, in July and August once the water got warm enough."

"What about your sister?" Mel shifted in the saddle on Daisy-May's back. Although the roofs of the ranch's outbuildings were still visible over the crest of a low hill, this was the farthest she'd ridden since her accident. Before stopping here, she'd held Daisy-May to a slow walk and had kept the conversation on easy, ordinary topics. Cole had followed her lead.

"She grew up on the ranch too, but Molly's always had different interests at heart." Cole patted Bandit's neck. "Not that she didn't work as hard as the rest of us, but whenever she had free time she wanted to hang out with her friends in town. She likes horses, sure, but she's more one for reading, movies and listening to music. In high school she also played volleyball so had a lot of practices."

"Whereas I was always out riding." Mel loosened her grip on Daisy-May's reins. The horse was as calm as the slow-moving creek. Unless Mel gave her a signal, Daisy-May wasn't going anywhere. "I tried to convince myself I didn't miss riding, but I did.

Without your help, I might never have gotten back on a horse again."

"I didn't do much." Cole patted Bandit again. "Even without me, living in a place like High Valley, I bet you'd have been riding again in no time. Once a horse person, always a horse person." Beneath the shadow of his hat, his blue eyes twinkled, and he gave her a teasing grin.

"I was crazy about horses but then…" Mel needed to talk to someone, and Cole was the obvious choice. "You want to ride on?" Maybe it would be easier to talk if she didn't have to look at him.

"Sure." Cole's smile widened. "Bandit gets bored stopping in one place."

Like his rider. Mel's stomach knotted. *Friends.* Cole had said they were friends and friends talked about important things with each other.

"You were saying you were crazy about horses?" Cole turned Bandit in a wide circle away from the creek and horses and riders meandered along a shaded path that wound through a stand of pine trees, the wind lifting the boughs in a gentle whisper.

"Always. I was the girl whose bedroom

was plastered with horse posters. As a teenager, I had a part-time job working at a local stable. Horses weren't a hobby. They were my life." Until they weren't. "My mom and stepdad didn't push me to compete. I wanted to. When I made the national team, it was the happiest day of my life."

"And then?" Cole's voice was low, muffled by the creak of saddle leather and clop of their horses' hooves.

"I got involved with Stephen. My ex-husband. He was on the team too and when we started dating, things happened fast. I fell head over heels for him and it was like a whirlwind." And she'd only recognized the warning signs that they weren't right for each other too late. She drew in a breath as they came out of the trees into pastureland again, still keeping the horses to a steady walk. "I thought he loved me."

"He didn't?" Cole drew Bandit closer to Mel and Daisy-May so the two horses walked side by side. From where she sat atop Daisy-May, Mel's left knee brushed Cole's right, making her skin tingle beneath her jeans.

"Not really. Stephen only loved the idea of me. I thought, we both did, that I had a chance of being a national show jumping champion. A chance of rising in the ranks in the world standings too. But after I had the accident, he…" She gulped, and Daisy-May turned her head as if to ask what was wrong. "We'd only been married a few months. Stephen said we should get married because it would help both of us focus. He wasn't the person I thought he was. What I didn't know then is he'd cheated on me, before and after the wedding. My pregnancy with Skylar wasn't planned. When I found out I was pregnant, he didn't want me or her."

"That…" Cole pressed his lips together and his expression darkened. "Is he still competing?"

Mel shook her head. "He started coaching soon after Skylar was born. He's done well. He got his champions all right. They just weren't me."

"Was he there when you had your accident?"

Mel nodded, memories of that day rolling over her. "My coach was called away to a meeting, but Stephen told me I could handle the jump no problem. I had to show the horse who was the boss. Even though something felt off and I'd only ridden that horse once before, I trusted Stephen. I was the newest member of the team and I didn't want to look bad in front of everyone." Instead, it had been extra bad because her husband had let her down in front of their friends and teammates. His voice was soft but accusing as he uttered the words that still haunted her.

Not good enough. A disappointment. Shouldn't have made the team.

"I finally said I'd try the jump, but as I was getting ready to do it there was a loud noise. Later, I found out it was a truck backfiring. The last thing I remember is the horse rearing and then I was hurtling through the air as the ground rushed up to meet me."

And when she'd woken up in the hospital, her life had changed forever.

"I'm so sorry." Cole's voice was gruff. He stopped Bandit and then when Mel stopped Daisy-May too he reached across both horses to take Mel's hand. "Stephen didn't deserve you *or* Skylar."

"No, he didn't." Mel straightened in her saddle. "It took me a lot of talking in therapy to understand that, but I got there in the end. The thing is, he always made me feel whatever I did wasn't good enough when he wasn't good enough himself. Forget about the horse world, he was never good enough as a man."

"He couldn't have been." Cole held Bandit's reins in one hand and clasped Mel's hand tight. "You and Skylar are better off without him."

"We are." Cole's hand in hers was warm and comforting. His touch made her feel safe too, in a way Mel hadn't in a long time. "I should have realized what Stephen was like and never married him in the first place. Instead, I got taken in because he was handsome, charming and said all the right things. He seemed to want the same things I did too. I still feel stupid."

"Not stupid. Never." Cole shook his head. "There was one blessing, though. Without Stephen, you'd never have had Skylar."

"True and I don't want to consider what my life would be like without her." Mel's heart swelled. "Yesterday when I pushed you to call and make those appointments with the counselor and physical therapist, I realized my fear of riding didn't just stem from the accident. It came from the memories of Stephen too. By not riding, I was still letting him have power over me."

"And now?" Cole's hat had slipped back on his head, and sunlight glinted on his light hair. Despite his superficial resemblance to Stephen, Cole was a far better man than her ex. A man who'd earn her trust and respect through his actions rather than expect it as his right.

"Any influence he had over me is gone for good. And he all but abandoned Skylar before she was even a year old. He's only seen her a handful of times in the last two years. He pays child support, but being a dad is about much more than money." Mel took her hand away from Cole's and eased Daisy-May into a walk again and then a slow trot, her heart pounding in time with the two-beat rhythm. "My mom and stepdad helped me go back to school to train as a physical therapist, and they helped with Skylar too. I'm grateful, but now I'm independent. I have a new job I love and a whole new life here."

"Good for you." Cole's smile warmed Mel as much as his hand had.

Although he and Bandit could outrun the

more sedate Daisy-May with ease, they let her set the pace. And Cole's expression and demeanor told her he was listening to her and what she had to say was important and meaningful. He also seemed to like her for who she was and didn't want her to be anyone else.

As the horses came over a low rise, Mel stared at the vast landscape that opened up in front of them, an expanse of grassland extending until the rim of prairie met the sky. The panorama was both endless and, like her life, filled with potential.

"No matter what Stephen does or doesn't do, I owe it to myself and Skylar to make the best life I can." Mel wasn't ready to canter or gallop but this slow trot felt as good, maybe even better, than winning one of those rosettes and shiny trophies she'd once set her sights on.

Like riding horses, the biggest and most important part of life wasn't about winning competitions. It was about figuring out who you were and what you valued.

Right here, right now, Mel felt at one with the horse and herself in a way she hadn't since childhood. She grinned as she glanced at Cole and Bandit and let Daisy-May pick up the pace, the horse's hooves thudding on the grassland. For this moment, she felt at one with this man too. The kind she and Skylar might need in their lives beyond friendship.

"Good job, Skylar." Joy patted the girl's shoulder as Skylar held up a horse finger puppet made out of yarn. "You too, Paisley." She admired her granddaughter's wool sheep.

Skylar took black, white and brown wool from one of the craft boxes in the middle of Joy's dining room table. When Bryce had asked if Joy could look after his kids when school let out early on the last day, she'd told Mel that Skylar was welcome to join them. "My mom says I can take riding lessons here this summer."

"That's great." Joy helped Skylar find the pattern to make a dog. Cam, Paisley's younger brother, had soon gotten bored with crafts and was playing with his toy cars under the table.

"I helped Skylar convince her mom." Paisley's voice was serious. "So did Uncle Cole.

He said since we were both helping with the cowboy challenge, Skylar needed to learn about horses and how to ride them. He also said it was like having a backyard swimming pool but not knowing how to swim."

"My mom laughed when he said that. Cole makes her laugh a lot," Skylar said. "I wish he was my uncle. He's nice and fun too."

"Do you have any aunts or uncles?" Joy helped Paisley put together the pieces of the portable wooden puppet theater her own children had played with. Dennis had made it for them for Christmas one year and Joy had helped him. Each night after the children were in bed, she and her husband had worked together in the small woodworking shop he'd set up in the basement. A room Joy still couldn't make herself go into. Dennis's tools were where he'd left them, as if he'd only popped out for a moment instead of being gone forever.

Her kids had loved this toy theater and now the next generation of Carter children enjoyed it too. Joy fingered the red velvet curtain she'd sewn from an end of material she'd once used to make cushions and stared out the dining room window. A soft rain pattered on her garden and the sky was a muted gray. The years had gone too fast. Like Dennis, Paul, her oldest, was gone too. Joy swallowed the lump in her throat.

"No uncles, but I have two aunts." Skylar's voice pulled Joy back to the present. "They're my mom's younger sisters. They live in California near where I used to live." As she glued the pieces of wool onto white construction paper to make a beagle dog, Skylar stuck her tongue between her lips in concentration. "My dad's never around, so I bet Cole would make a good dad, too."

"If he could ever maybe stick around in one place. That's what I heard *my* dad say to Uncle Zach." Paisley hung up the stage curtain along the small tension rod Dennis had fashioned.

"You shouldn't listen in on adult conversations. If you accidentally overhear something, you shouldn't repeat it either." Joy tried to make her voice firm.

"I wasn't listening in. I was standing right there." Paisley's tone was earnest. "My dad and Uncle Zach were helping me tack up Luna."

"Oh." Joy made a mental note to have a

word with her sons and the ranch hands too. Children were like sponges, listening, observing and copying everything the adults in their lives did. In this case, there was no harm done. Everybody knew Cole didn't like to be tied down, but what if Bryce and Zach had been talking about something else?

"Uncle Cole likes Skylar's mom a lot. I know because of how he looks at her when she's doing other stuff." Paisley set her sheep puppet in the middle of the herd of red cows she and Joy had made the last time they'd played with this theater.

"Yeah, he does." Skylar borrowed a miniature green tractor from five-year-old Cam and pushed it along the edge of the tablecloth. "I think my mom likes Cole too. She fusses with her hair whenever we're around him, and she never does that. It's weird because she always says it doesn't matter what you look like but who you are inside that's important."

"Your mom is right." But it didn't hurt to fix yourself up, if only to make yourself feel good. That's why Joy had asked Beth to help her choose some new clothes last year. She wanted to avoid falling into any ruts, so no drab colors and garments that no longer fit. Dennis had liked her to look nice too.

"You said your dad isn't around a lot?" Mel had never mentioned her ex-husband, and Joy hadn't asked. However, since Skylar had mentioned him, and if Cole and Mel liked each other, it wouldn't hurt to try to help them spend time together. Whenever Mel was due at the ranch, Cole came into the house a few minutes beforehand and changed his work shirt and jeans for clean ones he'd started leaving on the rail in the utility room. Her son had never done anything like that before, so together with Mel fixing her hair, it had to be a sign.

"Nope." Skylar pushed Cam's tractor again and made a finger puppet horse gallop alongside. "My dad travels a lot so he's usually too busy to see me. When my mom got the job here, she said it didn't matter where we lived because my dad could see me as easily here as in California. Even when my dad makes plans to see me, most of the time he cancels. I miss him, but it's no biggie." The edge of hurt in Skylar's voice told Joy it was a biggie indeed.

"You can share my dad if I can share your

mom." Paisley came around the table and squeezed onto the chair beside Skylar. "I miss my mom." Paisley's voice wobbled.

"We all miss your mom, but she'll always be in our hearts." Joy hugged her grand-daughter. Like Paul and Dennis, Bryce's wife, Alison, had also been taken too soon. Although Bryce had come out of the fog of grief that had enveloped him after Alison's death, it was still too soon for him to think about dating, let alone remarrying. "You'll always have a lot of people who love you. All of you." She included Cam and Skylar in another hug.

"My mom says it's good to share so yeah, you can share in her too." Skylar's voice was muffled. "I'd still like Cole for a dad, though. He listens to me. He also makes me feel special."

"You *are* special, and don't let anyone ever tell you otherwise." Joy drew in a breath and made herself speak calmly. No wonder Mel never talked about her ex. Even if a marriage didn't work out, the children should be a pri-ority for both parents. While Mel was a de-voted mom, a man who didn't value Skylar enough to make sure he was part of her life wasn't worthy of being called a father at all.

Joy had seen how Cole looked at Mel, too. Mel looked at him similarly. It also wasn't only Joy who'd noticed. Rosa and Beth had both remarked on it as well. The town's Fourth of July celebration was coming up. With help from Skylar and the Sunflower Sisterhood, it could be the perfect time for Mel and Cole to get to know each other better. They had nothing to lose and maybe everything to gain.

And while Cole had never made a secret of not wanting to settle down, if the right woman came along, he might change his mind. She glanced at Cam, who'd taken his cars and some of the puppets to the race-track he'd set up in a corner of the dining room. He was too little, but the girls were old enough to keep a secret.

"I have an idea to do something nice for Cole and Skylar's mom." Joy sat in another chair beside Skylar and Paisley, still squeezed together. "But I'll need your help to make it happen."

CHAPTER SEVEN

"Thanks for giving me a ride into town." Waving away Cole's offer to help her, Mel opened the pickup truck's door and hopped to the sidewalk in front of the Bluebunch Café.

"Not a problem. Picking up those extra barrels for the obstacle course is the reason you're late." From the driver's seat, Cole tipped his hat and glanced at Skylar behind him. "Me and Skylar will have fun with Zach and Ellie. Stay as long as you want. I'd give you a ride home too if my mom and Beth hadn't already offered." He gestured to the café, where a "Closed" sign hung from the window. "Enjoy making those crafts."

"Thanks." Mel glanced at Skylar too. "I'll be back in time to read you a story before bed. Be good and do what Cole and Zach say."

"I'm always good." Skylar gave her a cheeky grin.

"Love you." Mel leaned into the truck, kissed Skylar's forehead and patted Blue. The dog was buckled in beside Skylar in her booster seat, which Mel had moved from her car to Cole's truck when he'd picked her up after work.

"Go." Cole made a shooing motion. "We'll be fine. Zach texted me. He and Ellie have got the movie set up and popcorn ready to pop."

"I'm going." Mel settled her bag more firmly on her shoulder and moved toward the café. Only a month ago, and apart from work and things at Skylar's school, her calendar had been empty. Now, between the cowboy challenge and Sunflower Sisterhood, her time outside work had filled up.

She rang the bell beside the café door and the buzzer echoed. The Bluebunch had closed an hour ago and Kristi was hosting tonight's Sunflower Sisterhood meeting here. They'd be making decorations for the town's late summer Sunflower Festival. Mel didn't like being late, but the work on the cowboy challenge had taken longer than she'd expected. There hadn't been time for her to pick up her own car or do anything more than grab a fast-food dinner with Cole and Skylar when they got back to town.

"Here you are." After Kristi unlocked the café door, she wrapped Mel in a hug. "A few others were running late too so you haven't missed anything. We were only chatting and setting out the craft supplies."

"And eating the amazing poppy seed cake Kristi made and wanted us to try before she adds it to the Bluebunch menu." Rosa's voice reached Mel, followed by a burst of female laughter. "We saved some for you."

"That sounds great. I missed dessert," Mel called back as she tucked her hair behind her ears. While she usually wore it pulled up in a bun or ponytail, before leaving work she'd taken out the elastic to leave her hair loose so it curled in soft waves on her shoulders. Although Cole hadn't said anything, he'd smiled when she'd come out of Healing Paws after also changing from her scrubs into a denim skirt and floral-patterned vest top she'd paired with the pale yellow cardigan her mom had sent for her birthday a few days ago. Since she was so new here, she hadn't mentioned her birthday, but thanks to a small celebration with Skylar, it still felt like a special marker. She had a new town, new job and a whole new life.

"Surprise." Joy stood up from behind a table that held a cake with lit candles. A birthday banner was fixed to one wall and pink, white and green balloons hung on strings from the ceiling.

"What?" Mel glanced back at Kristi and around the group of women. Rosa and Beth clapped and joined the others in singing "Happy Birthday." "Today's not my birthday."

"We're a few days late, I know, but we wanted to celebrate you." Joy came around the table and hugged Mel. "Skylar told me because of moving you hadn't had a party, so I talked to Beth and we thought we'd have a belated celebration now."

"Wow. Thank you." Mel sat in the chair Rosa held out and admired the cake decorated with pink roses, green leaves and "Happy Birthday, Mel" written in green on the white icing.

"Cole helped us." Beth grinned as she passed Mel a cake knife. "Without you having to pick up those barrels, we wouldn't have had enough time to help Kristi get set up after closing the café."

"Cole didn't say a word. Skylar didn't either."

"We swore them to secrecy," Beth said. "Aren't you going to make a wish before you blow out the candles?" She stilled Mel's hand on the knife.

"I guess so." Mel's thoughts swirled. What could she wish for that she didn't already have? The lit candles shone around the circle of smiling faces. She took a deep breath, wished and blew out all the candles at once. She'd wished that she and Skylar would always be as happy here as they were right now.

Mel began to cut the birthday cake, and the knife slid through the creamy chocolate layers. "I thought you already had cake." She turned to Rosa. "You said something about poppy seed?"

"Oh, we did." Rosa patted her stomach beneath an orange dress with embroidered appliqué flowers. Like her striking whale-shaped silver pendant, the dress was undoubtedly one of Rosa's own designs. "Some of us missed dinner so that poppy seed cake was helping her with work. Kristi wanted us to taste-test it. She packed away several pieces for you and Skylar to have at home." Rosa's rich laughter rolled out again. "This birthday cake is for fun."

Mel's vision misted. "I don't know what to say."

"You don't have to say anything." Kate's smile was kind. "The Sunflower Sisterhood supports each other, not only our community. However, speaking of our community…" She pinged a fork against her glass of soda. "I'm happy to report that the voluntary summer placements for our seventh and eighth graders with special needs are going from strength to strength. With Mel's help, two of my students are starting at Healing Paws next week."

"That's great news." Joy's smile warmed Mel inside and out. Beth had told Mel that Joy's oldest son, Paul, had died in his early twenties owing to complications from cystic fibrosis. As such, support for youth with special needs was close to Joy's heart.

"My Lily has a placement at Tawny Ridge." Kate smiled at Lauren, the Carter cousin who, with her husband, ran the stud farm. "I don't know how I got such a horse-crazy daughter. It must be Ellie's influence."

"Ellie's coming along so well with her riding. She's entering three local horse shows this summer. I've told her it's to get experience, but she wants to win ribbons too." Lauren leaned toward Mel. "I saw your Skylar's name on my class list. I'm teaching the beginner's group that starts at Tall Grass Ranch this coming Saturday."

"Yes." Mel balanced a mouthful of cake on her fork. "Skylar's excited about those lessons."

"And you're not?" Lauren looked curious.

"She'll love riding, and I feel silly admitting I have reservations but…" Mel put her forkful of cake back on her plate. "She's my little girl. I want to keep her safe."

"I get it." Lauren made a sympathetic face. "I'm a mom too, and even though I teach, the first time my son got on his pony I wanted to haul him right off again. Although she didn't show it at the time, Beth told me she was the same with Ellie."

Beth nodded her agreement. "Even now, each time I see Ellie ride, and although I'm proud of her, I still worry about her getting hurt. Zach helped me realize how much she needs her independence. I'm trying not to let myself think about how I'll worry when she's old enough to drive a car."

Thank goodness learning to drive was much too far away for Mel to worry about with Skylar.

"No matter how old your kids are, the worry never stops." Joy glanced at Rosa, who, like her, had adult children. "I had a lot of sleepless nights worrying about the mischief Cole got into as a boy before he finally grew out of that phase. But that worry was nothing compared to what I went through each time Cole was in a rodeo ring. I didn't breathe easy until he'd text me to say he was fine. When that text didn't come…" Joy shook her head. "Now I want to keep him home safe, but I can't. He's long grown and makes his own choices. All I can do is hope he makes the right ones."

"And help him along when you can." Rosa exchanged another look with Joy that Mel couldn't read. "Now if all of you have finished eating cake, at least for now…" Everyone laughed as Rosa clapped her hands. "Tonight's meeting is to start making decorations for the town's Sunflower Festival. We've also had a last-minute request from the Fourth of July committee for extra red, white and blue rosette centerpieces to decorate the table with the raffle prizes." Rosa turned back to Mel. "Most of us are on both committees."

"That rosette centerpiece request came from me." Soft-spoken Diana reached under the table for a box filled with clear jars. Near Mel's age, she ran what had once been her grandparents' ranch and was a single mom too. "Between the Fourth of July, Sunflower Festival and haying season, I'm busy from dawn to dusk."

"That's a change how?" Joy raised her eyebrows, and all the women laughed, Mel included. "Whether we're running a ranch, our own business or working for someone else, we're always busy. Some of us are caring for children or elderly relatives too. As long as I choose it myself, I'd rather be busy than bored. I don't want to have time to brood on my troubles. Besides, with friends like all of you, those troubles are shared and, if not halved, more bearable."

"Hear, hear." Lauren raised her soda glass in a toast.

"Let's get going, ladies." Rosa clapped her hands again. "Rosette centerpieces with

Diana, and sunflower wreath-making with Joy."

"Making wreaths is tricky," Beth said to Mel as they moved toward the rosette centerpiece table. "Thanks to Joy and Rosa, I'm better at crafts than I used to be, but I've never made rosettes or used a glue gun before either." She looked doubtfully at the red, white and blue card, gold and blue glitter paper, wood sticks and hot glue guns laid out on a table by the café's front window.

"Neither of them are hard." Mel sat beside Beth and took pieces of paper for both of them. "I love crafts. I can help you if you want."

"That would be great. I have this fear of somehow gluing my fingers together." Beth laughed as she picked up the instruction sheet Diana had left at each place.

"I've made rosettes lots of times for Skylar's birthday parties." Mel passed Beth a pair of scissors. "Let's start by cutting out stars for the centers. There's a template so they're all the same size. See?" She held it up.

"I can do that." Beth's anxious expression eased.

"I bet you can pleat paper into a fan shape

too. You must have done it when you were in elementary school."

"I did." Beth chuckled.

"Using a hot glue gun is the trickiest part but you'll soon get the hang of it." Mel grabbed one for when they needed it.

"Like this?" Beth cut out a star from gold glitter paper.

"Perfect." Mel nodded as she arranged the different colors of scrapbook paper into the pattern shown on the instructions. "Once we pleat the paper and stick it together, we'll glue your star to the center. Then add the wooden stick as a stem, put it in a glass jar and we're done."

"Got it." Beth grinned as she cut out a second star.

Mel took another template and pair of scissors to cut out stars too, surrounded by the hum of friendly conversation and light laughter.

She'd always prided herself on being independent and rarely asking for help but maybe she'd missed out. If she took the risk of letting herself rely on these new friends, and with Cole too, could she and Skylar get something in return she'd never let herself imagine?

THREE HOURS LATER, Cole parked his truck in front of Mel's white-clapboard bungalow on a quiet residential street several blocks from the center of High Valley. "Don't forget your backpack or the horse picture you drew with Ellie." He turned off the engine and got out of the vehicle to help unbuckle Skylar from her booster seat in the back.

"I won't." Skylar gave him a gap-toothed grin. In the last week, she'd lost one of her front baby teeth, but, if anything, the temporary empty space in her mouth made her even cuter. "Thanks for looking after me tonight."

"I was glad to." Cole held out his arms, and Skylar wrapped hers around his neck as he lifted her out of the high truck to the ground. "I had fun." He unbuckled Blue's vehicle harness and grabbed the dog's leash before closing the truck's rear door.

"Me too." Skylar looked at Cole, the trust and affection in her expression tugging on a piece of his heart he'd thought was gone forever. "If you want, you could come over for dinner one night? My mom's a great cook."

"I'm sure she is, but she might not like you inviting me or anyone else." Cole straightened his cowboy hat and followed Skylar up the walk to Mel's front door, Blue pulling on the leash.

"Mom doesn't mind. She says I can have a friend over whenever I want. You're a friend, aren't you?" Skylar stopped in front of the white-framed screen door. Inside, a wreath of artificial greenery and white and yellow daisies hung from the half-open interior door, matching the colors of the real flowers in the boxes on either side of the front windows.

"Well, yes, I'm a friend, but your mom has to plan to have dinner guests." Cole took off his hat and pushed the bell beside the screen. This house was one of the older ones in town, built in the 1920s. Last year, the new owner, who also owned the Squirrel Tail Ranch, had renovated it, intending to use it as an in-town retirement property. For now, he was renting it out, and Mel said she'd been lucky to find it when she and Skylar were looking for a place to live.

"There you are. Right on time." Mel opened the door and gestured them inside. "I got home a few minutes ago. I have cookies and—do you not want to come in?" Mel hugged Skylar as Cole stepped back out onto the small porch. "I made a pitcher of lemonade earlier."

"Of course he wants to come in. Blue too." Skylar grabbed Cole's hand and tugged it. "He's coming for dinner too. You said I could invite anybody I wanted."

"I did but—"

"I need to check the horses before bed. I should head home." Cole spoke at the same time as Mel, and Skylar glanced between them.

"Of course." Mel looked at Cole's hand in Skylar's. "It's late. You need to have a snack and get to bed, young lady." Although Mel's voice was bright, it had an edge of what might have been disappointment. "Skylar was right to invite you. You're welcome to come for a meal. What about supper the day after the Fourth of July? I'll be off work."

"I don't have camp that day either so I can help Mom make you something." Skylar squeezed Cole's hand before dropping it. "Do you like chocolate cake? My mom makes the best chocolate cake ever."

"Skylar." In the soft light of the front hall, Mel's cheeks reddened. "I'm sure Cole's mom makes chocolate cake too. Mrs. Joy is a wonderful cook and baker."

She was, but although his mom had made lots of cakes for Cole, a woman and her daughter never had. "That sounds great. And chocolate cake's my favorite. As for checking the horses, if you're okay with Blue coming in too, a half hour later won't make a difference."

"Yeah, my mom wants Blue too. She loves dogs. I wanna show you the puzzle I'm doing and after you can help put me to bed." Skylar dragged Cole fully into the hall, and the screen door closed behind him. "He's great at reading stories."

"You read to Skylar?" Mel closed the inner door as Cole pulled his boots off.

"He read me lots of stories. Some of mine and Ellie's when she was my age too." Skylar dropped her backpack on a hall chair and unclipped Blue's leash. "We read together."

"Only a few books." Cole's face got warm. "Skylar said she was supposed to practice her reading this summer, so we read together after watching the movie. Zach and Ellie were cleaning up the kitchen and they didn't need extra help."

"Thank you for that. Reading with Skylar. I always put books in her backpack." Mel stopped at the entrance to the living room and gestured toward a tan-colored sofa topped with blue and white scatter cushions.

"No problem." Like Skylar, Cole had struggled with reading and his oldest brother, Paul, had helped. While Paul couldn't take away the sting of the other kids who'd called Cole names, he'd sat and read with him for months. After school, in a break from doing barn chores and at bedtime. Finally, what had been a jumble of incomprehensible letters began to make sense. Too embarrassed to admit he had a problem, Cole had never asked for Paul's assistance. But in his quiet manner, Paul had understood what Cole couldn't say. And in the years since his brother's death, Cole missed and thought of him every day. Maybe helping Skylar was a way of paying Paul's kindness forward.

"Well, I really appreciate it." Mel's smile warmed Cole. "I'll get you a glass of lemonade while Skylar shows you the puzzle we're working on."

"Then I want Cole to read me a chapter in the book about the pony club Paisley lent me. He makes excellent horse noises." Skylar tugged him farther into the living room. "See? The puzzle's right here."

Cole tossed his hat on the sofa and sat beside it as Skylar pointed to the half-completed puzzle on the wooden coffee table.

"It's San Francisco. Where I used to live." Skylar waved the box showing Cole the picture of the completed jigsaw. "My grandma sent it to Mommy and me."

Cole reached for Blue to settle him on the floor. "Do you need some help? I used to like doing puzzles."

"Sure." Skylar clambered up on Cole's other side and gave him a container with the extra puzzle pieces. "My grandma took me for a ride on a trolley car once." She pointed to the picture.

"This one might be the missing piece for it." Cole held up a piece in red, gold and white. "What do you think?"

"It fits." Skylar squealed as she slotted the piece into place and then rummaged in the container as Cole glanced around the room.

Although Mel was renting this house and had lived here less than eight weeks, it was a well-loved home.

A framed watercolor painting of farm fields in summer hung on the wall between two armchairs covered in the same fabric as the sofa. A brown teddy bear with a pink scarf around its neck occupied a child-size rocking chair by the gas fireplace. Several library books were stacked on an end table below a goose-necked reading lamp. And a pair of adult-size green knitted slippers sat by one of the chairs as if Mel had just taken them off.

"I found another one." Skylar added a puzzle piece to complete the Golden Gate Bridge.

"Down, boy." Cole grabbed Blue's collar as the puppy made a move to join them on the sofa. "You're doing great, kiddo." He helped Skylar find more puzzle pieces to slot into place as she chattered about Ellie, Paisley and Paisley's pony.

Unlike him, Mel hadn't hesitated. She'd jumped feetfirst into making a new life. She'd thought about what she wanted, and what was best for Skylar, and she was determined to get it.

Had he ever thought about what he truly wanted? When he was a kid, all he ever wanted was to ride rodeo, but he'd never thought about a life beyond it. He'd also gone along with the crowd because it was easy. Maybe at heart he wasn't the good-time guy and joker and troublemaker he'd always thought he was. But if he wasn't, who was he?

Skylar giggled and nudged Cole's arm, pulling him out of his thoughts. "Blue wants to help us."

"He's still a puppy so he's looking for something to chew, more likely. Here you go." He dug in his jacket pocket for a toy bone and gave it to Blue.

He'd never let himself imagine having a home like this one or, except fleetingly with Ashley, a family either. But what if instead of living up to a reputation that maybe nowadays was only in his own head, he tried to change it? He stroked Blue's floppy ears. With a woman like Mel and girl like Skylar in his life, he could be a better man. Cole admitted he wasn't making the most of his life. That had to change, starting now.

As Mel came into the room, he got to his feet and took a tray with glasses of lemonade and a plate of cookies from her.

"You two are doing great with that puzzle." Mel beamed at him and patted Skylar's shoulder.

Skylar beamed too and, as she offered him an oatmeal raisin cookie, Cole's heart swelled.

Maybe he'd also been too quick to discount having a wife and family of his own but he could change that too.

This house didn't only feel like a home. It was one where *he* felt at home in a way he never had before. It was the kind of place—and family—that could welcome and nurture him and where he could imagine himself staying for a while. Maybe even forever.

CHAPTER EIGHT

"STAND STILL FOR ME, PLEASE. You're wriggling like you have ants in your pants." Mel laughed as she applied sunscreen to Skylar's face and neck. "I know you're excited but—"

"Course I'm excited. It's our first Fourth of July in Montana." Skylar gave another skip, and Mel almost dropped the tube of sunscreen. "Mrs. Joy and Paisley told me all about it. After the parade, there's games, a picnic, a pie-eating contest and fireworks tonight in the field by the baseball diamond."

"There you go. All done." Mel adjusted Skylar's pink bucket hat. "It's going to be a hot and sunny day so make sure you keep your hat on. We'll have to look for shady spots too." Mel put the sunscreen back in her bag and stepped farther under the awning in front of Healing Paws. After a Fourth of July pancake breakfast at the American Legion Hall, she and Skylar had stopped at the clinic to help add finishing touches to the parade float entry. Something was up with Skylar, though, and it was more than Fourth of July excitement.

"Today's already a scorcher." From her seat in a folding lawn chair by the clinic's front door, Carla fanned herself.

"Are you sure you're okay?" Mel dug in a cooler for a bottle of water and passed it over. Only a week from her due date, Carla looked as if she was going to give birth at any moment.

"I'm fine. I've told this baby he or she needs to hold on because I can't miss Fourth of July." Although Carla laughed, her husband, who'd also helped with the parade float, looked worried. "Just in case, my mom's looking after our other two today. They're watching the parade near her house so the little one can still have his nap."

"I remember those days." Joy, who'd arrived with Paisley, Cam and Beth, greeted the group. "Although I thought the baby and toddler years would never end, they did, all too soon." Beneath a white cowboy hat, Joy's expression was pensive.

"Where's Cole?" Skylar hugged Joy and linked arms with Paisley.

"He's been working on the ranch's parade entry, but he should be by soon." Joy took a pair of aviator sunglasses out of her bag and put them on. "I asked him to meet us here."

Skylar and Paisley giggled and whispered together behind their hands.

"What's the big secret?" Mel stared at the girls.

"Nothing." Skylar giggled again.

"They're excited, that's all." Joy turned to talk to Beth and several women from the Sunflower Sisterhood who were already chatting with Carla.

Mel shaded her eyes and glanced along High Valley Avenue. The parade route began at the far end of the street that bisected High Valley in two. Middle school kids rode scooters and bikes from one side of it to the other, distributing candy, coupons and other small items donated by local businesses.

"Sorry I'm late." Cole appeared at Mel's side in his usual boots and a pair of crisp jeans with a short-sleeved blue chambray shirt that showed his muscled forearms. "I needed to help Zach get the horses hitched up to the wagon and—what is it, you two?" He crouched to Skylar and Paisley's level as the girls' giggles grew louder. "Do I have mustard or something on my face?"

"No." Skylar shook her head. "I saved a space for you to watch the parade. Right here beside my mom." She pushed Cole closer to Mel.

"Skylar." Mel tugged on the edge of her daughter's hat to get her attention. "There's plenty of space for all of us to watch the parade. Cole can stand where he wants."

"But it's nice and shady here. You don't want him to get sunburned, do you?" Skylar stood at Cole's right, giggling more. "After the parade, I signed him up to play games with us."

"What a wonderful idea." Joy patted Skylar's shoulder. "You're a kind girl to include Cole so he's not on his own."

"How could I be on my own? The whole family's here." Cole's face was as red as Mel's must be. "Besides, as soon as the parade ends I should get back for chores."

"I already arranged with one of the ranch hands to do the chores in the horse barn too so you can enjoy the whole day." Joy beamed at Mel and Cole. "They take it in turns to work on holidays, so it's fine." She took a quick peek up the street. "Is that the high school marching band, I hear? We take a lot of pride in our small-town charm." She spoke into Mel's ear as the band noise increased. "High Valley is known for its July Fourth parade. The whole town gets involved. Wait until you see the ranch float. Ellie's helping Zach drive our old farm wagon, and she decorated it along with Kate's daughter, Lily, so…"

As Joy talked on, Mel snuck a glance at Cole. He stared straight ahead, absorbed by the antics of a clown waving to the onlookers and handing out red, white and blue balloons.

Skylar, never subtle at the best of times, couldn't have been more obvious. Knowing Paisley, she was likely in on whatever crazy plan Skylar had come up with too.

Cole took blue and red balloons from the clown and gave them to Skylar and Paisley. "You want one too?" He grinned at Mel, the smile, as always, transforming his face, making him look more boyish.

"Of course." She took a red balloon by its

string and grinned back. She'd tried to suppress her attraction to Cole, but if only for today, what might happen if she let down her guard and let herself have fun?

"Look at the band, Mommy." Skylar waved her balloon as the high school marching band wearing matching blue polo shirts, red shorts and white sneakers led the parade playing "The Star-Spangled Banner."

Mel nodded and waved at a dark-haired girl playing the cymbals who lived down the street from them.

Standing in front, Skylar and Paisley oohed and aahed at each parade float as it passed.

"Squirrel Tail Ranch went all out." Cole pointed to a pickup truck pulling a low-bed trailer with a miniature red barn draped in American flags and bunting. Teenagers dressed in sparkly denim shorts and matching flag-patterned tops walked alongside handing out bags of popcorn, light-up flags, flashing wands and glow bracelets all featuring the ranch's logo.

"When Shane came by to fix a leaky tap at my place, he told me the Fourth of July is his favorite holiday." She grinned at the older man as he tossed a patriotic beach ball to Joy who caught it with a laugh. "He brought a bunch of those giveaways for Skylar. We're lucky to have such a good landlord."

As the Healing Paws float came into view, Mel, Cole and everyone else cheered. Mel's boss, the clinic's owner, and her husband sat in a decorated wagon surrounded by their three basset hounds. Two of the dogs wore American flag bandannas and the other sported a stars and stripes bow tie.

"Blue's such a goof. I'd never get him into a costume riding on a float." Cole chuckled. "He'd see a bird or squirrel and be off, taking any costume off too."

"Never say never." Mel took photos with her phone. Her boss had asked to get some pictures for clinic advertising. "He's still a puppy. Dogs mature."

"Maybe." Cole shook his head as several clowns on stilts and riding small motorbikes wove behind the Healing Paws float. Following them was the library's parade entry with children dressed as characters from American history, including Abraham Lincoln, George Washington, Uncle Sam and the Statue of Liberty.

The crowd roared their appreciation for the volunteer fire department as Cole's younger brother, Bryce, tooted the air horn and waved from the driver's seat of a shiny red fire truck.

"Here's the Tall Grass Ranch float now." Joy touched Mel's arm as Paisley and Skylar squealed in excitement. "Cole and Zach gave that wagon a fresh coat of red paint. Doesn't it look good?"

"It sure does." Mel admired the vintage wooden farm wagon with the Tall Grass Ranch logo in black lettering on the sides and pulled by two draft horses. Zach sat on the high driver's seat holding the horses' reins as beside him Ellie waved to the crowd.

"My grandpa remembered his dad using that wagon for ranch work. It's a big part of our family's history," Cole said.

"Now it's making new history. Ellie and her friends did a great job of decorating. That flag is awesome." Mel pointed to the wagon covered in hay bales topped with a giant American flag, and red, white and blue ribbons matching ones braided into the horses' manes and tails.

"We finished the flag fifteen minutes

before the parade started." Cole's expression was wry. "The base is made of chicken wire with balled-up tissue paper glued on. When a chunk of paper fell off, we had to re-glue it. Talk about a last-minute panic. Ellie was almost in tears, Zach tried to calm her down and I was gluing paper and making sure nothing spooked the horses."

"Even with all the parade noise, those Clydesdales are so composed." Mel marveled at the well-matched team.

"I trained Autumn and Clay from when they were colts." There was a note of quiet pride in Cole's voice as he studied the brown horses, a breed used for heavy farming work. "I'd trust both of them with my life."

"I'm sure they trust you too." Mel's voice caught. Horses had good people sense and recognized leadership.

"That's the goal." Hidden by the crowd, Cole's warm hand reached for one of Mel's.

Beneath the brim of his cowboy hat, he half turned and gave her a slow and intimate smile. Along with Cole's gentle pressure on her hand, Mel's insides went soft and warm. The day had hardly begun, but it was already the best one she'd had in a long time.

COLE COULDN'T REMEMBER when he'd last taken an entire day off work, even the Fourth of July. When he wasn't riding in a rodeo, he'd been traveling, practicing or doing something else related to his job.

Cole also couldn't remember when he'd last had this much fun. He'd had plenty of excitement, sure, because riding rodeo was an almost nonstop adrenaline rush. But neither riding rodeo nor any of the dates he'd ever gone on had been as enjoyable as today. "Are you ready?" Standing shoulder to shoulder with Mel, he bent down to check the scarf that tied his right leg to her left.

"As ready as I'll ever be." Her eyes twinkled before she glanced at Skylar and Paisley, who'd also paired up for the three-legged race. "What about you, girls?"

Skylar gave her mom a thumbs-up.

At the far end of the line of competitors, the mayor blew a whistle and they were off.

"We should have practiced beforehand." Mel hobbled at Cole's side as the two of them tried to stay upright. "Look at Skylar and Paisley go."

"They're closer in height." Cole guided them around a hillock in the middle of the town's soccer field. "Even if we come in last, it's still fun."

Mel stumbled to one side and laughed as Cole held her upright. "We are last."

"Still better than the balloon toss." Cole eyed the finish line by the chain-link fence. "I still think that balloon was defective. I'd hardly let go of it when it popped."

"Focus." Mel's tone was playful. "Otherwise we'll be disqualified here too. You'll wish you'd chosen another partner."

"Never." He grinned and nudged her elbow. "Besides, we still have a chance to catch up."

"Whoa." Mel swerved to avoid two small boys who veered in front of them.

"Hang on." Cole tried to keep Mel from falling but instead she tumbled to the grass, pulling him with her. "You okay?"

"Sure." She was laughing so hard she could hardly speak as she pushed her glasses farther up her nose. "We've truly lost now."

"It doesn't matter." They'd landed face-to-face, and Cole stared at Mel, mesmerized by her smile and the expression in her eyes as they met his. "Mel, I…" He moved closer and took her hand. "Today, with you, is the best and—"

"You missed seeing me and Paisley win." Skylar appeared by their side. "Why are you still lying on the grass?"

"Just catching our breath." Mel's face turned a pretty shade of pink. "Good for you for winning."

"We're doing the scavenger hunt next but it's only for kids." Skylar still stared at them curiously.

"Maybe the three-legged race should only have been for kids too." Mel laughed again as she untied the scarf binding her to Cole, and he helped her up.

"I still enjoyed it." Cole brushed grass off his jeans, missing Mel's closeness.

"I did too." As Paisley and Skylar ran off to join the scavenger hunt, Mel held Cole's gaze and, as she smiled at him, he felt like he'd been handed the biggest prize of all.

"Want to get ice cream?" He cleared his throat, all of a sudden aware they were the only two left on the field.

"Sounds good."

As they walked toward the ice cream van on the edge of the town's Meadowlark Park,

Cole nodded and smiled at people he'd gone to school with or who'd been friends of his folks.

"Hey, Cole. Good to see you back. Let's catch up soon."

He waved to a guy he'd played football with his junior year who was setting up a game of watermelon bowling.

"Cole Carter?"

As they joined the line for the ice cream truck, a white-haired man in a casual checked shirt and chinos turned to speak to him.

"Yep, that's me. Nice to see you, Reverend Ralph." Apart from his white hair, the minister at the Carter family's church when Cole was a child looked much the same.

"You too, Cole. I was sorry to hear about your dad. He was sure a fine man."

"He was." As Cole introduced Mel, his heart squeezed. Could he ever be the kind of man his dad had been? "I didn't know you still lived in town."

"I don't. My wife and I retired to Missoula but we came back for July Fourth. Brought our oldest daughter and her family with us." He indicated a small group chatting with the fire chief. "I've thought of you a lot over the years."

"In what way?" Cole stiffened. Here came the reminder of his past and in front of Mel too.

"Remember when the decorated tree caught fire at that Christmas Eve service? What grade were you in? Second, maybe third?"

"Second." Cole spoke through gritted teeth. "I shouldn't have been fooling around. I didn't mean to—"

"It was an accident and turns out you did me a favor." With a kind smile, Reverend Ralph waved away Cole's apology. "Everybody pulling together to put out the fire and rescue the service brought the church community together. Besides…" He gave an embarrassed laugh. "If it was anyone's fault it was mine. I should never have put an advent wreath with lighted candles so close to excited Sunday school kids. I learned my lesson for sure."

"I bet you did." Mel joined in the joke.

"Nothing wrong with being a lively kid. My youngest grandson, Zeke, is the same. You folks enjoy your day." Reverend Ralph patted Cole's shoulder in a fatherly way before taking his ice cream and rejoining his family. As Cole and Mel ordered ice cream and then walked into the park, Reverend Ralph's words echoed in Cole's head.

All these years, people had talked about that Christmas tree going up in flames and he'd blamed himself. Instead, it had been a simple childhood mishap that had even had a good outcome. Maybe he was the only one who'd been hard on himself, unnecessarily as it turned out.

He finished the last bit of chocolate ice cream and crunched on the cone. At his side, under a sprawling shade tree, Mel ate her own ice cream. She'd chosen local blueberry and now her lips were tinged blue.

"Your mom looks like she's having fun." Mel's voice broke into Cole's thoughts and she gestured to where his mom sat at a picnic table drinking a soda across from a gray-haired man whose back was to them. "Isn't that Shane Gallagher, whose house I'm renting?" She finished her ice cream and wiped her mouth with a napkin, taking away the blue stain.

"Looks like him." Cole dragged his gaze away from Mel and how her rose-pink lips curved into a sweet smile that made his knees go weak, to look where she'd pointed.

Although his mom was only talking to the guy, it was weird seeing her with a man who wasn't his dad. "Since he and his son bought the Squirrel Tail Ranch, Shane's gotten involved in a lot of things around town."

"From how he's leaning in to talk to her, I suspect he'd like to get involved with your mom too."

"He's a widower, but no, even if he's interested in Mom, my dad was the only man for her like she was the only woman for him." That's what they'd both always said.

Mel shrugged. "With your dad gone, and you and your brothers and Molly grown up, your mom might be lonely. If she could find happiness with someone else, why not?"

"I guess so but…" Cole watched as Shane gave his mom a hand to help her up from the picnic bench. He didn't drop her hand right away either, but instead held it and leaned closer to her again. Cole had held Mel's hand during the parade, but that was different, wasn't it?

"Don't stare. You'll embarrass them." Mel cupped Cole's chin and turned his head to face her. "Shane seems like a nice man. Because your mom talked and drank a soda with him doesn't mean she's going to marry him. Beth said it's good to see Joy getting out again. I expect your mom will miss your dad for the rest of her life, but that doesn't mean she has to hide out at the ranch."

"I want her to get out. All of us kids have been encouraging her to get involved in things again." However, Cole had never considered that one of those things might be another man.

"I understand it's strange to see your mom with someone else. I felt like that too when my mom started dating my stepfather. Mom will never forget my real dad, but Pete makes her happy. I want that for her. For them both."

"I want my mom to be happy too." Like Cole wanted his own happiness if he could let himself believe in it.

"Look." Mel pointed to Kristi from the Bluebunch Café, who stood near the bandstand beyond the picnic area and held a microphone. "She must be going to announce the raffle prizes. Skylar and I bought a bunch of tickets. I never win anything, but it's raising money for a great cause. Your mom told me the town's been fundraising for the past three years to get enough money to make the arena lobby and ice surfaces more accessible for wheelchair users and others with mobility issues."

"I bought tickets too." No matter where he was, Cole always supported any efforts that helped people with disabilities. Like being Skylar's reading buddy, it was something else he could do in Paul's memory. "The only thing I ever won in a raffle was a beer mug with a flower bouquet made out of beef jerky."

"That's nice, I guess." Mel laughed.

"It was okay at the time." Cole laughed too. "I still have the mug with the name of the prize's sponsor around somewhere. I ate the jerky as a snack as I traveled from rodeos in Texas to Arizona."

They watched and clapped as Kristi announced prizes and, with aid from the mayor, drew the names of winners.

Beth, Skylar, Paisley, Cam and Ellie joined Mel and Cole, the children holding cones of pink cotton candy.

"Are you doing okay, kiddo?" Mel adjusted Skylar's hat so it better shaded her face.

Skylar nodded and her eyes were bright

with excitement. "Today is the most fun ever. I won an awesome prize at the scavenger hunt too. See?" She dug in a pocket of her shorts to show Mel a pink eraser shaped like a rabbit and a toy store gift certificate.

"That's fantastic." Mel grinned and gestured to Skylar's cloud of cotton candy. "I don't want to know how much sugar you've had today but the Fourth of July only comes once a year."

"And I'll brush my teeth extra good tonight." Skylar giggled and leaned into Mel to give her a hug.

Seeing the love the two of them shared made Cole's heart warm. What would it be like to belong with others and be part of a family that way?

"Next up is this gourmet picnic basket donated by the Bluebunch Café." His mom, now giving Kristi a hand, displayed the basket that had been set out with the other raffle prizes on a long table covered with a red tablecloth.

"Kristi showed me that basket earlier. I told Zach I wanted to win it because it includes so many of my favorite treats," Beth said as they all sat on the grass. "Those rosette centerpieces Mel and I made look good." She pointed to the table behind Kristi and Joy.

"If *you* win the basket, you can share it with my mom." Skylar gave Cole a meaningful look.

Mel shook her head at her daughter and made a severe face, but Cole suppressed a laugh. As the day had gone on, Skylar and Paisley had done everything possible to push Mel and him together. Little did they know he wanted to spend time with Mel anyway.

"We have a winner." Kristi's voice boomed through the loudspeaker. "Cole Carter. Come on up and have your picture taken for the newspaper. Are you going to share that basket with the lovely lady you're sitting with? Why don't you and Melissa McNeil come up together? Mel's new in town, so let's show her a big High Valley welcome."

"Shall we?" Cole's face warmed as he held out a hand to Mel.

"Skylar? Paisley?" As everyone nearby clapped, waved and cheered, Mel ignored Cole's outstretched hand and stared at the two girls.

"We didn't have anything to do with it. Honest," Skylar said.

"Go on." Beth clapped too and gestured to where Kristi stood, now holding the basket in her arms, the mayor and Cole's mom beside her waving and cheering. "I'm happy to keep an eye on Skylar so you and Cole can eat together and watch the fireworks too."

"Go on, Mom." Skylar beamed. "I want to stay with Mrs. Beth and Ellie."

Mel scrambled to her feet and finally took Cole's hand. "We've been set up."

"We have." Her hand felt as good in his as it always did but Mel looked as awkward as Cole must. Choosing to spend time together was one thing but being dragged into the town spotlight was more than a little uncomfortable. "I know how these things work. Smile and play along for now. Everyone wants a show, so let's give them one," Cole whispered in Mel's ear as she straightened her clothing.

"Okay." Mel's face was bright red.

Skylar looked innocent, as did Paisley, with matching sweet-as-pie smiles. Maybe they *didn't* have anything to do with this setup, but the raffle draw had been fixed.

Sooner or later, he'd get to the bottom of who had done that fixing. He'd always been able to take a joke but this one had gone too far because it had upset Mel.

Cole squeezed Mel's hand and gave her a reassuring smile as, still holding hands, they jogged toward his mom, Kristi and the mayor. "It's meant in fun and we're friends. Besides, I'd like to eat with you."

"Yes, you're right. I'd like to share the picnic with you too." Mel shrugged as if shedding off her embarrassment.

But as Cole took the basket from Kristi, and they posed together for the newspaper photographer, Cole with one arm around Mel's shoulders, being together like this felt a lot more than friendly.

Instead, it felt like they were a couple. Maybe even one that was meant to be.

CHAPTER NINE

Sitting together on a plaid picnic blanket in the town park, Cole passed Mel half of the last piece of Kristi's poppy seed cake, which they'd decided to share.

Kristi was a nice woman and around Cole's age. When she'd first moved to town, his mom had made a point of introducing them. Although they'd met up for coffee, there was no romantic spark, and he and Kristi had slipped into an easy friendship instead.

Now he'd slipped into friendship with Mel too but, with plenty of romantic sparks, there was nothing easy about it. Spending the day with her had been enjoyable, but he hadn't needed his mom and others to make such obvious attempts to set them up. Before things went any further, he needed to take a stand.

"I'll talk to my mom. She needs to stop interfering. We're adults and can manage our own lives."

"I'll talk to Skylar too." Mel stretched her legs out on the blanket. She'd kicked off her sandals earlier and her toenails were painted with white-and-yellow daisies, echoing the small tattoo on the inside of her wrist. "I've never known her to lie to me, but I can't shake the feeling she wasn't telling me the whole truth about this picnic basket."

"My mom means well."

He glanced at Mel tidying up the picnic things. Before today, every town event he'd attended as an adult he'd been at a loose end. With Mel and Skylar, he'd been a real part of things. "No matter what my mom, Skylar, Paisley or anyone else tried to do, I liked spending time with you today. I like spending time at the ranch too but today was... different." The word he'd almost used was *perfect*. However, he'd stopped himself because maybe it hadn't been as good for Mel as for him.

"I liked spending time with you today too." Mel set the wicker basket aside. "So did Skylar." She glanced across the park where her daughter sat in a big group in between Paisley and Cam with Cole's mom, Beth, his brothers and various Carter cousins and other extended family. "The fire-works will start soon. I should—"

"Stay here and watch the fireworks with me? Skylar's fine. My mom or Beth will let you know if there's a problem." Cole breathed in the familiar scent of hot dogs, grilled hamburgers, fries, popcorn and smoke from the barbecue near the park's picnic shelter.

"Okay." Mel sat back on the blanket and gave him a half smile. "As a single mom, I'm used to always being 'on call.'"

Although Cole didn't have to answer to anyone, since returning to the ranch he'd felt needed in a manner that was new. On the rodeo circuit, lots of people had depended on him but it was about work. Nobody had needed him—or cared about him—in the way Skylar and Mel needed and cared for each other. "Skylar's lucky to have you."

"I'm lucky to have her too." Mel wriggled her toes in the grass. Her toes were as cute as the rest of her.

"What's with the daisies?" He gestured to her feet and wrist.

"I got the tattoo after Skylar was born. In some traditions, daisies symbolize child-birth and motherhood. They can also mean a new beginning. I'd lost my riding career. My husband wasn't around and I had a new baby and was trying to figure out how to be a mom. This tattoo reminded me that life still held hope and good things, even if I didn't know what they'd be."

"That's special." And Cole liked getting to know parts of Mel she might not share with everyone else.

Mel nodded. "Daisies mean a lot to me. They grew wild on my family's ranch in Alberta. My dad used to call them a 'noxious weed,' but my mom liked them. My younger sisters and I picked bunches for her every summer." Mel's voice hitched.

Cole moved closer to her on the picnic blanket and covered one of her hands with his. "It sounds as if you loved that ranch."

"I did." Her gaze locked with his. "We lost it a few months after my dad died. There was a drought, the crops failed and since my folks were already close to the financial edge, the bank foreclosed. When we left the ranch for the last time, I promised myself I'd never be in a situation of losing my home again. That's why I became a physical therapist. It's a steady, secure job."

A cloud scudded across the rising moon to plunge the park into shadows. Neither ranching nor riding rodeo could ever be described as a steady, secure job, but Cole had never thought of doing anything else. It wasn't like he had a college degree to fall back on either. "I hear you're doing great at Healing Paws." He swallowed the bitter taste in his mouth.

"Who says?" Mel's expression was both pleased and curious.

"Carla, for one. Also anybody whose animals you've treated." He forced a smile and kept his hand in hers. He couldn't give Mel the safe and secure home she needed. "Small-town life. People talk. Gossip, sure, but a lot of folks here are kind and care about others."

"That's good to hear. I like High Valley. So does Skylar. The school is wonderful and she's making a nice group of friends."

"You think you'll stay?" As the barbecue smoke dissipated, Cole inhaled the sweetness of grass from nearby fields. He'd have recognized that scent blindfolded as specific to High Valley and the ranch—the aroma of home, family and roots.

"Of course." Mel's tone was tinged with astonishment. "I only made such a big move because I wanted to find a place I could call home for a good long time. As soon as I can set aside enough money for a down payment, I want to buy a house here too. Renting is temporary."

The first fireworks lit up the sky in a red, white and blue spiral with an accompanying snap, crackle and boom. When he visited High Valley, Cole bunked in one of the cabins his grandfather had built for the ranch hands. Or, if all the cabins were full, he stayed in the bedroom he and Zach had once shared in the big ranch house. Unlike some cowboys, he'd saved most of the money he'd earned riding rodeo so he had a nice nest egg tucked away. He'd never thought of using it to buy a home of his own, but what if he did? And what if he could share that home with someone like Mel?

"Look." Mel drew in an awed breath. "I didn't expect a small town would have such an elaborate fireworks display." With her free hand, she pointed to the sparklers dancing above them, also in red, white and blue, as children darted around the park, shrieking with happy excitement and waving small American flags.

"Montana's known as Big Sky Country.

We go big in a lot of things around here."
The size of the land, the ranches and people's hearts too. After Ashley had broken things off with him, Cole had kept his
heart safe. Maybe his heart had even gotten smaller because he hadn't let himself
care about anyone or anything apart from
his mom, immediate family and the horses.

But while he hadn't been paying attention,
and in only a short time, Mel and Skylar had
become part of his life and heart too.

"Did you see that, Cole? Look, there's another one. They're so pretty." Skylar's words
tumbled over each other as she skidded to a
stop and sprawled on the blanket in front of
him and Mel as the sky exploded in a panorama of colors and light.

"They sure are." His throat tightened as
she chattered about the fireworks.

"Slow down and take a breath, sweetie.
We can't keep up with you." Mel laughed,
took her hand away from Cole's to smooth
Skylar's flyaway hair and give her a high
five.

"Mrs. Joy said the last firework is always
the biggest. Last year it was red, white and
blue stars in the pattern of our flag." Skylar

twisted her head around to talk to Cole. "I want to share it with you."

He wanted to share it with Skylar too. "Sit between us so you have the best view." He shifted on the blanket to give Skylar space. She nestled beside him. Over Skylar's head, Mel gave him a soft smile. Although Cole hadn't planned it, he was caught up in something with her—and Skylar too.

He couldn't fight it either. Mel reached behind Skylar's back to tuck her hand into Cole's again. Her hand was soft, strong and capable and fit like it belonged there. Like Skylar fit against his shoulder. Just for tonight, he'd let himself feel that new feeling; one of being part of something special and wonderful.

Although he couldn't give Mel and Skylar his whole heart, he could give them part of it. Would that be enough?

JOY PASSED THROUGH the open door of the Camp Crocus Hill office, following Ellie and Lily. The two girls rolled their wheelchairs down the wide asphalt ramp as Joy spotted Beth ahead of them. Last summer, Beth and Ellie had come here to camp, and now they weren't only part of the camp family but part of the Carter family too.

"Have you seen Cole?" Joy caught up with Beth and they both stopped where the ramp forked into two. One paved path led to the main part of the summer camp with the visitor parking area, cabins and dining hall, and the other led to the paddock where campers took horseback riding lessons.

"He was in the small barn with Zach when I was there half an hour ago." Beth gestured to it on the far side of the paddock. "Those horseback riding lessons are so popular we're going to have to hire more staff."

"That's a good problem to have." Joy returned Beth's smile. After some tough years, both the ranch and Camp Crocus Hill were doing well and that was in part thanks to Beth's business expertise.

"It is." Beth and Joy watched as Ellie opened the paddock gate, and she and Lily joined Lauren by several horses that had already been saddled.

"Having so many kids apply for volunteer placements at Camp Crocus Hill is good too. It should also mean we'll be able to hire some of those volunteers as camp counselors when they're older."

"Ellie already has her name on the list. For now, though, she loves helping with the riding lessons. Living here is a dream come true for both of us." Beth's voice caught.

"For me too, having you here. When Molly comes home in a few weeks, the whole family will be together again." Although Joy would never forget the ones who'd been taken too soon, she tried to focus on the family she still had. Compared with many others, she was lucky.

"There's Cole with Ellie and Lily now." Beth pointed to the paddock. "I need to get a move on. I promised Zach I'd help him with the tractor order. I should be able to negotiate a nice discount with that new sales guy."

With a laugh and a wave, Beth jogged along the path leading to the parking area where she'd left her car, and Joy moved toward the paddock. Beth and Zach were a good team. The kind of team Joy and Dennis had been. If only her other kids could have that kind of life partnership too.

She reached the paddock fence and waved at Cole. He usually had breakfast at the ranch house after early chores, but this morning his chair had remained empty. The horses had been cared for as usual so he hadn't overslept. More likely he was avoiding her.

"Mom?" His expression was wary. "I don't usually see you out here at this time of day. Weren't you scheduled to be working in the office?"

"I was but I asked one of the camp counselors to cover for me." Joy studied her son. Shaded by his cowboy hat, his eyes were dark shadowed and his mouth was unsmiling. "You missed breakfast."

"I brought fruit and cereal bars from the cabin and ate in the barn." Cole moved a halter from one hand to the other. "I need to finish up a few things here and get back to the main barn and—"

"I'll help you." Joy opened the paddock gate. "I expect you want to talk to me as much as I want to talk to you. Avoiding issues doesn't make them go away."

"Yeah." Cole's cheeks flushed beneath his sandy beard stubble as they walked to the barn in silence. This smaller barn, painted the same cheery red with white trim as the other ranch buildings, was only used for

Camp Crocus Hill. It was a place to store tack and, if needed, stable the horses used for riding lessons in case of injury or bad weather.

"What do you need me to do?" Joy indicated a wheelbarrow, pitchfork, broom, gloves and line of barn boots by one of the walls. "I'm not dressed for mucking out stalls, but I can sweep or spread fresh straw."

"I've already cleaned the stalls, but you can help with new bedding."

"Fine." Joy replaced her sandals with a pair of boots and drew on a pair of gloves. "What do you want to say to me?" Cole didn't look like Dennis, but like his dad, when something was bothering him, the only way to get it out was to be direct.

Cole heaved a bale of straw toward the nearest stall. "What do you think you were doing pushing me and Mel together yesterday?" He broke open the bale, then grabbed a pitchfork and fluffed the straw. "If I wanted to spend time with her, I would have."

"I only wanted to nudge you two together. Mel and Skylar are good for you." Joy took another fork and began spreading the straw across the textured concrete floor of the stall, bedding it deeply.

"I'm an adult. I can manage my own life." Cole poked at the straw, again avoiding her gaze.

"You can." Joy chose her words with care. Even when your child was an adult, you didn't stop being a parent but you had to go about it differently. "I worry about you. You as good as hide out in the horse barn and from the look of you, you're not sleeping well. Yesterday, you said you were going to head back to the ranch as soon as the parade ended. I wanted you to have some fun."

Cole added more straw to the stall, distributing it evenly from the center to the edges. "I *did* have fun. I didn't need you and the others trying to set me and Mel up. Skylar and Paisley didn't come up with all that by themselves. And the picnic basket? Come on."

"You seemed to enjoy eating the contents of that basket." Joy suppressed a smile. "You and Mel looked like you enjoyed watching the fireworks together too." Seeing the two of them together, and even more when Skylar joined them, they'd seemed like a happy family.

"That's not the point." Cole grabbed a feed bucket, hitting it against the wooden stall door with a dull clang.

"So what *is* the point?" Joy moved to the next stall to spread more straw. "At first, I promised myself I wouldn't interfere but now I have to. You're drifting. I don't want you to be one of those people who can only think about what they did in the past. You did well in rodeo, and I'm proud of you for making a success of it, but now you need to make a new path."

"You think I'm not trying? I'm working on the cowboy challenge. I'm running the horse barn and I'm spending time with Mel and Skylar. What else do you want?"

"I want you to be happy. Yesterday with Mel, you had a light in your eyes I don't think I've ever seen before. It was good." Joy set her pitchfork aside and put an arm around her son's stiff shoulders. "I also want you to find work that's meaningful to you. Not something someone else asks you to do and not ordinary daily chores either. Work where, in some part of it, you can hold your head high because it's something you want to do and you're proud to do it."

"I've been thinking about horse training. Rodeo stock contracting too." The tightness in Cole's shoulders eased a fraction.

"Those are both great ideas." Joy let out a breath. "Whatever you decide, I'll support you. We all will." If Cole found a new sense of purpose, maybe her restless son would finally settle down. "As for Mel and Skylar, while I *do* think they're good for you, I want to be sure *you're* good for them."

"What do you mean?" Cole stepped away from her embrace.

"You're my son and I love you. Always and unconditionally, but..." She paused. "If you want to truly deserve a woman like Mel, you need to step up. She and Skylar need someone who's going to be there for them. Not only for fun times like Fourth of July but for the hard patches too."

"I can be there for hard times." Cole's voice was low.

"I know you can." Joy moved closer to him again. "It's time you let everyone else see what I see in you. If you don't, I fear you'll always regret it." She patted his shoulder.

"I want to try." Cole's words came out in a choked whisper.

"I'm here to help." Joy swallowed a lump of emotion. "Whenever you need a sounding board, you can come to me. Even though you're an independent adult, I'll always be your mom. However, I've said my piece and from now on, I'll try to keep my nose out of your business."

She held out her arms, and Cole walked into them like he'd done as a little boy.

After several long moments, he cleared his throat and grabbed another bale of straw. "You looked friendly with Shane Gallagher yesterday."

"He's sweet. A real gentleman too." Joy's cheeks heated and she busied herself with gathering up scattered tack. Dennis had only been gone a few years and she'd been married to him for more than half her life. It was too soon to be thinking of another man.

"If he asks you out, you should go." Cole leaned on a pitchfork and gave her a teasing grin before he sobered. "If I'm hiding out in the horse barn, maybe you've been hiding out too. Dad wouldn't want that."

"No." Joy hung a trail rein on a metal

hook. "We had so many plans but now your dad's gone and I... You're right. I *have* been hiding out." Joy needed to set an example for Cole and all her kids. Especially when life was tough, you had to go on. She couldn't call out her son for drifting without taking a hard look at herself too. "Shane asked if I wanted to go kayaking with him next week. He and his son are adding kayak rentals at Squirrel Tail."

Cole laughed. "Squirrel Tail isn't a ranch, it's a resort. When I picked up Paisley from that birthday party, you should have seen those manicured lawns. They already offer wildlife safaris and meditation retreats, next thing you know they'll be adding a spa."

"Don't knock it." Joy laughed too. "Beth says it's good to diversify." And maybe not only in business but in life as well. "I've never gone kayaking, but it sounds fun." She also wanted to get to know Shane better. As a friend to start and perhaps something more. He'd lost his wife and she'd lost her husband, and neither of them was in a rush.

"You should go." Cole took a deep breath. "Gotta admit it was strange to see you yesterday with a man who wasn't Dad, but if you want to spend time with Shane, I'm okay with it. I know you don't need my permission but make sure he treats you right."

"I will." Joy suppressed a smile. Shane had mentioned his kids were protective of him too.

"You're old enough to make your own decisions. We both are but...aw heck." This time Cole held out his arms and Joy stepped toward him.

And into a hug that held love, hope and forgiveness. Things Joy needed as much as her son.

CHAPTER TEN

MORE THAN HE'D ever wanted anything before, Cole wanted to prove he was worthy of Mel and Skylar. All day as he'd gone about his ranch work, his mom's words had reverberated in Cole's head. He wanted to step up, and as the saying went, actions were louder than words. He had to show he meant what he said, starting now.

He stood on Mel's front porch and rang the bell, holding Blue's leash and a bunch of flowers with his other hand. "Hey, Skylar." He greeted the little girl as she opened the screen door and bent to pat the dog.

"Come in." Mel appeared behind her daughter. A white apron patterned with yellow daisies covered her jean shorts and a bubblegum-pink T-shirt. Her hair was pulled back in a high ponytail and what appeared to be a blob of chocolate frosting dotted her chin.

"We made you chocolate cake and I

helped." Skylar tugged on Cole's arm before unclipping Blue's leash when he indicated she could. "We're all in the backyard."

"All?" Cole glanced at Mel as he gave her the yellow-and-white daisies mixed with greenery the florist had wrapped in paper. "I didn't know you were having a party."

"We're not. We weren't." Mel put a hand on his arm, and Cole's skin tingled. "But when Mrs. Shevchenko called to ask about her dog, I found out she'd spent the Fourth on her own. She only lost her husband six months ago, so I asked her to join us." She buried her nose in the bouquet of flowers. "These are beautiful. Thank you."

"Mom also invited the lady who lives across the street from us. We met her when we moved in. She gave me a puzzle book and stickers." Skylar whisked Cole through the hall and into the kitchen. "So now it's a party."

"Mrs. Moretti was alone on the Fourth too. She said she knew you. Isn't that nice?" Mel followed them into the kitchen and opened a cabinet door to retrieve a tall vase.

Cole's stomach twisted. He hadn't seen Angela Moretti in years, but she'd worked in the main office at the high school all the

Carter kids had attended. Between the ages of fourteen and seventeen, Cole had spent too much time in that office waiting to see the principal so he'd also seen way too much of Mrs. Moretti. *Nice* undoubtedly wouldn't have been the word she'd have used to describe him.

Mel unwrapped the flowers and filled the vase with water as Skylar went ahead out the back door to the patio at the rear of the house. "I hate the thought of anyone being alone for the holiday. I didn't think you'd mind."

"I don't." Despite that initial sharp stab of disappointment at having to share Mel and Skylar with anyone else. "What *I* think is you're one of the kindest people I've ever known." Mrs. Moretti notwithstanding, this dinner was Cole's chance to redeem his younger self. He smiled and went out the door to greet the other women.

Half an hour later, he'd taken over barbecuing duties, leaving Mel to chat and watch Skylar play with Blue or splash in an inflatable paddling pool.

"That sure smells good." Mrs. Shevchenko appeared at Cole's elbow. She carried a pasta salad in a plastic container and set it on the nearby picnic table. "Between her job and Skylar, Mel works so hard. It's nice to see her relaxing and off her feet. I hope we didn't interfere with a date for you two. Those flowers are sure pretty. Mel showed them to me when I went inside with her so she could point me toward the bathroom."

"Not at all." Cole flipped several burgers on the grill. The flowers were a thank-you for a casual meal between friends and Skylar was always going to be there too. There was nothing "date-like" about it. But did he want to ask Mel on a date? And if he did, would she say yes?

"You always were a good boy at heart." Mrs. Shevchenko patted his arm. "You've turned into a good man too." She darted a glance at Mrs. Moretti.

"I suppose lots of kids act out." As Angela Moretti studied him, Cole straightened his shoulders. He wasn't a teenager expecting a lecture. There was no reason for him to act like one. "Make sure you don't overcook those burgers." Mrs. Moretti shifted her focus to the grill. "My digestion isn't what it used to be and there are few things worse for it than dry, tasteless meat."

"Yes, ma'am." Cole adjusted the barbecue's heat and smothered a smile,

"I'm sure the burgers will be fine, Angela." Mrs. Shevchenko piped up again. "Cole is Dennis Carter's son and Dennis knew his way around a grill." She chuckled and passed Cole a plate to begin serving. "Don't mind Angela." She lowered her voice. "Not that it's an excuse but her husband's death hit her hard. Her heart hurts more than her digestion."

"I want Cole to cook hamburgers for us all the time." Half an hour later, Skylar pushed her empty plate aside and rubbed her stomach. "I'm stuffed."

"Maybe Cole will share his grilling secrets with me." Mel laughed and gave Cole a playful wink as she stacked their used plates. "Are you too 'stuffed' for chocolate cake, Skylar?"

"No." Skylar hopped off the picnic bench and tugged Mel's arm. "I'm never too full for cake."

"I didn't think so." She gathered up the bowls holding leftover salad. "Come help me get the cake and dessert plates. No, no." She waved away the offers of help from Cole and Mrs. Shevchenko and Mrs. Moretti. "You stay put. You're guests."

"Those burgers were quite tasty." After Skylar and Mel had disappeared inside the house, Mrs. Moretti broke the awkward silence.

"Of course they were." Mrs. Shevchenko folded her paper napkin on her lap. "Haven't Mel and Skylar made a wonderful job of this garden?" She gestured to the thriving vegetable patch fronted by a row of sunflower plants.

"They sure have." Cole recognized an intentional change of topic when he heard one and listened as the two women debated the merits of different types of fertilizer.

"Is everyone ready for cake?" Skylar darted ahead of Mel and set a blue picnic plate and fork at each place. "Mommy and I made it specially and she let me decorate it."

"Aren't you clever?" Mrs. Shevchenko admired the white frosting topped with multicolored sprinkles.

"Mommy showed me how to use a grown-up spatula." Skylar beamed at them.

"You did a wonderful job, sweetheart." Mrs. Moretti's voice held a warmth Cole had never heard there before.

"You sure did." Cole added his praise to the others as Mel cut the cake and served them each a piece.

He took several appreciative bites and stated, "This is the best chocolate cake I've ever had." Having finished his cake so quickly, he set aside his fork and turned to Mel. "Truly."

"Told you so." Across from him, Skylar grinned, her mouth smeared with white frosting and chocolate crumbs.

"It's a family recipe. My grandma taught me to make it." Mel's face pinkened with pleasure as Mrs. Shevchenko and Mrs. Moretti murmured compliments too.

As dusk fell, Cole breathed a sigh of relief while, alone in Mel's compact kitchen, he loaded plates and cutlery into the dishwasher. Mel was saying goodbye to Mrs. Shevchenko and Mrs. Moretti by the side gate beneath the open kitchen window, and Skylar had taken Blue to her bedroom to pick out a book for Cole to read to her. Thanks to Mrs. Shevchenko, Skylar and Mel keeping the conversation on easy topics, Mrs. Moretti hadn't mentioned anything to make Cole uncomfortable and the evening had gone better than he'd expected. Although he'd have liked to have had some time alone with Mel, maybe they'd have time to hang out for a while after Skylar was in bed. He closed the dishwasher and grabbed a cloth to wipe the countertops. He wanted to talk to Mel about that rodeo over in—

"I must say I was surprised to see Cole Carter here." Mrs. Moretti's voice drifted from behind the honeysuckle that edged the path between the kitchen window and gate.

"He's a friend." Mel answered her as the gate squeaked open.

"You're new here so I'm of the mind to give you a bit of advice. For your sake, and Skylar's too, you need to be careful who you make friends with. In high school, well, if Cole didn't make trouble, it sure found him." Mrs. Moretti made a tsking sound, and Cole gripped the cloth into his fist. "It was such a shame for his parents and brothers and sister. I suppose most families have one bad apple."

"Cole has been nothing but kind and respectful to me as well as Skylar." Mel must be standing nearer the kitchen window because her voice was clearer. "I wouldn't let anyone spend time with my daughter who I had concerns about."

The tightness in Cole's chest eased.

"Mel's right." Mrs. Shevchenko joined in. "We all have things in our pasts we'd rather not be reminded of, even you, Angela."

"I only meant—"

"I know exactly what you meant. I'm also not so old I don't remember what happened our senior year of high school."

"I…you… It was nothing, Nina." Mrs. Moretti made a gasping noise like she'd been thrown from a horse and lay winded on the ground.

"We all gave you a second chance, so Cole deserves the same, don't you think? Whatever he did or didn't do in school is neither here nor there. Most of it was only boyish pranks anyway. What matters is who Cole is and what he does now. If you or anyone else has anything to say about him either to his face or behind his back, they'll have to deal with me." The gate squeaked again. "Thank you for a lovely evening, Mel."

"You're welcome. Let me know how

Pixie…" Mel's voice faded, together with the women's footsteps.

"I got some new library books and I—Cole?" Skylar tugged on his hand. "Are you okay?"

"Yeah, fine." He made himself rinse the cloth in cold water, hang it over the faucet and smile at Skylar. "Let's see what you've got to read."

But as they sat together in the living room, side by side on the sofa, and Skylar showed him her books about horses and ponies, Cole couldn't shake the memory of what Mrs. Moretti had said.

Despite how he'd been welcomed back to High Valley, she likely wasn't alone in thinking of him that way. He'd only been unlucky in hearing her. The big question, and one that continued to haunt him, was could he truly start over in a place where his past was so much a part of his present?

"I FOUND SKYLAR'S cuddly rabbit toy. She forgot it under the picnic table." Mel came into the living room and sat in her favorite comfy chair across from Cole. He perched on the sofa with Blue napping at his feet. Skylar's library books were still scattered across the coffee table. "She can't sleep without that rabbit. My mom gave it to her when she was a baby and... What's wrong?"

"Nothing." He stacked the books and avoided Mel's gaze.

Mel sat cross-legged in her chair and studied his slumped shoulders. "I don't believe you." Since they'd spent all that time together on the Fourth of July, she was more attuned to Cole and something had clearly unsettled him. "I may not know you well but I like to think I know when you're upset about something. I talked to Skylar and told her I didn't want her coming up with any more ideas to get us together. I hope she didn't say or do anything more."

"No." Cole shook his head and gave her a wry smile. "I talked to my mom too. She and the Sunflower Sisterhood were behind that picnic basket raffle. Although I didn't like how they went about it, along with Skylar and Paisley, in a way they did me a favor. It was a great day."

"It was." And Mel had decided to enjoy the time she and Cole spent together, not analyze it. "So is your back hurting or—"

"No. The physical therapist is helping a lot with my back pain." He looked at Mel briefly. "The counselor… He's helping with the rest."

"Good." If Cole didn't want to talk to her, she didn't want to push him, and it was getting late. "I should—"

"I heard what she said." Cole's voice was thick with pain.

"What who said?" Mel glanced around the quiet room.

"Mrs. Moretti." He swallowed, and his Adam's apple worked. "When you were saying goodbye to her."

"Oh." Mel leaned forward. "Then you also heard what Mrs. Shevchenko and I said."

"I did but Mrs. Moretti's right. I caused trouble in high school. I'm not proud of it but it's the truth. I skipped school whenever I thought I could get away with it." Cole's expression was grim. "I hardly ever did homework. I talked in class and talked back to teachers too. I broke a bunch of glass test tubes in the chemistry lab and the teacher needed stitches. That one was an accident although nobody believed me."

"I guess—"

"No." He shook his head. "I need to tell you the truth. All of it. As a Halloween prank, I wrapped the trees outside the school in toilet paper. I didn't know it was the day before a bunch of people from the school board were coming to make a special presentation with newspaper photographers and everything. You name it, I did it."

"Were you sorry afterward?"

Cole shrugged. "I guess so but I never knew why I acted out. Looking back, I wanted attention but that wasn't the only reason."

"No?" Mel was out of her depth but at least Cole was talking to her.

"School was easy for everyone but me. Except for sports or wood shop, I struggled."

"You said before reading was hard for you. Was that part of it?"

"Maybe." Cole patted Blue. The dog had woken up and nosed his leg. "I hadn't really thought about it before. If I'd been concentrating on reading or doing my studies, maybe I wouldn't have come up with so many bad ideas to occupy my time."

"But you feel genuine remorse for what you got up to, then. That's important. That shows your true character."

"It does?" Cole raised his head and the haunted expression in his eyes caught Mel's heart.

"Sure." She moved to sit beside him on the sofa, and Blue snuggled between them. "I also heard your mom say you grew out of getting into mischief a long time ago. Nobody, except for someone like Mrs. Moretti, thinks of you like that now. Instead, everybody knows you're smart with horses and ranching and rodeo. You're also a good son, brother and uncle. You're great with Skylar too, and after only a few times of reading together her comprehension and ability to read both aloud and to herself has increased a lot."

"Good for her." Cole gave Mel a half smile. "Zach and Bryce got scholarships and went to college. Molly did too. Now she's even going to graduate school."

"If that's what they wanted, that's great. Did you want to go to college?"

"No, never." Cole's smile broadened. "I like being outdoors and working with animals. I'd hate being cooped up in a college classroom. All I ever wanted was rodeo but now…" He straightened. "I'm figuring out what I want to do next."

"My mom always said we each have our own path but the important thing is to 'bloom where you're planted.'" Mel had held to that advice throughout her life.

Cole took Mel's wrist and traced her daisy tattoo. "Maybe I'm a weed."

"So? Weeds provide ground cover to prevent soil erosion. Without weeds, riverbanks and shorelines would slide into the water." Cole's thumb was warm on Mel's skin and as he circled the outline of her tattoo, her breathing sped up. "Weeds also help fertilize soil and repel pests."

"Go on." Cole's voice held a smile. He linked his fingers with hers and moved closer so his light breath brushed her cheek.

"Weeds are part of nature's ecosystem. They have their place like everything else does." Cole eased Blue off the sofa, and his shoulder bumped Mel's as he settled close beside her.

"And?"

"Weeds attract bees and butterflies too." She was rattling on like a biology textbook, but Cole's closeness excited her as much as it put her off-balance.

"You picked daisies, what your dad called a 'noxious weed,' for your mom."

"You remembered?" Unless it was something to do with him, Mel's ex had rarely listened to her, let alone remembered anything meaningful.

"Of course." Cole's voice deepened. "I picked daisies for my mom too. Still do now and again. There's a big patch of them down by the creek."

There was a new and unexpected intimacy between them. "That's so nice." Awareness hummed and Mel reached for Cole's hand. "Do you—"

"I wanted—"

"You first," Mel said as they spoke at the same time.

Cole squeezed Mel's hand before letting go of it to pat Blue. "I wanted to ask if you're free next Saturday. There's a rodeo over near Butte, and I thought we could go to it to get ideas to help finalize plans for cowboy challenge activities. What do you say?"

"A rodeo?" Mel blinked. There'd been a connection between her and Cole. Not only physically with that brush of their shoulders and touch of hands but emotionally too. However, instead of exploring it, he'd changed the subject. "I have next Saturday off work, but I don't want to bring Skylar to a rodeo so far away. It would be too long a day for her." Mel would like to spend a day with Cole, though. "Maybe—"

"I already thought of that and talked to my mom. She said she'd be happy to look after Skylar if that would help." Cole picked up Blue, and the sleepy pup nestled into his shirtfront.

"I don't want to impose." Mel didn't want to take advantage of Joy's good nature.

"Mom said you might say that, so she said to tell you it wouldn't be an imposition." Cole shifted farther away on the sofa, and Mel missed his nearness. "Mom thinks a lot of Skylar. Since Bryce has volunteer firefighter training that weekend, Mom's also looking after Paisley and Cam. It will be fun for the three kids to play together."

"That's super." There was no reason for Mel not to go to a rodeo with Cole. As he'd said, they'd get some good ideas for the cowboy challenge, the reason they were spending time together in the first place.

"Great. We'll have to leave early in the morning and we won't get back until late.

Mom said if it's okay with you, Skylar could sleep at the ranch too like Paisley and Cam are doing."

"Skylar would love that. She's been asking to have a sleepover with Paisley, and staying at your mom's place will make it extra special." Mel gathered up Skylar's scattered library books.

"I'll leave you and Mom to organize the details." Cole got to his feet, still cuddling Blue. "I have early chores tomorrow so I need to get a move on. Otherwise, the alarm will be going off almost as soon as I'm in bed."

"Of course. Next Saturday's a date." Mel stood too and put a hand to her mouth. "Not a date, date. I meant I'll put it on my calendar." Why was she all of a sudden so awkward around Cole? It absolutely wasn't a date, date. She hadn't needed to explain.

"Yeah." Cole grabbed his hat from the end of the sofa.

"The last time I went to a rodeo was in Alberta when I was little."

She'd sat on her dad's lap as he'd told her about the different events. Her mom and younger sisters had stayed home, so it was one of the rare times Mel had had her dad all to herself. Although she only remembered snatches of that long-ago day, she'd never forgotten the sense of safety and security encircled in Dad's arms. She remembered his warm laugh too when he'd let her try on his cowboy hat and it had slipped over her forehead. And she remembered the scents of horses, hay, dust and the special one that was her dad, a mix of saddle leather, sandalwood and cedar aftershave.

"Nowadays, rodeo is big business, but this one is a small-town event so it won't be as glitzy as some." In Mel's narrow hall, inside her front door, Cole put on his hat and dug in the front pocket of his jeans for his keys.

"I've never been one for glitz and glamour." Mel had had enough of that with her ex-husband.

"Me neither." Cole retrieved his key ring and as he turned to open the screen door, his gaze caught Mel's and held. "Thanks for dinner. Thanks for listening too."

"You're welcome." There was that connection between them, even stronger this time.

He tipped his hat, went out onto the porch and down the steps to his truck.

Long after they'd waved goodbye to each other, and the truck's taillights had disappeared around the corner at the end of her street, Mel stood at the door looking out into the summer night. Despite what Angela Moretti had said about him, Cole *was* a good man and he deserved a second chance. High Valley was Mel's second chance but what if there were other chances for her here too?

CHAPTER ELEVEN

"WE'RE NEARLY THERE. Only ten miles to go." Cole gestured to the sign beside the highway. He and Mel had left the ranch as the sun nudged the eastern horizon. Now, several hours later and many miles farther west, the landscape was bathed in bright golden light. Along with the green and gold fields, indigo-blue sky and humpbacked ridge of the distant mountains, if Cole felt at home anywhere, it was here.

"It's beautiful." From the passenger seat, Mel let out a soft breath. "Until I moved to High Valley, I'd forgotten how much I love the West. San Francisco's a great city, and there's pretty country north of there where my mom and stepdad live, but not like this."

"Wide-open spaces are either in your blood or they aren't. That's what my dad used to say. He was neighborly, but he never wanted to live in a place where he was squashed in with those neighbors. He said he needed room to breathe."

"Not a problem out here." Mel's voice held a smile.

"No." Cole glanced over at her. "I'm the same. Since Molly always hankered for city life, my sister couldn't be happier living in Atlanta. Cities are fun to visit, but being crammed in with millions of people to live? Not for me." He turned his attention back to the highway. Empty of other traffic, the sinuous paved thread meandered through the landscape, bisected by a yellow line down the middle.

"Our dads sound a lot alike. Mine said he was born to live and work on this kind of land. Dad taught me to respect it too. To understand the weather and rhythm of the changing seasons." She hesitated as if trying to find the right words. "He talked about a lot of things I only understood much later when I was older. Like he was just one in a long line of stewards of the land. As much as he could, he wanted to protect it and set an example for those that came after. He also said it was important to acknowledge and honor the peoples who lived here first.

Our history is new here but theirs goes back thousands of years."

"Is that why you asked Rosa and her family to get involved in the cowboy challenge?" Cole studied the vast landscape cradled by an endless sky dotted with puffy white clouds. There was something about being away from High Valley and in the confines of the truck that inspired confidences.

"Yes. It may seem like a small gesture, but acknowledging traditional territories is a welcoming practice. My Canadian aunt, my dad's older brother's wife, has Indigenous ancestry so I've learned from her. Now I'm learning from Rosa too."

"I'm learning from her as well." Cole had never thought much about history until lately; returning to his hometown had opened his heart and his eyes.

"You must have been to lots of cities with rodeo. Which one's your favorite?" Mel drank from the purple water bottle she'd tucked into the middle console.

"It's a toss-up between Forth Worth and Calgary. Both places have a fantastic rodeo culture and fun nightlife too, but when I competed in Calgary I won. The whole family traveled up to Canada to watch me ride. That made it extra special." It had been one of the best weeks of Cole's life. Not only had he done well doing something he loved, but the people he loved most had been there to cheer him on. Ashley, too, and back then he'd thought she was the woman he'd spend the rest of his life with. He pushed away the lingering hurt. Ashley was long gone, and he'd moved on too.

"My mom and stepdad used to watch me compete." Mel turned away from Cole to look out the passenger window. "Right from the start, and no matter if the horse show was big or small, they were always there. In some ways, I feel like I let them down."

"How?" Cole signaled to take the exit to Twin Creek Plateau, the town where the rodeo was being held.

"When I made the national team, it was what I'd worked toward for so long. I'd have a chance to compete in major international events. Then I got hurt, and it was all over. My stepfather, Pete, had spent so much money to help me keep riding and for what?" Mel picked up her backpack from the truck's footwell and hugged it like she did Skylar.

"Did he and your mom ever blame you?" Cole slowed the vehicle as they joined a line of others waiting to enter the rodeo grounds.

"No. They were great. All they cared about was me being okay. My ex-husband sure blamed me, though." Her voice hitched.

"From what you've told me it sounds like you're the one who should be blaming him." Cole tightened his grip on the wheel and stared at the top-of-the-line horse trailer in front of them. A man who'd treated Mel and Skylar the way Stephen had was a man who deserved a lot more than blame.

"I *have* blamed Stephen, not that it made a difference." Mel's voice was artificially bright. "It's fine. Montana's a fresh start. I miss my family a lot, but Mom and Pete are talking about visiting Skylar and me later in the summer. Pete's happy I'm riding again. When he and Mom called last night, I told him how supportive you've been."

"You're doing a great job all on your own. I've only given you a bit of encouragement." Cole parked the truck at the far end of a grassy field half-filled with other pickup trucks and larger show trucks, as well as horse and livestock trailers. While some of the trailers only held horses, many were much bigger and contained living quarters too. The kind of trailer Cole used to call home and that was now parked behind a barn at the ranch. He should sell it but he couldn't bring himself to place the ad, at least not yet.

"Don't be so modest. If not for you, I might not have ever gotten back on a horse. I told Pete that too." Mel bumped Cole's elbow in a playful gesture.

"Did you tell him you're doing Western riding?" After bumping Mel's elbow back, Cole shut off the truck's engine and grabbed his own backpack from the rear seat.

"Not yet, but I will." Mel replaced her sunglasses with a pair of regular glasses, Cole's favorite ones with green frames. "All Pete truly cares about is horses being treated well. I'm sure the type of horse or riding wouldn't matter to him."

Cole got out of the truck and set his hat firmly in place. He'd never met Pete so he couldn't judge, but hearing about the guy was a reminder he and Mel came from different worlds. "Before the rodeo events start, I'd like to look at some of the stock. I know a guy who's a stock contractor and he said he'd show us around." It would also delay the reality of Cole having to be at a rodeo as a spectator not participant.

"Sure. That sounds good." Mel tucked her phone into her bag. "I got a text from your mom and Skylar's fine. They've baked chocolate chip cookies, and now they're going to the horse barn to help Zach and Ellie clean and organize tack."

"Great." It *was* great. Warmth spread through Cole. Mel and Skylar had already been let down by one man. But now Skylar was becoming part of Cole's family, he had to make sure he didn't let her or Mel down again.

"No wonder your mom says she worried when you were in a rodeo ring." From her seat beside Cole in the packed grandstand, Mel stared at the cowboy in the center of the dusty arena who'd wrestled a steer to the ground. Somehow he'd managed to get the animal to lie on its side with all four feet in the same direction. "The speed alone is terrifying." She pressed a hand to her chest.

"That steer must weigh two or three times as much as the cowboy."

"Steer wrestling's the fastest event in rodeo. If you know what you're doing, neither the speed nor the animal's weight matters." Cole laughed as he clapped and cheered.

"Is that why you liked it best?" She glanced at Cole from beneath the brim of the white cowboy hat Joy had lent her. Now Mel was living in the West, she should buy a cowboy hat of her own but a proper one was expensive and Skylar's needs came first.

"I like speed, sure, but in steer wrestling you have to be precise. It involves skill and strength, as well as timing." Cole studied the cowboy with a practiced eye. "That guy's new and still green. If he ever hopes to have a chance in a rodeo with a large purse, he needs to work on his technique. A purse is the money you get if you win," he clarified at Mel's puzzled expression. "That cowboy there was slow reaching the steer and off-balance too. You're supposed to slide down the side of a galloping horse, not almost fall off."

Mel nodded as she listened, learned and

tried to understand. This world was Cole's and he was at ease here in a way she'd never seen him before. In worn jeans, a blue-and-white-checked snap shirt and dark cowboy hat, he looked the same as the other men, but there was something different about him too. Maybe it was how he carried himself with an air of assurance and command he didn't have at the ranch.

After meeting Cole's friend Heath, a fifty-something stock contractor from Colorado, they'd found seats in the stands to watch the roughstock events. Those were things like bareback riding and bull riding where competitors were scored on both their own performance and that of the animal. Then they'd watched timed events including roping, barrel racing and now the last few steer wrestling competitors. "I get why Paisley wants to learn barrel racing." Mel had watched in admiration as women riders had raced around barrels in a set pattern, at one with their horses as they navigated rapid turns at breathtaking speed. "I only hope Skylar doesn't get the same idea. I'm worried enough about her learning to ride a nice, quiet pony like Luna."

"You let her take riding lessons, though." Cole rested one booted foot on the back of the empty seat in front of them. "If she wants to try barrel racing or anything else, you'll make the right decision for her when that time comes."

"I suppose." Mel bit back a sigh. "My mom didn't want me to do show jumping. The more she pushed me to try something less risky, like dressage, the more I resisted." Yet, if Mel had focused on dressage, sometimes likened to horse ballet, she might not have gotten hurt and she could still be competing. She'd likely never have studied physical therapy, though, moved to High Valley or met Cole and been here at this rodeo. One choice had changed her life in unimaginable ways.

"You can guide them all you want, but in the end most kids will do what they're set on. We're both examples of that. All you can do is try your best to keep Skylar safe and you do that already. You're a great mom." Cole's voice was serious.

"I appreciate the thought, but how do you know if I'm a good mom or not?"

"I've seen enough already. Plus, I had a good mom. I know what one looks like."

Cole smiled warmly and covered Mel's hand with his. "Skylar's healthy and happy and that says a lot about the kind of mom you are. Trust yourself."

"I'm working on it." In parenting and everything else.

"What did you think of the Western dressage?" Cole kept a hold of Mel's hand as, after the steer wrestling ended, they got up from their seats to follow the crowd to an exit.

"I liked it." There had been a small display before the main rodeo events started. "From the little I saw, it's similar to English dressage but with Western tack. You'd also never see English dressage riders wearing Western clothes, but some of the principles seem to be the same. I want to learn more about it." Maybe even try it herself although the idea was too new for Mel to talk about it with Cole or anyone else.

"Hang on." With his free hand, Cole grabbed his phone out of his pocket and read a message. "One of the cowboys I know from the circuit texted me. He and a bunch of others are getting together for an after-party at a local honky-tonk. We could get a meal and listen to music. There's a good band playing. What do you say?"

"Sure. We need to eat before driving back." It wasn't a date. It was only getting a meal with a group. "Since Skylar's sleeping over at your mom's, I don't have to be home at a specific time."

Her daughter was also having so much fun with Joy and Paisley, it seemed she hardly missed Mel. Despite the brief flash of hurt, one of the reasons she'd moved to High Valley was to make new friends and have Skylar be part of a community. Now that was happening, she'd focus on being grateful. Skylar would always need her, but in different ways than before.

Cole smiled again. "Then let's go have some fun." He helped her down the narrow arena steps, his hand still tucked in hers.

Fun. Except for occasional weekend brunches with her mom and sisters, for almost seven years, Mel's fun had had something to do with Skylar. While Mel was an expert in free and fun things to do at home, often involving making play dough, slime or blanket forts, before the Sunflower Sisterhood and today with Cole, she'd missed going out for an evening with friends. While she didn't want to think about her life without Skylar in it, she also missed times to talk about things that weren't to do with children.

Cole's calloused hand in hers was a reminder of the work he did and passion for horses and animal welfare she also shared. That passion had been evident when he'd talked to Heath, the stock contractor. "I've never been to a honky-tonk."

"Well, let me tell you all about it. I guess you'd call it a restaurant, bar and music venue." Cole dropped her hand to loop an arm around her shoulders and tug Mel close. "But you can't call yourself a Montanan, even an adopted one, if you haven't been to a honky-tonk. My grandpa loved this song called 'You're More at Home in a Honky Tonk' and it's real, old-time country and western." Cole sang a few bars and laughed. "I remember Grandma Carter putting the music on and him and Grandma dancing to it when I was a kid. He'd swing her around the living room and she'd laugh and kiss his cheek. My dad would dance with my mom too."

The warmth in Cole's deep voice made

Mel's stomach quiver with unexpected excitement, as if her birthday, Christmas and Skylar's birthday had all come at once. She didn't know what was happening between them but whatever it was, it felt good. And even before they reached Cole's truck to drive the short distance to the honky-tonk, Mel also knew it felt right.

CHAPTER TWELVE

COLE FINISHED HIS perfectly grilled steak and drained the last of his soda. Across the table from him, Mel was talking to Heath and two of the women who'd competed in barrel racing. Her expression was animated, as if she was genuinely interested in what the others were saying. Cole already knew Mel wasn't the kind of person to put on an act, but in spite of her Alberta roots, he'd still worried she might be uncomfortable in a honky-tonk. She'd spent most of her life in California and, as far as riding went, she'd only just gotten back on a horse. However, she fit in here, as well as with his friends.

"Let me buy you a beer." Phil, a cowboy Cole had often competed against—and usually beaten—came up to their group and gestured to Cole's empty glass.

"No, thanks. I'll have another soda." Cole glanced at Mel, still talking to Heath and now asking him questions about a prize bull's Texas bloodline. Who'd have thought she'd be interested in something like that? Although Ashley was a barrel racer, and grown up in a ranching family in South Dakota, Cole had never talked to her about stock contracting. She'd never asked either. But here was Mel holding her own with a guy like Heath who, Cole could tell, was impressed by her too.

"Gone soft, have you?" Phil finished his beer and signaled to the server for another one, along with a refill of Cole's soda.

"No, but I'm driving." Unlike some of the other guys, Cole had never been a big drinker, but with Mel today he'd stuck to soda. He'd never do anything to put her or Skylar at risk.

"Is your retirement permanent or are you planning on coming back to rodeo?" Phil studied Cole and his gaze was shrewd. "Never thought I'd say it but I miss you. The circuit's not the same without you livening things up."

"You don't miss me winning?" Cole tried to joke. He'd considered Phil a friend, as well as competitor, but maybe he'd been wrong about the friend part. As for retirement,

Cole's doctor said it should be permanent, but that was none of Phil's business.

"Without you around, I take home more prize money, sure." Phil glanced at Mel and gave Cole a knowing smile. "She's sure a pretty lady. Her name's Mel too. What do you think your old Mel would have made of you hooking up with her?"

"Stop it." Cole stood to face Phil. "Her name is Melissa and she's a friend. We're not dating. As for Mel Garcia, he'd have liked her."

She was the kind of woman his mentor Mel would have called a "keeper." Cole should have paid more attention when Mel Garcia had had reservations about Ashley. Instead, he'd been caught up in what he'd thought was love. With hindsight, and although Cole still resented what Ashley had said about him not being dad material, she'd done him a favor by breaking things off between them.

"I was only joking." Phil grabbed his beer glass from the server and passed Cole a fresh soda.

"It wasn't funny." Cole had never been comfortable with a lot of things the other cowboys talked about, but he'd gone along with it. Being here with Mel was different. "I was raised to respect women. Would you talk like that about your mom or sister?"

"No." Phil rolled his eyes. "You used to be fun."

Maybe Cole used to be silly too. "Drop it, okay?" Phil wasn't any different from some of the other guys here but, all of a sudden, he was seeing them in a different light.

"If you say so." Phil rocked back on his heels. "You've changed, bro. When that steer took you down, it broke more than a bunch of bones." He shook his head. "Maybe it broke you too?" He gave Cole a mocking smile.

Cole clenched his fists. The guy he used to be would have knocked the smile off Phil's face without thinking twice. But now? He glanced around the table, which had fallen silent. Other cowboys and competitors, Heath and Mel, all watched him.

Behind her glasses, Mel's eyes were anxious before she stared at her empty plate.

In that instant, Cole knew what he had to do. He unclenched his fists and eyed Phil. "You're right, the accident changed me in a whole bunch of ways and some of them are for the better." He took a shaky breath, the urge to hit the guy still coursing through him. "Now I know what's important. And it's not what's on the outside. What's truly important is what's on the inside." He looked around the table again. "It's about taking a stand for what you believe in, about apologizing when you're wrong. Most of all, it's doing the right thing, including changing who you are when you should."

In the silence, a lone clap sounded and was joined by others. Mel clapped too, her eyes shiny, and she wore a wide smile that wrapped around Cole and made him feel ten feet tall.

Phil muttered something about getting another drink but when he moved toward the bar nobody called him back or joined him either. As the band returned from its break and launched into a Texas two-step, Cole held out his hand to Mel. "Join me?" He gestured toward the dance floor filled with couples.

She smiled, murmured something to Heath and took Cole's hand.

Until tonight, Cole had always focused on what he'd lose by giving up rodeo. But what if instead he let himself think about what he might gain in retirement? For a start, he could have a whole new way of life. And what if, as part of that life, he let himself hope this woman might have feelings for him too?

"You did a hard thing, but Phil had it coming." In the middle of the wooden dance floor that adjoined the honky-tonk's restaurant and bar, Mel held one of Cole's hands in hers with her other hand resting on his shoulder. He kept his hand on her upper back as he showed her the pattern of the dance. Two steps quick and two steps slow following the beat of the music at an even pace. "You also did the right thing."

She'd seen how Cole had struggled to curb his temper. Yet even though Phil had pressed him, Cole had kept his cool. He'd stopped, taken a breath, held his ground and then let Phil walk away. Better yet, he'd then asked her to dance.

"I tried." He steered Mel into the center of the group, the faster and more experienced dancers circling around them.

"I mean it." She felt the music through the soles of the boots, which, like the hat, she'd borrowed from Joy. "I'm proud of you."

Cole dipped Mel to the beat, the twang

of a guitar melding with the words of what Cole said was a song by Clint Black, "A Good Run of Bad Luck." Maybe that song was more than one to dance to. Perhaps it was a metaphor for what they'd both been through. Bad luck had shaped them, though, and led them here to a fresh start and some overdue good luck.

"I did what I needed to." His smile was stiff.

Under Mel's hand, his shoulder was solid and well-muscled, and for a big man he was light on his feet as he guided her expertly around the floor. She relaxed in his embrace, and as he increased the speed of the two-step, he pulled her closer so her hair brushed his chin. Mel's body tingled, and warmth spread from the top of her head to the tips of her toes.

As he gave Mel an unexpected twirl, she laughed before tripping over his boots.

"Oops. I've got you. I won't let you fall."

"I know. It's fine. Sorry for being clumsy." A man like Cole wouldn't let her fall on the dance floor or, if he had anything to do with it, off the back of a horse either. This kind of dancing was a lot like relationships. You had to depend on your partner and lead and follow each other. You also had to communicate with each other and work as a team. All the things she and Stephen had never done.

"You're not clumsy. You're beautiful."

"I...thanks." Her voice squeaked, and she hoped he didn't hear it. She moved closer to Cole as the song changed to a slow waltz. Shania Twain's "From This Moment On" was a wedding first-dance favorite Mel recognized.

She thought of how it had been only her and Stephen and a few friends and family at the courthouse for their wedding because Stephen was leaving the next day for a competition in Europe. Looking back, it was one of the many times she'd gone along with what he wanted.

No more. She was a new person now, one who'd learned to stand up for herself and what she believed in. Like Cole had done with that Phil guy.

Her chest got tight as she and Cole danced together and the music with those achingly romantic lyrics swirled around them. They danced without speaking, in sync with each other and the music. As the last notes of the song faded, Cole didn't move away. Instead, he still held her close and rested his chin on top of her head for several endless seconds.

Feelings old and new swept through Mel, connecting her to Cole in a way that went beyond friendship.

"It's getting late and we have a long drive home." Cole's voice was husky as he led her out of the crowd to the edge of the dance floor.

"Yes." Mel tried to work moisture into her dry mouth. "Thanks for today."

"Thank *you*." His smile was gentle and intimate. "I've had a great day."

"Me too." The best day Mel could remember having in a long time. "We got lots of good ideas to finalize cowboy challenge activities." That was the reason they were here, she reminded herself.

"Yeah." As they reached their table in the restaurant, Cole said goodbye to his friends, and Mel fumbled under her chair for her backpack.

"It was good meeting you." Heath took the backpack, stood and handed it to her. "If you're ever going to be near our place in Colorado, give me a call. My wife and I would be happy to have you stay with us." He opened his wallet and gave her his card, flipping through a folder interspersed with family pictures. Earlier he'd mentioned he and his wife had three daughters, all of whom were married with children of their own. "Our grandkids would have fun with Skylar. We've got a whole setup for them. Ponies, of course, but I built them a playhouse and miniature barn too."

"That sounds terrific." Mel tucked Heath's card in her own wallet beside a picture of Skylar. As she stepped away from the table, leaving Cole to finish his goodbyes, Heath followed her to a quiet corner near the door.

"I mean it." Heath's blue eyes were intent. "I think about Cole a lot. His mentor's death, coming so soon after his own dad's passing, hit him hard. And then the accident." Heath paused and darted a glance to one side. "Cole never talks about what happened, but that steer almost killed him. I was there and..." He rubbed a hand across his face. "I've told Cole whatever he needs, I'm there for him. Now I'm telling you because he's always been so independent. I get the sense he might listen to you more than me."

"I'm sure that's not true. I haven't known Cole long." Mel's face warmed.

Heath's deep-set eyes crinkled as he

smiled. "Even if he doesn't recognize it yet, you and your little girl are good for him." He patted Mel's shoulder in a fatherly gesture. "I'm not asking you to go behind Cole's back but if you have a chance, let me know how he gets on, won't you?"

"I will." The backs of Mel's eyes prickled. Heath was about the same age her own dad would have been if he'd lived. He even resembled her dad with his stocky build, no-nonsense manner and loping cowboy gait. "If you're interested, you and your wife could come to the cowboy challenge. I expect Cole would like to see you there. I would too." And she meant it. There was something about Heath she instinctively trusted.

"I might do that. We could make a long weekend of it."

"Good." Mel smiled at Cole as he joined them.

"Take care, son." Heath clapped Cole on the shoulder and nodded to Mel.

"Heath likes you." Cole let the door of the honky-tonk swing shut behind them. Gravel crunched under their feet as they walked the short distance to his truck parked in a corner of the lot.

"I like him too." It was cooler outside and the air was fresh. Overhead, the enormous sky was hung with a carpet of glittery stars. "He seems like a good man."

"He's the best." Cole clicked the automatic unlock on his key fob, opened the passenger door for Mel and she hopped in. "He's a good stock contractor too. Knows his stuff."

Mel fastened her seat belt as Cole joined her in the truck and started the engine. "I enjoyed talking with him." He was different from most of the other men she'd met today. His pride in his wife and family for a start, but he also had a sense of being grounded in who he was, what he did and where he came from. In twenty odd years, could Cole be that kind of man too?

As they pulled out of the parking lot and joined the highway heading east, back to High Valley and the Tall Grass Ranch, Cole reached over and held Mel's hand in his.

In the soft darkness, the cool night air rushed in through the half-open windows, bringing with it the scent of wildflowers, horses and pine trees.

Mel didn't need to talk and it seemed Cole didn't either. Occasionally he glanced across at her and smiled. The kind of smile that made her warm all over again.

And still he held her hand, driving with his other one on the wheel as the truck's headlights illuminated the ruler-straight two-lane highway, only the hum of the engine and occasional whoosh of a vehicle coming from the opposite direction breaking the comfortable silence.

Today hadn't started out as a date but somewhere along the way, especially after they danced together, it had turned into one. But Mel wouldn't put a name to it or the new feelings connecting her to Cole. Not only were they too new, but those feelings were also too precious.

CHAPTER THIRTEEN

AT HER DESK in her den office, Joy closed the bulging file folder that held her notes for the Sunflower Festival and set it on top of the other folder with cowboy challenge information. It was now the first week of August and the golden summer days were slipping by, but unlike the past few summers, Joy was savoring them. Before, she'd counted each day on the calendar as one more day without Dennis. Now, while she still thought of her husband each morning when she woke up, and each night at bedtime, as well as numerous times in between, most often she was able to look forward to the day.

Between her work for the Sunflower Festival, cowboy challenge, the ranch and at Camp Crocus Hill, she was busy. And nowadays, instead of using busyness as a coping mechanism for grief, being busy was part of living her life again.

Making sure she had her tote bag, she got up from the desk and walked through the family room to the main hall and out the front door to the wide porch. In the summer, this porch was her favorite place. That's why she'd asked Shane to meet her here. What she hadn't counted on was her sons currently being outside the main barn working on the old tractor.

She returned Bryce's wave and stood by the porch railing. She was a grown woman who could see and do what she wanted. She didn't need her boys hovering over her.

"Are you all ready for your date?" Beth came around the side of the house carrying a feed bucket.

"It's not a date. Shane and I are only going kayaking." Except the flock of butterflies taking flight in Joy's stomach felt a lot like a date, at least what she remembered from long-ago teenage dates with Dennis. She'd also fiddled with her hair and taken longer to choose what to wear than if she'd been going out with a female friend.

"When an attractive man asks you to go out with him, it's definitely a date." Beth gave Joy a teasing grin as she stopped at the bottom of the porch steps by Joy's wild-flower garden. "It's also a date when that man takes his vehicle to the car wash beforehand and picks up a picnic lunch from the Bluebunch Café." Her eyes twinkled. "I saw Shane in town earlier when I dropped Ellie off at Rosa's studio."

"Oh." Joy loved High Valley and had never wanted to live anywhere else. However, in such a small community, you didn't need to do more than sneeze and folks knew about it.

"Shane Gallagher's a nice man." Beth sobered. "And you're a nice woman. Whether you call it a date or not, it's great to see two nice people going out together. Molly agrees with me."

"Molly?" Joy's daughter wasn't coming home until next week for the cowboy challenge. How had news of Joy going out with Shane reached Molly in Atlanta?

"I *may* have mentioned you going kayaking with Shane when I video-called Molly last night. I sent her some pictures from the Fourth of July and Shane was in a few of them." Beth had the grace to look sheepish. "When Molly asked who he was, I told her."

As Shane's blue SUV pulled into the long

drive that led from the road to the ranch house, Joy moved down the porch steps. It was fine. She was fine. Even though she hadn't been on a date with a man who wasn't her husband in more than forty years, she had no reason to be nervous, despite those butterflies.

"Have fun, Mom." Cole gave her a hug as Shane parked in front of the house. While Joy had been talking to Beth, Cole, as well as Zach and Bryce, had left the work on the tractor and now stood near Beth in front of a patch of pink coneflowers.

"What are you all doing here?" She glanced at her boys. "I…you…" Shane got out of the driver's side of his vehicle, and Joy plastered a smile on her face. Two kayaks, one blue and the other green, were fixed to a roof rack on top of the SUV. Both kayaks had a graphic of a squirrel and Squirrel Tail Ranch in discreet black lettering.

"We're looking out for you." Cole squeezed her shoulder before releasing it. "Whenever any of us kids went on a date, you and Dad would stand here waving us off. You always had to meet our dates too. Although I hated it, it was still kind of cute. We knew you loved us and cared about what we did and who we were with."

"You were teenagers." She almost hissed the words in Cole's ear before she greeted Shane and introduced him to her sons and Beth. As Shane opened the door for her, she slid into the passenger side of the SUV.

"Sorry about that." After Shane had come around the vehicle to sit beside her in the driver's seat, stopping partway to speak to Beth, Cole, Zach and Bryce, Joy dug in her tote bag for her sunglasses. "My family's protective." If they weren't adults, and apart from Beth, she'd have grounded the lot of them, without even knowing what they'd said.

"It's fine." Shane glanced over as he started the vehicle and his smile was warm, as well as caring. He not only smiled with his mouth but also his eyes. "Today, this... It's new for me." He put the truck in gear and as they turned in a circle in front of the ranch house, Joy's sons and Beth all waved. "Not the kayaking." Shane joined Joy in waving back and also beeped the horn. "But it's been a lot of years since I was out with a woman who wasn't my wife or one of my daughters." Beneath the brim of a white cowboy hat, his expression was anxious.

"Me too. I mean, with my husband or sons." Joy settled into the comfortable cushioned seat. "Although kayaking is new for me too." She glanced out the window at the familiar fields that had been worked by generations of the Carter family. Along with the sunflowers near the house, the grain was doing well this year. However, Joy had been a ranch wife long enough to know you couldn't count on anything until the crop was safely harvested and sold.

"I felt like a teenager again getting ready to come and pick you up." Shane stopped at the entrance to the ranch and waited for a truck with a horse trailer to pass before turning onto the highway. "If you think your family was protective back there, you should have heard my son." Shane's laugh rumbled. "We're lucky to have kids who care about us, though."

"We are." Joy laughed too. "Tell me what I need to know about kayaking."

"Beyond making sure you wear a life jacket and sunscreen?" Shane laughed again, his broad shoulders shaking beneath a white

T-shirt with a Black Angus cattle graphic on the front. "That was Bryce's contribution."

"Why am I not surprised?" Joy shook her head. "He has young kids but still…"

"Zach asked me what time I planned to have you home, and Cole said I needed to watch out for garter snakes because you're scared of them."

"And Beth?" Joy gave Shane a sideways glance.

"All she said was have fun."

As Joy joined in with Shane's easy laughter, the butterflies in her stomach settled. Her family was part of who she was. A man who couldn't accept that and them wasn't a man she wanted to spend time with. But when they'd talked on the phone in the past few weeks to arrange today's outing, Shane had made it clear her family wasn't an issue and his family was important to him too.

She'd never thought she could find another man like Dennis, but she'd been wrong. Joy didn't need another Dennis in her life. The love she had for her husband could never be replaced and she didn't want it to be. However, maybe there could be a new man and a different kind of love.

She wouldn't know unless she tried—starting with giving a good man like Shane a chance.

COMING OUT OF the gully that marked the midpoint in the cowboy challenge's adult trail-riding course, Cole eased Bandit into a trot. Now, several days before the event, he and Mel were doing a final run-through of the various activities.

The big horse looked over his shoulder as if to ask Cole whether they could speed things up even more. "Not right now, buddy. We need to wait for Mel and Daisy-May. They don't like to race like you."

Cole understood where Bandit was coming from. Although he loved his family and the ranch, the past ten weeks was the longest he'd stayed in one place since he'd graduated from high school. Like his horse, and although there were lots of good things about life here, Cole still had an instinctive need to run. "Are you still doing okay?"

"Yes." Mel rode around the edge of the gully to join him. She was on Daisy-May who, along with Princess, was the most even-tempered horse in their stable. Unlike

Princess, though, who was only used for riding lessons at Camp Crocus Hill, Daisy-May was also accustomed to ranch work. "I've been thinking about the cowboy challenge." Under Mel's riding helmet, her expression was determined. "I want to take part in a demonstration event."

"What kind?" Cole stared at her and drew Bandit back to a walk. Mel looked cute in her jeans, green T-shirt with a white daisy on the front and borrowed boots, but she looked good in anything she wore. Since that day at the rodeo, and especially after they'd danced together, they had a new connection. Although he didn't want to analyze it, that connection had a lot to do with trust, and Cole knew he both wanted and needed Mel in his life.

"Western dressage."

"Are you sure?"

"No." Mel walked Daisy-May alongside Cole and Bandit. "But I have to keep pushing myself. Getting on a horse again and riding with you is a big first step but now I need to do more. I want to prove to myself, and Skylar too, that I've truly conquered my fear."

"I'm proud of you." Emotion surged through Cole and if they hadn't been on horseback and with Mel still easily startled, he'd have hugged her.

"Hold that thought until I do it." Mel patted Daisy-May's neck.

"You will." Cole dragged his gaze away from Mel's hands. That first day he'd met her, he'd thought she had gentle hands as well as capable ones. Now that he knew her better and had held her hands in his, he knew they were all that and more. His own hands tingled as he gathered up Bandit's reins and guided the horse toward a low rise of land bisected by a small creek.

Daisy-May drew closer to Bandit as Mel guided her horse toward the rise of land too. "Although I mostly competed in show jumping, early on I did a lot of dressage too. Seeing Western dressage at the rodeo got me thinking about doing something similar here." As Daisy-May picked her way up the rocky hill, Mel's leg brushed against Cole's.

From only the brief touch of her leg, Cole's leg now tingled too. "You haven't had time to train with a horse." Bandit stopped at the edge of the creek when Cole indicated.

"No, but I talked to your mom. I've also been watching Western dressage events online." Mel gave him a brief smile as she halted Daisy-May too. "Your mom's been doing some Western dressage work with her horse for fun. She loves it. As she put it, she wants to keep riding into her seventies and even eighties, but she doesn't want to jump anymore. Like trail riding, dressage is a bit more sedate. It's about trust too and working one-on-one with your horse over time."

Cole had always been good at developing that trusting bond with horses. It was people he struggled with. "What do you want to do and how can I help?"

Their two horses stood and waited side by side, so close that Mel's left leg almost touched Cole's right one again. Under her helmet, hair had escaped from her ponytail to curl around her face. Mel wasn't conventionally pretty, but her face had both sweetness and character. The kind of face that belonged to a woman a man could count on for a lifetime.

Cole stilled. He couldn't be falling in love with Mel, could he? No. What he felt for her was different from what he'd felt for Ashley.

But that hadn't been a true and lasting love. He swallowed and tried to pay attention to what Mel was saying.

"So, you see, if your mom took Daisy-May and me through a short lesson, I'd get to ride in public, and we could showcase the Western form of dressage here. Your mom could show what she's been doing with her horse, Cindy, too. What do you think?"

What he really thought was Mel was turning him upside down and inside out to leave his stomach in more of a churn than any of the rodeo tricks he'd done on horseback. "Sure. Sounds—that's good." Cole managed to smile.

"Really? You're not just saying so?" Mel's voice was anxious. "A couple of friends I used to ride with are coming to the cowboy challenge. They'd already arranged to visit me that weekend anyway. I haven't told them I've started riding again. The demonstration will be a surprise." Her words came out in a rush and her face turned pink.

Cole leaned across to pat Mel's shoulder. A friendly gesture, he reminded himself. "I think it's great." He also thought he was in big trouble and it had nothing to do with the cowboy challenge, horses or anything else he might have had some control over. For the first time in his life, a woman had snagged his heart as well as his soul. Without him noticing, Mel had gotten behind the walls he'd built up to protect himself to know the real Cole.

"Are you okay?" Mel studied him with a concerned expression. "You don't seem yourself. I hope you haven't had too much sun. You were working out in the fields all morning and we've been riding in almost full sun too. Once we get across the creek, we'll find some shade in the trees."

"I'm fine." Cole grabbed his water bottle from Bandit's saddlebag and took a long drink. He was more himself than he'd ever been. More scared than he'd ever been too. Being churned up with emotions old and new, and letting himself think about what he might truly need, was harder than facing the biggest, orneriest bull.

"All right." Mel raised her face to the sky. It was another perfect Montana summer day with bright sunshine, warm temperatures and high puffy clouds in a deep blue sky. "Do you want to cross the creek first or shall I?"

"Bandit and I will go first." Distracted by the sweet curve of Mel's cheek and how those curls of hair framed her face, Cole stuffed the water bottle back in his bag. "Daisy-May's steady on her feet but I want to make sure you'll both be safe. You never know what might turn up with spring runoff."

"Spring runoff? It's August."

"See those rocks over there?" Cole was rambling, still trying to collect his thoughts. He thought he wanted to run, but maybe he wanted to do something else entirely. Something that would keep him here at the ranch and close to Mel and Skylar.

"Fine." Mel's expression was still concerned but now confused as well. "It's hardly even a creek. More a trickle of water."

"You should see it in the spring. Melted snow comes from the mountains and it's a creek then all right, almost a river." Cole guided Bandit through the water and, once he reached the other side, he wheeled the horse around and gestured for Mel and Daisy-May to follow. "What do you think about…?"

He stopped and drew in a breath. Mel and Daisy-May were crossing the creek all right but as they came up the low bank, Mel grinned and leaned closer to one of Daisy-May's ears. The Appaloosa kicked up her hooves and took off at a canter that verged on a gallop.

Cole laughed and urged Bandit to follow, giving the horse his head. As they flew across the grassland, Bandit's hooves thudding on the dry ground, Cole recognized another feeling. One he'd almost forgotten but which, instead of being scary, was good.

For the first time in a long time, he was happy.

CHAPTER FOURTEEN

"THIS IS WONDERFUL." Mel took an end of the colorful cowboy challenge "Welcome" banner Rosa had made and used a nail and hammer to attach it to one of the wooden poles Zach and Cole had set up earlier. "It's a work of art." She passed the hammer and another nail to Rosa so she could attach the opposite end of the banner to another pole.

"My mother always said if you're going to do something, do it as best you can." Rosa's dark eyes twinkled.

"My mom says something similar." Along with using the talents you'd been given and trying again after failure. Mel took several steps back and studied the banner.

Through her job at Healing Paws, the cowboy challenge and now riding horses again, Mel was both using her talents and trying again. If only her mom and stepdad could have been here this weekend but with Pete's elderly mom's birthday on Sunday, they opted to stay close to home and celebrate with her. While they'd visit another time, Mel still had her friends, Becky, Lisa and Lisa's husband, Jorge, here.

"Unless you need anything else, I promised Joy I'd join her and Molly to help in the cookhouse. Kristi's already got the wood-fired stove going to bake bread and biscuits like the ranch cook would have. I bet we'll have folks lined up out the door there. We should raise extra money for the animal rescue by selling Kristi's baking and Joy's old-fashioned lemonade too."

"Joy's sure excited to have Molly home for the week." When Joy had returned to the ranch yesterday after picking Molly up at the airport, the older woman had radiated happiness.

"Family being together again is the best gift of all, but Joy and Dennis never held their kids back." Rosa took her tote bag from where she'd left it beneath the banner. "Molly wanted to be a nurse and working in a large city hospital was her dream. Joy would have loved Molly to stay nearby and work in one of the local hospitals but she knew she had to let her go. Even with Cole riding rodeo, Joy had to do the same, despite how much it scared her."

"That's what I try to do with Skylar, but it's hard." Although Mel wanted to raise Skylar to spread her wings and lead an independent adult life, she didn't like to think about her living far away or doing work or other activities that would involve a lot of risk.

"I'm lucky. So far my kids have stayed around here, but my youngest is talking about moving to New Mexico. His divorce hit him hard and he wants a change." Rosa tweaked the bottom edge of the banner, which rustled in the light breeze. "Whenever Wes talks about moving, I smile and nod, but I still see the little boy he used to be." She sighed. "Kids grow up too fast."

Even in the few months they'd been in High Valley, Skylar had grown and changed too. Soon she'd be seven and then eight and before Mel knew it, a preteen. "Just when I think I've got a handle on where Skylar's at, she changes again and everything is new."

"That's how it is, honey." Rosa sighed and then laughed. "Even when they're grown, your kids don't stop changing." She brushed her hands on her jeans. "I also need to find my husband. He and his dad are organizing the storytelling tent, and I brought along a bunch of supplies so folks can make dream catchers and other crafts." She patted Mel's arm. "The cowboy challenge is going to be a huge success. Don't forget to relax and enjoy it."

"I'll try." Mel would enjoy it more once that Western dressage demonstration was over. "I sure appreciate everything you've done." As soon as Mel had asked, the Sunflower Sisterhood had opened their hearts and hands to do everything Mel and Cole needed.

Rosa's smile was gentle. "Days like this one bring us together and make us a community. You're hosting it on the ranch, and the animal rescue's benefiting from the money raised, but it's about more than money. It's about belonging. I hope you feel you belong too."

"I do." Mel glanced at Skylar, who, along with Paisley, Cam, Ellie and several other children and young teenagers, helped volunteers from the animal rescue put up more event signs in front of the main barn.

Cole was outside the barn too and, together with Zach and Bryce, giving a vintage tractor and other old farm equipment a final polish. From his perch on the tractor's high seat, he waved a cleaning rag at Mel and she waved back.

"It's showtime." Lauren, who was overseeing the youth cowboy challenge participants, including those taking part from Camp Crocus Hill, pointed to a cloud of dust in the distance.

"Yes." Mel pressed a hand to her rolling stomach. She and Skylar had joined the Carter family for breakfast at the ranch house, but Mel had been so nervous she'd only managed to eat one of Joy's delicious blueberry pancakes. Now she wished she'd stuck to a piece of dry toast instead. "Here goes." She stepped forward to wave the driver of the first pickup truck, also towing a horse trailer, to the parking area in an open field behind the main barn.

From then on, the day was a blur as Mel darted to and from the stables and event registration area and answered questions from participants and spectators. Around midday, she paused briefly to eat the packed lunch Joy insisted on and watch Cole lead the children's lasso event. Paisley was the quickest and most accurate to lasso a rocking horse with a pink Hula-Hoop, and Mel joined the rest of the Carter family in clapping and congratulating her.

A half hour later, they all cheered on Skylar too. With Lauren holding a lunge line, and as part of a group of beginning riders, Skylar held Paisley's pony to a walk around the small paddock. Then it was on to the trail riding and encouraging Zach as he and his horse, Scout, took part, followed by the cutting competition.

"Wow." Mel watched in awe as horses and riders raced against a clock to separate cows from the rest of the herd.

"The horse has to think for itself in cutting events." Joy pointed to a brown American quarter horse that had just topped the scoreboard. "Skipper has the best 'cow sense' of any horse in this area."

Mel nodded. While things she remembered from her ranching childhood were coming back, she still had a lot to learn.

"There you are." An hour later, Cole joined Mel by the fence that encircled the pasture where individual demonstration events had been held throughout the day. "Except for a few words, I don't think I've talked to you since breakfast."

Although they hadn't had a chance to talk, she'd been conscious of Cole whenever he'd been nearby, a kind of sixth sense that was new. She adjusted the white cowboy hat she'd bought that was similar to the one she'd borrowed from Joy. "It's been so busy I've barely sat down all day."

"It's been a success too." Cole rested his tanned forearms on top of the fence next to Mel's, and the closeness made her skin prickle with awareness. "Because of you."

"Because of both of us." Cole's arms were strong but also gentle. The kind that could wrestle a steer as easily as hug a child. She'd seen him consoling Cam earlier when the little boy had tripped over a tent peg and fallen over, grazing both knees.

Cole gave a self-deprecating grin. "Even Mrs. Moretti has come around. Did you hear Mrs. Shevchenko talking up the event to her and what you and I did to make it happen?"

"I did. The two of them even pitched in to help serve lemonade and biscuits at the cookhouse. And Mrs. Moretti talked to the animal rescue manager about adopting a senior dog." Mel briefly clasped Cole's hand. "No matter what you did in the past, everyone here appreciates who you are today."

Mel hadn't missed the curious looks she and Cole had attracted, or Angela Moretti's pointed references to how a good woman would be the making of Cole Carter.

"You ready for the Western dressage demonstration?" Cole studied the fenced-in field where Joy and Lauren had already set up a small dressage arena.

"No, I'd never be ready. I haven't ridden a horse in front of anyone but you in more years than I want to admit." She forced a smile. "But I'm going to give it my best shot."

"Good for you." Cole's voice had an unexpected intimacy. "Daisy-May will keep you safe, and I'll be right here too."

"I know." She touched his hand again, its warmth and inherent strength giving her comfort and courage. "I haven't had a chance to introduce you to my friends either." She waved at Becky, Lisa and Jorge, who'd found seats in the middle of makeshift bleachers. "Lisa came second nationally in show jumping last year. Becky competes internationally in dressage and Jorge played polo for Argentina."

"Wow." Cole's eyes widened and he gave a low whistle. "Impressive group."

Mel's breath hitched in her throat. What had she been thinking inviting them here, let alone attempting a dressage lesson in front of that kind of audience? "I've only met Jorge once before, at his and Lisa's wedding, but Becky, Lisa and I have been friends for years. We met when we first started competing in California." When Mel had left the horse world, though, the threads of that friendship had frayed. "They're staying in the area this weekend because Jorge wants to check out some horses at a stud farm an hour away. Since Becky was visiting Lisa, she came along."

"It must be great to see them."

"It is." Except, and without meaning to, her friends also reminded her of a life she didn't want to think about. "Since my house is small, they booked bed-and-breakfast at Squirrel Tail. Skylar's in her element. Lisa and Becky are her adopted aunties." And when her daughter had won her first ribbon for participation in the beginner's pony showcase, Becky, Lisa and Jorge had clapped and cheered as loud as Mel. "I guess it's time." She indicated Joy, who'd led Cindy and Daisy-May into the ring.

"It doesn't matter what happens out there.

What's important is you're trying." Cole took Mel's cold hands in his warm ones. "You're also setting an example for Skylar and every other kid. You're showing them what it means to be brave and face your fear. So you failed in the past? You can always try again."

"What if I fall off?" Mel's whole body felt chilled, and she clutched Cole's hands.

"You haven't fallen off with me so far." His steady blue gaze helped settle her nerves. "But even if you do, I'll be right there. If I can't catch you, I'll pick you up."

"You'd do that for me?" Now her voice shook along with her hands and legs.

"Always. Now get out there so you and Daisy-May can show what you're made of." He leaned closer and his warm breath brushed her cheek. "I believe in you." His lips hovered over hers for an instant. Then, as if realizing they had an audience, he took a quick step back. "Believe in yourself."

"Okay." She couldn't let herself think about that almost kiss right now. She had a job to do and she had to focus on it. Mel straightened and squared her shoulders. She'd competed in front of much bigger crowds than this one. She'd ridden expensive horses at prestigious shows and, thanks to Pete's generosity and support, she'd had the best equestrian training money could buy.

Despite all that, nothing had ever been more important than today.

She opened the gate, went into the pasture and walked over to greet Daisy-May, rubbing the horse's head and ears in her favorite spots.

Astride Cindy, her seal-brown mare, Joy's smile was warm and encouraging. "You ready, honey?"

"Yes." Mel swung herself up into Daisy-May's saddle. All of a sudden she *was* ready. She glanced at Cole where he stood outside the pasture gate. He nodded and tipped his hat, holding her gaze with his.

The spectators didn't matter. Even her friends didn't matter. The next fifteen minutes were only about Mel and this horse working together in partnership. A human-animal connection she'd never found any other way and now, thanks to Cole, she'd begun to reclaim.

COLE GRIPPED THE top bar of the gate as he tracked Mel on Daisy-May. Horse and rider trotted around the corner at the far end of the dressage arena, their movements in sync. By now, they were almost through the demonstration, which had been flawless.

Pride thrummed through his body. He'd known Mel could do it but, up until she'd been astride Daisy-May, he hadn't known if she believed it too. Then her gaze had connected with his and he'd seen the determination in her eyes and on her face. The self-belief too. And now, in the past fourteen minutes, she'd proved to herself and everyone else what a true horse person looked like. Even though she wouldn't win a ribbon, she was a champion in how it counted most.

His mom gave the last command and demonstrated with Cindy, and Mel and Daisy-May followed. Now both horses and riders made a final circuit of the arena and when the clapping started, Cole's was loudest of all.

"Look at Mommy go." Skylar appeared beside him and jumped up and down, her blond pigtails flying beneath the pink cowboy hat Mel's mom and stepdad had sent her.

"Yeah." Cole patted the top of Skylar's hat. Emotion choked his throat and the backs of his eyes burned. "I'm real proud of her."

"Me too." Skylar's smile stretched from

one ear to the other. "My daddy said Mommy was finished with horses but I guess he was wrong."

"He sure was." Cole bit back other things he could have said about Mel's ex-husband. His folks had taught him never to badmouth others and he wouldn't start now. Besides, today was about celebrating Mel and he didn't want her ex casting a shadow over it. "Look. Your mom's finished the demonstration and she's waving to you to come see her." Cole opened the gate for Skylar to go through.

"You have to come too." Skylar pulled on his hand.

"I… You go on. Your mom won't want me crowding her. She's with her friends." The two women and Jorge had already joined her.

"You're her friend too, and Mommy wants you most of all." Skylar stared at him and her blue eyes were solemn.

"Okay." Cole swallowed and followed Skylar into the dressage arena.

"There you are." Mel stood at Daisy-May's head and patted the horse's neck. "I was telling Becky and Lisa how much you've helped me." She indicated the two women who stood on Daisy-May's other side, and Jorge who was talking to Joy.

"You did great all on your own." With the way Mel looked at him, Cole's heart swelled and he felt a new kind of satisfaction, one that was different from anything he'd experienced in rodeo.

"Meet Cole Carter." Mel introduced him to her friends, who smiled and greeted him. "He's a rodeo champion." She patted his arm. "Cole has the best understanding of horses and how to work with them of anyone I've ever met." Mel tugged him into the small circle, which Jorge had now joined.

"Coming from Mel, that's a true compliment." Jorge stuck out his hand for Cole to shake.

"Thanks." Cole returned the handshake.

"We missed Mel when she stopped competing." Lisa, a willowy brunette with brown eyes, studied him. "I'm happy she's back riding again."

"We all are." Becky's voice was firm. A redhead, Becky was dressed in jeans and a simple white T-shirt. However, she carried a black tote bag that Molly had whispered to Cole earlier cost as much money as a good horse.

As the conversation swirled around him, Cole held Daisy-May's reins and rubbed the horse's warm side. Unlike her friends, who now talked about people and places he'd never heard of, Mel was at home in the world of High Valley. She'd also easily bridged the worlds of English and Western riding.

"Cole took me to a rodeo too." Mel's voice broke into his thoughts. "It was a lot of fun." She looped one arm through his. "That's where I started learning about Western dressage."

"What did you do in the rodeo?" Jorge drew Cole into the conversation too. "We have a type of rodeo in rural areas of Argentina. There was one near where I grew up. I've heard of cowboy polo too. Riders use western saddles, and it's played in a smaller arena."

Cole looked around the circle of faces, Mel's the brightest of all. They were rich horse people, but nobody was mocking or judging him. Instead, they were interested, and Mel especially was trying to make him feel included and accepted in her life before she'd moved to High Valley.

He took a deep breath. "Until a few months ago, I was a professional rodeo cowboy. In

American rodeo that means I took part in a number of events at different rodeos around the country. A lot of years, I made the national finals too."

As he described the different events, and as Jorge, Lisa and Becky not only listened but asked questions, Mel beamed with pride, encouragement and affection. All of it for him.

Today, she'd faced her fears and let him into her life in a way that was new. Now, in celebrating what she'd achieved, and what they'd achieved together in making the cowboy challenge a success, Cole had to face his own fears.

He was finally ready to share them with Mel too.

CHAPTER FIFTEEN

THAT EVENING, Mel glanced around the family room in the ranch house where the Carters, Sunflower Sisterhood and others had gathered for a buffet supper. Along with Mel and Skylar, Joy's hospitality had extended to Mel's friends, Shane Gallagher and his son from the Squirrel Tail Ranch, and Mrs. Shevchenko and Mrs. Moretti.

"I love big gatherings. My husband did too." Joy paused by the stone fireplace that divided the family room from the kitchen and dining room. She held a tray with empty glasses and used paper napkins. "Dennis would be glad I'm back to hosting everyone again."

"It's a fun party." Mel said.

"You and Cole did a wonderful job today and I'm proud of you both."

"It was a pleasure." Mel looked to where Cole stood at the far end of the room with Zach and Bryce. Together with his brothers, he'd not only helped Joy but moved among the guests, more at ease than Mel had ever seen him.

"If you want, we can keep working on Western dressage together. You should get your own horse too. I can ask Shane to keep an eye out for you. He's better connected with that world than I am these days."

"That would be great, although I think Skylar wants a pony first." Mel's heart swelled as she glanced at her daughter, who sat on the floor with Paisley. The two girls and Cam were playing with Cam's wooden farm set.

"I'm sure she does, but it won't do Skylar any harm to use our ponies here for the next while." Joy's expression was firm. "She needs to learn more about riding and pony care first before she has the responsibility and privilege of owning her own animal. You, on the other hand, are an experienced rider. Daisy-May is a wonderful old girl, but you need a horse you can work with over time."

Mel did and today had reminded her how much she missed that kind of partnership. "You're right."

"Of course I am." Joy's smile broadened.

"As a mom, you always put your kids first. I did too, but sometimes it's better for those kids if you also do something for yourself."

Mel's throat clogged. "My mom says things like that." While she loved her new life in High Valley, she missed her mom. Although they didn't look anything alike, Joy and her mom were what her mom would have called "cut from the same cloth."

Joy gave her a gentle hug. "You let Shane know what you can afford and he'll start looking for a horse for you." Her voice hitched. "I was as proud of you today as if you were one of my own kids. If your mom could have been here, she'd have been proud of you too. Shane took a video of us if you want to send it to her."

"I'd like that." Mel returned Joy's hug before moving away to say goodbye to Becky, Lisa and Jorge. Her friends needed to make an early start the next morning so were leaving directly from Squirrel Tail.

"What a day." Ten minutes later, Cole joined Mel on the front porch as she waved until Lisa and Jorge's rented SUV disappeared around a curve in the long driveway. "It was a good one, though."

"It was." Mel untied the white sweatshirt with the Tall Grass Ranch logo she'd looped around her waist and shrugged into it. "Everyone else is helping your mom clean up, and Skylar's watching a movie with Paisley and Cam. Ellie and Lily are hanging out with them. Ellie wanted to call it babysitting but Skylar wasn't having that idea. Sometimes my daughter is six going on sixteen."

"She's independent. I don't know much about kids but that's good, isn't it?" For once without his usual cowboy hat, the evening sun touched Cole's face and gleamed on his dark blond hair.

"It is and I want Skylar to be independent." Mel sighed. "When I saw her on Paisley's pony today, she looked so grown-up." She'd reminded Mel of herself too in how she gripped Luna's reins and the look of determined concentration on her face as she'd guided the pony around the small course. "I'm not ready to let her go."

"You don't have to." Cole looped a consoling arm around Mel's tight shoulders. "Lauren had Skylar on a lunge line and it will be a while yet until she's ready to ride on her own. It's the same with being her mom. That lunge line will still be there. It's only looser than it used to be."

"How did you figure that one out?" Mel stared at Cole's profile as he leaned against the porch railing. The man she'd at first thought was a good-time, joking cowboy had hidden depths. Each time he let her see another side of who he truly was, she liked him more. She was increasingly attracted to him too.

"My dad." Cole's voice was low. "He said that to me once. I was seventeen and couldn't wait to leave the ranch and High Valley. I'd been hauled into the principal's office again. I don't remember what I'd done but Mrs. Moretti called my folks to come get me. When we were walking out of the school, my mom went ahead to the truck but my dad held me back." Cole moved to the edge of the porch by the steps and stared at Joy's sunflower field. "Dad said he understood I wanted to ride rodeo but I had to finish high school first. He also said I had to man up and make the best of it instead of causing trouble like a silly kid. If I couldn't settle down, Dad was going to keep me on a tight lunge line until I showed him, my mom and my teachers I could work with them instead of against them."

"Did you?"

"Eventually." Cole gave a short laugh. "What I didn't realize is as long as you have your folks, that lunge line is there. You may not feel it, but whenever you need a bit of guidance, if you're lucky your mom and dad are there for you. My dad had a way of talking sense to me. I lost that when he died. My mentor, Mel, tried but he died too. I lost both of them in fourteen months. My dad's accident first and then Mel's heart attack."

Mel hooked her arm through Cole's in a silent gesture of comfort. Beth had told her how Cole's dad had been killed in a tractor accident. Although nobody in the family would ever get over it, they were slowly learning to live with it. Like Mel and her family had learned to live with her dad's death, the grief still there but its rawness having faded with time to be overlaid by loving memories.

"You must miss them both."

"I sure do. When I heard your name was Mel, my mentor was the guy I thought of. His real name was Manuel. I made a fool of myself the day we met assuming you were a man too. I hope you know how embarrassed I felt."

"It was an easy mistake and one lots of people make." Mel tried to reassure him. "I've been thinking. When we were at the rodeo, you called me Melissa a few times with your friends. I liked it." She took a deep breath. "Maybe, if you don't mind, you could call me Melissa more often? Mel reminds you of your mentor and I... Well, I'd like to be separate from him."

"I'd like that. Melissa's a pretty name and it suits you." Cole's words came out in a rush. "You're a good person. A great person, in fact. I couldn't have made the cowboy challenge a success without you."

"Teamwork." Those butterflies in Mel's stomach were back and her pulse raced.

"Yeah." Cole shifted from one foot to the other. "With Ellie and Lily looking out for Skylar, if you have time I'd like to show you something."

"Sure." Mel licked her lips. "I'll text Ellie I'll be a while. Skylar's so wound up with excitement she needs to settle before bed."

She grabbed her phone and sent the message. "What do you want to show me?"

"My favorite place on the ranch." Cole grinned. "We can watch the sunset from there too. It's stunning seeing that deep red ball slip behind the mountains."

"I'd like that." One of Mel's hands went into Cole's, the movement natural, and they walked down the porch steps, past Joy's garden and toward the main barn.

As Cole kept hold of her hand, in that instant Mel realized she'd be happy to follow him anywhere. While they'd take turns leading and following, like two well-matched horses in harness, she wanted them to move through their lives together. Sharing, growing and loving too.

"Here." Five minutes later, Cole led Mel around the far corner of the main barn and toward a stand of tall trees. "See?"

She drew in a soft breath. "It's a tree house. Skylar's never mentioned you had one."

"The kids haven't been allowed to play here since last fall. A windstorm took off the tree house roof so when it needed to be replaced we took the time to repaint and fix a bunch of other things too. Until this week, it's been a construction zone."

"It's wonderful."

"Three generations of Carter kids have played in this little house. The trees were planted by Joe and Laura Carter, who started the Tall Grass Ranch more than a hundred years back. My grandpa built the first tree house for my dad and his sisters, and Dad fixed it up for my brothers, Molly and me. Now it's for Bryce's kids and we hope it'll go on for another generation too." Cole patted the tree's sturdy trunk where a ladder led up into the wooden house nestled in the branches. "You go first and I'll follow."

Mel let go of his hand and put one foot on the first rung of the wooden ladder. "My sisters and I would have loved a tree house of any kind but especially this one. It looks like a fairy-tale castle come to life. It even has a turret."

"That's my grandma's influence." Cole chuckled as he followed Mel up the ladder. "She always painted it white with green trim too so now whenever we repaint it we do so in her memory."

Mel reached the tree house proper and moved across the main room, exclaiming at the window details, and the small table and chairs Cole and his brothers had made for Paisley and Cam. "Which window faces west for the sunset?" Mel turned in a wide circle, the last rays of sunlight picking up reddish tones in her pretty brown hair.

"That one there." Cole indicated and moved with her. "Hang on." He dug in a front pocket of his jeans for a small brass key, put it into a lock in the window frame, turned it and the window frame slid inward, becoming a door. Through the wide opening he gestured to a wooden platform big enough for the two of them to sit side by side. "We keep it locked because Cam's still small enough to get ideas about jumping off, but my grandparents and my folks used to watch sunsets from here too."

"Wow." Mel's eyes widened. The sky was streaked with shades of blue, pink and gold, and the orangey-red sun hung above the distant mountains.

Cole sat at the edge of the platform and gave Mel his hand as she sat too. "No matter what else is going on in the world or my life that view never changes." Although Cole hadn't recognized it until recently, it was a view that grounded him and gave him a sense of peace.

"I can see why this is your favorite place. It's magical. Looking at this view, and how the open land meets the endless sky, makes my own life and problems seem small."

"Never small. Mel—Melissa." Cole cleared his throat. "What you did today by taking part in that dressage demonstration was amazing. You inspire me." He shifted closer so his jean-clad thigh brushed against hers. "It's not just on horseback either. Who you are and what you do makes me believe I can change and be a better man."

Her smile as she reached for his hand and clasped it warmed Cole down to his bones.

"Cole looped his free arm around the soft curve of her shoulders. "You already know I pulled pranks as a kid. Riding rodeo made me grow up, but that troublemaker past somehow still spilled over into my relationships. I can't even call them *relationships* really. Casual dating more like. The one time I tried to commit to a real relationship, a few years ago, she—her name

was Ashley—didn't believe I could so…
That was that." The words rang hollow, the
pain he still felt reverberated in his chest and
throughout his body.

"I'm sorry." Mel's voice was low.

Cole had been afraid she'd try to convince
him he was wrong and his feelings didn't
matter. Instead, her simple acceptance was
like a healing salve to his wounded soul.

Mel leaned nearer and her warm breath
brushed his cheek. She smelled of sweet
prairie grasses mixed with a flowery scent.
Roses or was it peonies? No matter, her
sweetness came from inside more than any
body lotion or perfume.

"Somehow, I have to come to terms with
retiring from rodeo. I've been avoiding it,
but I have to figure out a real future for
myself beyond being a rodeo cowboy." He
leaned nearer to her too and held her close.
"A future beyond working in the horse barn
and ranch projects thought up by my brothers and Beth."

"You've mentioned stock contracting a
few times. Is it something you want to look
into more?" By Mel's voice and expression,

it was clear she not only accepted him for who he was but wanted to help him too.

"Maybe. When I talked to Heath at the rodeo, he made stock contracting sound interesting and rewarding. It wouldn't have the same adrenaline rush as rodeo, but it could be the new path I need."

"It's a shame Heath and his wife couldn't come to the cowboy challenge, but if they visited here another time, you'd have more time to talk and ask him for advice."

"Yeah. He had a good reason, though. Nothing better than a new grandbaby, even if the little one came a few weeks early." As the last sliver of red sun dipped behind the mountains, leaving behind a purple-gray twilight with the first stars gleaming in the big sky, Cole straightened. "No matter what I end up doing for work, I was wondering about something else too."

"Sure, what?" When Mel had changed after the dressage demonstration, she'd taken her hair out of its usual ponytail and now it brushed her shoulders in loose waves and curled around her heart-shaped face. He liked it when she wore her hair down. And even in that oversize ranch sweatshirt and jeans, she was beautiful.

"Until now, I could never commit to anything or anybody. But when I'm making that future beyond being a rodeo cowboy, I hope it's one you and Skylar will be part of." His fingers tingled as he took his hand away from hers and slid a strand of hair away from her face, the silkiness slipping through his fingers. "There's something important between us and I want to explore it. I hope you feel that way too."

"I do." Her breath hitched. "I've felt it for a while now. It's new and it's different, but it's important and special." In the dusk, her eyes behind her glasses were huge in her pale face. "I care about you a lot, Cole."

"I care about you a lot too. Melissa." He grinned and then sobered. This wasn't a time for teasing or to joke because he was afraid of his feelings. It was a time to mark what he hoped would be the beginning of the rest of his life.

He'd wanted to kiss her for weeks but, like today before the dressage demonstration, they'd always had an audience. While that wouldn't have mattered to him before, with

Mel he'd held back because he wanted their first kiss to be private and special.

As he tilted his head toward hers, she moved too and their lips met. And it was a kiss that was everything he'd wanted and hoped for. One that was sweet, gentle and, in its own way, a promise. Not only for today but, if he was lucky, for forever. He'd changed, he was sure of it. The old Cole would always be a part of him but alongside this new, better and more adult one. And with Mel's help, he truly had a chance to start over.

CHAPTER SIXTEEN

FOUR DAYS AFTER the cowboy challenge, Mel still had a spring in her step and, whenever she looked in the mirror, a light in her eyes that was new. Her job was going well, Skylar was happy at summer day camp and High Valley was their forever home. In the past few days, Mel had spent most of her free time with Cole, riding horses together, having dinner at her place with Skylar, talking and some more kissing too. Most importantly, though, they'd talked about the future. His, hers and theirs.

After driving out to the ranch to drop off Skylar to spend the day with Paisley, she let the door of Healing Paws slide shut behind her and dug in her purse for her work lanyard.

"Who is first for me today? Oh, hi, Molly." She stopped in front of the reception desk to greet Cole's sister.

"Surprise." The pretty blonde smiled and waved. "The temp covering Carla's maternity leave called in sick. Since I worked here part-time during college vacations, the owner asked if I could fill in at short notice. It's been nonstop busy since we opened. You're lucky you started later."

"It's good of you but it's your second-to-last day in Montana." Mel looped the lanyard around her neck.

"I know." Molly's smile slipped. "I'm only filling in for a few hours. I stayed in town last night to catch up with a high school friend so it wasn't a big deal. I'm going back to the ranch after lunch."

"Your visit has gone too fast." Mel studied the animal-themed calendar atop the reception counter. "It will be September before we know it."

"Yes." Molly sighed and fiddled with a stack of file folders. "I didn't expect to, but I miss the ranch. Montana, High Valley and the horses are part of who I am."

"Your mom said you ride in Atlanta." Mel studied Molly more closely. Although she didn't know her well, the younger woman didn't seem her usual bubbly self.

"When I have time. Between work and my master's program I don't get a chance to do a lot of that. I love pediatric nursing and my classes too, but Atlanta doesn't feel like home." Molly fiddled with the folders again. "Besides, I'm not riding my own horse and mostly everyone there does English, not Western riding. There's a certain attitude, you know." Molly rolled her eyes and glanced around the now-empty waiting room. "I went to the stables not too long ago and one of the other women had a saddle that cost more than I earn in a few months of work and the way she looked at me..." Molly grimaced.

"Just because some people can be snobbish, you shouldn't let it spoil your enjoyment of riding. There are lots of wonderful people in the horse world too." Like Shane Gallagher, who in the past few days seemed to have made it his personal mission to find Mel the perfect horse for her budget and lifestyle.

"Your friends who came to the cowboy challenge were great. It's... Forget I said anything." Molly gave her a bright smile.

"If you're sure." Mel half turned as the

clinic door opened and Kate came in, followed by Lily, who rolled her wheelchair up to the desk.

"Yes, it's fine." Molly came out from behind reception to greet Kate and Lily. "The kids are in the back. Mel can show you." She inclined her head toward Mel. "Three of Kate's students have their last volunteer placement day here today. From everything I've heard, those placements the Sunflower Sisterhood organized have been fantastic."

"They have." Mel greeted Kate and Lily too.

As Kate smiled and told them about all the placements she'd lined up for Saturday afternoons in the fall, her straight black hair, cut into a crisp bob, swung from side to side.

"You're a force to be reckoned with," Mel said. "I've hardly done anything to help with those placements whereas you and the others are making them happen."

"We're a team." Kate gave a quick nod. "You had the cowboy challenge and the Sunflower Festival is coming too. Give yourself a break. Skylar is also younger than most of our kids." She glanced at Lily and her expression was fond. "Thanks for letting Lily and Ellie babysit Skylar. I appreciate you trusting them."

"Why wouldn't I?" Mel gazed at Kate in astonishment as Molly returned to the desk to answer the clinic's phone.

"You'd be surprised." As Lily wheeled across the waiting room to talk to a woman with a golden retriever who'd come out of the treatment area, Kate's smile slid away. "When I needed help with Lily when she was younger, it was hard to find a babysitter able to care for a child with special needs. It's also hard when your special needs teenager is looking for babysitting jobs herself."

"Skylar loves Lily and Ellie and those girls are great with her," Mel assured Kate. "Skylar hasn't stopped talking about that scavenger hunt with toys Lily organized for her."

Kate's expression was grateful.

"Mel?" Molly stood from behind the desk again. "Sorry to interrupt, but it's Cole. He couldn't reach you on your cell so he called the clinic."

"Sure." Mel took the phone from Molly. "Hey, Cole. What's up? Is—"

She listened and gripped the phone tight,

her palms all of a sudden clammy. "I'll be there as soon as I can."

"What is it?" Molly took the phone's handset from Mel's limp fingers.

"It's Skylar. She was riding Paisley's pony. She fell off and I don't know what…" Her voice cracked as the waiting room and the other women's worried faces blurred together.

Skylar was the most important person in Mel's life. She couldn't lose her. Not now. Not ever.

AT THE RANCH HOUSE, Cole sat on the family room sofa and rested his elbows on his knees, his head in his hands. He'd promised Mel and his mom he'd look after Skylar and Paisley while his mom took Cam for a haircut. When the girls had asked to ride Paisley's pony, he hadn't thought anything of it. It would only be for an hour in an enclosed pasture and he'd keep Luna on a lunge line.

Everything had worked out fine, and he was about to suggest the girls untack the pony and come inside with him for a cold drink and snack. However, thanks to that old bull letting out a bellow that could be heard clear across the creek, Cole had glanced away from Skylar for a split second. Luna yanked on the lunge line and the next thing Cole knew, Skylar was facedown in the dirt. Paisley was screaming and the pony stood between the girls snorting and blowing in distress.

"Skylar's fine." Mel came into the family room and sat beside Cole on the sofa. "She's only shaken up. The paramedics checked her out and Molly did too."

"You're sure?" Cole's throat was raw and his eyes gritty. It was only midday, but he felt he'd lived a lifetime in the past hour.

"Absolutely." Mel touched his arm until he looked at her. "We need to keep an eye on Skylar for the next twenty-four hours but she should be back to her usual self the day after tomorrow. She had the wind knocked out of her. Since she was wearing a helmet, and as far as the paramedics and Molly can tell, she didn't hit her head, there's no risk of a concussion."

"I promised I'd take care of her." Cole suppressed a groan.

"And you did." Mel's voice held concern but not judgment. "You can't watch kids every single minute. You heard the bull roar, and you checked to make sure he wasn't making a beeline for the riding arena. I'd have done the same. Skylar being thrown was an accident."

"Yeah." But why did trouble follow Cole around like Montana gumbo mud stuck to his boots?

"Your mom invited me and Skylar to stay here tonight so if there's any problem Molly is nearby." Mel gave him a small smile. "Having a pediatric nurse in the family is great. Molly was so caring, and she's up there in the guestroom now helping Skylar settle. To distract them, your mom took Paisley and Cam for ice cream at the Bluebunch Café, and Zach got Luna calmed down. Everything's under control."

"Except that bull." Cole grimaced. "I told Bryce we shouldn't buy him, but my brother insisted. Big Red has been a menace since the day he walked out of the stock trailer. I'm selling him at the next auction for sure."

Mel scooted closer. "Don't be so hasty. Did you ever think something must have spooked Big Red too?" Her lips twitched as if she was trying to hold back a laugh. "Out of everyone, shouldn't you be the one to give him another chance?"

"I suppose so." Cole rubbed at the tightness in his neck. "Bryce shouldn't be trying to manage the stock. He's got a degree in crop science. Ask him about plants and he's your guy. He's transformed the agricultural part of the ranch business, but when it comes to animals, apart from horses, they aren't his strength. Zach's great but he's busy juggling everything else."

"Maybe Bryce and Zach really need to have you around." Mel's steady gaze held Cole's. "If so, and if you're thinking of becoming a stock contractor, where better than here?"

"Maybe." The same thought had crossed Cole's mind more than once, especially in the past few weeks, but would his brothers take him seriously? Bryce and Zach were both college graduates whereas he'd barely scraped through his senior year of high school. He knew more about livestock than both of them, though, and as his folks had always said, not all learning came from books.

"Think about it." Mel grinned. "You asked

me my thoughts about your life after rodeo so that's what I'm doing. If you took him in hand, Big Red might surprise you. I heard Zach say he's healthy and a good breeder."

"He is." And Cole couldn't blame the bull for Skylar taking a tumble off Luna. Mel was right. It *was* an accident. He and his siblings had fallen off ponies, and later horses, a bunch of times when they were kids. Except for Bryce once breaking his collarbone, no harm had been done. Riding here on the ranch wasn't the same as riding rodeo, or in the kind of competitions Mel had. "Does Skylar want to keep riding?"

"Yes." Mel exhaled. "It would take more than what happened today to keep her away from horses. She's still more upset about Luna being scared than falling off herself."

"That's good, I guess." He put his arm around Mel and hugged her. "I was right there in seconds of Skylar landing on the ground. She was responsive the whole time."

"And you called the paramedics and they got to her right away too. Even before me." Mel nestled into Cole's side and rested her head on his shoulder. "I had to let Skylar get back on her bike the first time she fell off, and I'll let her get back on Luna too. Skylar needs to live her life."

Cole's throat constricted. He needed to live his life too, and Mel was a part of it, for which he was grateful.

"Skylar's dad wanted me to get her back on a horse today. I told Stephen later this week is soon enough." Mel shook her head. "Empathy's not one of his strong suits. He rarely listens to medical advice either."

"You called him about Skylar?"

"Even though I didn't want to, I had to. He'll always be her dad." Mel's voice was tinged with sadness. "For Skylar's sake, I promised myself I wouldn't talk badly of him. Until she's old enough to tell him herself, I also vowed I'd let him know about things going on in her life. If he wants to be involved, I won't stop him, although he's usually too busy."

"Many parents wouldn't be so generous." That quality was the things he liked most about Mel.

"I try. Sometimes it's hard but it's for Skylar, and I'll always do what's best for her." Mel linked her fingers with Cole's. "When I talked to him, Stephen said he'd fly up here to see Skylar next weekend. He'll be in Denver on business so he can make a quick trip. I didn't want him to get her hopes up, but he insisted on talking to her and so... He promised he'd be here."

"Will he stay at your place?" Something that felt a lot like jealousy needled Cole.

"No way. My house is a Stephen-free zone." Mel's laugh was forced. "He's booking two nights at the Squirrel Tail Ranch. I better warn Shane. Stephen has high expectations and he can be demanding." She hesitated and made a face. "If his expectations aren't met, well... I also have to ask Shane not to mention to Stephen he's looking for a horse for me. I don't want Stephen interfering in anything to do with that."

From what Cole had seen of Shane, the man was more than capable of handling even the most difficult guests. Although kind, he had a no-nonsense manner along with an innate confidence that reminded Cole a bit of his dad. Was that one of the reasons his mom liked Shane so much? She insisted the two of them were just friends, but as well as taking her kayaking, Shane had also taken

Joy for dinner at Ruby's Place, the fanciest restaurant in town.

"I'm sure Stephen's visit will be fine." Cole pushed away thoughts of his mom's romantic life. He wasn't sure at all, but Mel didn't need anything else to worry about.

"I hope so. He's talking about buying Skylar a pony. I told him she hasn't been riding long enough but, as usual, he wouldn't listen." Mel shivered and Cole hugged her again. "Do you have boarding space if Stephen insists? Knowing him, he's likely to turn up with a horse trailer in tow and no advance notice."

"I'll make space." Cole tried to reassure her. "You want me to charge him more than usual?"

"That wouldn't be right." Mel's rigid stance eased. "Thanks for making me feel better, though. Nowadays, I wonder what I ever saw in Stephen, but I was young and he was charming. Like a lot of women, I was taken in by good looks, romantic gestures and what I thought was love."

Like Cole had been taken in by Ashley. He knew better now because his feelings for Mel were different and stronger. It didn't matter Stephen was coming to town. Maybe he wouldn't even have to see the guy. Besides, it would be nice for Skylar to see her dad. From the sounds of it, he didn't pay much attention to her.

"No matter what happens when Stephen visits, I'm here for you and Skylar. I hope you know that."

"I do." Mel gave him a quick kiss on the cheek. "Promise me you'll forget about Skylar's mishap?"

"I'll try." Except that was easier said than done. Cole would put today behind him but quelling the doubts today had sparked would be much harder. Out of all the mistakes he'd made in his life, he'd never made one that had put a child in danger.

Mel might have forgiven him, but could Cole truly forgive himself?

CHAPTER SEVENTEEN

"THERE YOU GO, GIRL." On Saturday afternoon a week later, Cole patted the top of the pony's head before leaving the stall and latching the door. "You'll soon settle in."

The pony, Christabel, stared at him with soft dark brown eyes before she pawed the straw and stuck her nose into the grain bucket Cole had left for her.

"She sure is pretty." Bryce studied the animal as he left Luna's stall two doors down. "That white coat with brown spots makes her look like a pony in a story I used to read to Paisley." He grabbed a broom and swept up loose straw. "Paisley's never been the jealous type, but she wouldn't be human if she didn't wonder why a kid who's only been riding a month needs a top-of-the-line horse from a top-of-the-line breeder."

"Nothing but the best for Skylar." Cole jerked a thumb toward the closed barn door.

"That's what her dad said. He's still out there in the paddock talking to her about core stability and strength. She's six. Riding should be fun, but he's going on like he expects her to be a national or world champion."

"I hear you." Bryce patted Cole's shoulder. "Who knew the guy was such a big deal? Mel sure kept that close to her chest."

"Mel mentioned Stephen to me a while ago but she's not the kind to make a big deal out of it." Cole stacked empty feed buckets along a wall and resisted the urge to kick one of them.

"Unlike him." Bryce shook his head. "You'd gone to fix up the stall, but when we were unloading Christabel, Stephen barely stopped talking. All about his national and world show-jumping titles and the expensive horses he owns."

"He's won a lot as a competitor and now coach."

"In the equestrian world, sure." Bryce's close-cropped light brown hair framed a square face with serious blue-gray eyes. He'd always been the quietest of the brothers, but since his wife, Ally, passed, he'd gotten even quieter and much of the light had gone out of him. "He can't have been such a success with Mel, though. How long have they been divorced?"

"Since Skylar was a baby. Mel said Stephen left soon after Skylar was born." Cole tried to shrug as if it wasn't important and mask the anger that had risen as soon as he'd met Stephen and which hadn't yet subsided.

"There you go." Bryce swept up the last of the straw. "From how Skylar was acting, I got the impression she doesn't see much of her dad. Christabel is likely a guilt present. If Stephen's trying to buy Skylar's love, she'll soon see through him. Kids are smart. Sure, they like getting presents, but nothing can replace spending time with folks who love them." Bryce's voice hitched, and he busied himself checking the water buckets Cole had already filled.

"Paisley and Cam are doing okay, aren't they?" Cole studied his brother's hunched shoulders.

"As okay as possible without their mom." Bryce raised his head and the sadness in his eyes was like a punch to Cole's stomach. "Ally was their world. She was my world too. Mom helps, and now Beth and Ellie are there for them too, but nobody can take their mom's place. They miss her and always will." He cleared his throat. "I'm doing the best I can."

"That's all you can do." Although the circumstances were different, that's all Cole could do too. "Paisley and Cam are great kids and I'd be—"

The barn door banged open. "Cole?" Skylar's voice rang out and footsteps pounded along the wooden floor.

"Hey, kiddo." He held out a hand so Skylar wouldn't skid past him. "What's up?"

"Daddy's taking me to buy a saddle and other tack for Christabel." Skylar's blue eyes shone and her hair was in two tight braids. "He says it's an early birthday present since he can't be here for my birthday next month. He doesn't know where there's a good store here. I said I'd ask you."

"Of course." Over Skylar's head, Cole exchanged a glance with Bryce. "There's a place the other side of town but…" He paused. "You're welcome to borrow tack from us until you get more of a feel for riding."

"I know but my dad…" Skylar's smile

slipped and she looked over her shoulder to where Stephen stood outside the barn door.

"What's taking so long to get information?" Ignoring Cole and Bryce, Stephen came into the barn and directed the question at Skylar.

"I'd better give you the details myself." Bryce greeted Stephen. "Skylar's still learning where places are around here. Also, my daughter's seven and has lived here all her life but she wouldn't be able to tell you about that tack store."

Stephen didn't return Bryce's smile. "I appreciate everything you and your family are doing for my little girl." He patted the top of Skylar's head and nodded at Cole. "Mel's told me about all of you and the ranch."

She had? Cole stiffened. From everything Mel had said, and unless it was something to do with Skylar, she never talked to her ex-husband. And earlier, Stephen had barely said two words to Cole when he'd arrived with Christabel in a shiny dark green horse trailer.

"Skylar's a wonderful friend to my daughter, Paisley." Bryce's voice was mild but his stance was wary.

"Paisley's my *best* friend." Skylar giggled and tugged on Stephen's hand. "Find out where the store to get the saddle is, Daddy, and afterward you said we could do whatever I want. I want ice cream at the Bluebunch Café. Ms. Kristi always gives me an extra scoop of chocolate. That's my favorite, and she knows the lady who makes it."

"Sure." Stephen's phone chirped and he pulled it out of his pocket and glanced at the screen.

"Can you come back for the Sunflower Festival?" Skylar tugged on his arm again as Stephen continued to look at his phone. "Mommy and Mrs. Joy and lots of others are organizing it."

"I...no. Sorry, Sky." Stephen still didn't look at his daughter. "I'll be in Europe and...the name and address?" He gestured to Bryce.

"Of course." Bryce gave him the details. "If the owner doesn't have what you're looking for, she should be able to order it in. Mel or one of us could pick it up for you."

"Thanks." Stephen's smile didn't reach his eyes.

"Along with Christabel and paying for me to join pony club, Daddy got me a necklace too. See?" Skylar pulled it out from beneath her pink T-shirt. "It has a blue stone because that's the birthstone for my birthday in September."

"It's pretty." Cole bent to look.

"Tomorrow we're going to a water park that has all kinds of rides and other fun stuff. We're spending the whole day together." Skylar beamed at Stephen.

"That sounds exciting." Cole smiled at her.

"Daddy says I can have my birthday party at the Squirrel Tail Ranch. Remember that party I went to with Paisley?" Without waiting for Cole to answer, she darted to Christabel's stall to say goodbye to the pony before following Stephen out of the barn.

"Skylar's a kid with a new toy," Bryce said as he made sure Christabel's stall was latched. "Once her dad leaves, she'll soon settle down again."

"You think so?" Cole's stomach rolled. He couldn't compete with Stephen. The guy could give Skylar whatever she wanted.

"It may take a few days." Bryce's smile was wry. "I don't envy Mel trying to get her back on track. Kids like and need routine. When that routine gets disrupted, watch out.

Mel will handle it and won't let Skylar get too far out of line. As for the rest of it?" He studied Cole. "Stephen isn't here. You are."

"How does that make a difference?" Cole pressed a hand against his churning stomach.

"You have to ask?" Bryce bumped Cole's shoulder, the gesture taking Cole back to childhood when Bryce had been the little brother who'd followed him everywhere. "If Mel liked Stephen, she'd still be married to him. She isn't. I've seen how she looks at you. She likes you, bro. You like her too."

"I do." And Cole wasn't shy to admit it.

"For Skylar, a man like Stephen is fun. What she's too young to understand is that he isn't likely to be there when she needs him. Being a dad isn't just for the fun stuff like buying presents and taking your kid to water parks and for ice cream. It's showing up day after day for everything. The good along with the harder parts."

"You think I can do that?"

"I *know* you can." Bryce's voice was gruff. "Without you, that first year after Ally died would have been a lot worse. You helped me to keep going and get out of bed each morning."

"I didn't do much. Pulling out of a few rodeo competitions wasn't a big deal."

"It was to me." Bryce hugged him. "You texted or called me every day for months too. No matter where you were or what you were doing. I knew I could count on you."

"That's what family does." It was how Cole's folks had raised all their kids.

"That's what *our* family does." Bryce gave him a half smile. "And that's part of the reason Mel likes you. Skylar does too. If you have it, spending money is easy. Giving of yourself is a lot harder. You're serious about them, aren't you?"

Cole nodded. Although he'd only just realized it, he loved Mel and Skylar with his whole heart and soul. But was he worthy of a woman like Mel? She'd already been hurt once. And although Bryce might dismiss it, money *was* important. Stephen was a superstar in the equestrian world. He was also suave, successful and good-looking. Compared with him, what would Mel want with Cole? A rodeo cowboy who wasn't even riding rodeo anymore.

"SKYLAR WAS SO excited about going to the water park with you. How do you think she feels now? Not only did you cancel on her, but you also canceled at the last minute when she had her things all packed."

Standing in the small front hall of her house, Mel crossed her arms in front of her chest and tried to steady her breathing. She'd told Cole her home was a Stephen-free zone and it should have been. However, she didn't want to have this conversation on the front porch in view and earshot of her neighbors. Since Skylar had stormed into the house and slammed her bedroom door minutes after Stephen had arrived to pick her up for their day out, Mel had to talk to her ex and find out what was going on.

"She'll get over it." Stephen jingled the keys to his rental car. "I have to catch an earlier flight than I planned. Something came up with a horse and one of the team's riders. You know what it's like."

"All I know is you've let down a little girl who was counting on you." Why had Mel ever found this man attractive? He was handsome, sure, but that was only on the outside. On the inside, where it truly mattered, he was selfish, self-absorbed and didn't care about anyone's feelings but his own. "Skylar's your daughter. She should come before anything and anyone else. You hardly see her as it is. When you do, you usually change or cancel plans like you did today. Coming here to pick her up isn't the time to tell her you're on the way to the airport instead. You could have called."

"Yeah, well…" Stephen shifted from one foot to the other and studied his polished tasseled loafers instead of meeting Mel's gaze. "You'll explain it to her, won't you?"

"Explain what?" Mel held on to her temper by a thread. "You messed up here, not me."

"I did but…" Stephen's shoulders slumped. "I'm sorry. For everything. Not only today. Seeing you here, you're doing great. Skylar's happy and that's because of you."

Mel stood stiff. Stephen had never apologized to her before, for anything, but in this case the person he needed to apologize to was Skylar. "Being a dad is about more than paying child support and buying Skylar a pony and all the rest of it. It's about being there for her when she needs you and putting her first."

Like Cole did. The realization slid through Mel and left her with a warm glow. Happiness, contentment and a fundamental sense of rightness too.

"You're right. I guess I need to step up." At least Stephen looked ashamed. "I'll talk to Skylar."

The tightness in Mel's chest eased as she gestured down the hallway toward Skylar's closed bedroom door. "You'll always be her dad, and she loves you."

But, and like Mel, Skylar loved Cole too. Mel truly loved him. The kind of love that was strong, deep, lasting and nothing like the superficial feelings she'd once had for the man who stood in front of her. Beneath his charm and surface polish, Stephen was awkward and the most important parts of his character were either broken or had never developed in the way they should.

"I love Skylar too." Stephen cleared his throat. "And I…"

He stopped as Skylar's bedroom door crashed open and she came down the hall, her small face red and tear-stained.

"Hey, sweetheart." Mel hugged her daughter and Skylar clutched Mel's waist. "Your dad's really sorry he has to leave." Over Skylar's head, Mel stared at Stephen, willing him to do the right thing.

"I sure am, Sky." Stephen crouched to Skylar's level. "I'll make it up to you, I promise."

"How?" Skylar sniffed and rubbed a hand across her eyes.

"I'll rearrange my schedule so I can come here for your birthday, how about that?" He cupped her chin in one hand. "It's only a few weeks away. We can go to the water park then."

"Whatever." Skylar's voice was small and flat.

"In the meantime, you'll have lots of fun with Christabel."

Stephen glanced at Mel as if asking her to help him out but she shook her head. This situation and Skylar's disappointment were all his fault. Before, she'd always tried to smooth things over, but from now on she was done. Stephen had to own his mistakes, keep his commitments and do the work he needed to build a genuine loving relationship with Skylar.

"Cole said Christabel is the prettiest pony he's ever seen. He's going to look after her for me when I go back to school and can't see her every day." Skylar leaned against Mel, her body warm and trusting. "And Mommy and Mrs. Lauren and Mrs. Joy and Ellie are all going to help me learn to ride Christabel and care for her too. Even mucking out her stall."

"That sounds fine." Stephen's voice cracked as he pulled Skylar into a hug. "I'll be back before you know it. I already talked to Mr. Gallagher about you having a party at his ranch."

"Mommy and Mrs. Joy and Paisley will help me plan my birthday party. I don't want a horse riding party at the Squirrel Tail Ranch after all. I want one here. At home." Skylar straightened. "You can come if you want but if you get busy I understand." Her childish voice held resignation, not malice, and for an instant sounded almost adult. She took Mel's hand. "You better go, Daddy. You don't want to miss your airplane."

Mel swallowed a hard lump of emotion.

Did Stephen know what he was really missing? If he didn't change his ways soon, by the time Skylar was a teenager there might not be a place for him in her life.

"Yes, right." Stephen got to his feet. "Be good and look after your mommy." Stephen patted the top of Skylar's head at the same time as the girl twisted away.

"I will. Cole will help me look after Mommy too."

Was there a certain smugness in Skylar's tone? "Cole and his family are good friends but Skylar and I look after each other." Mel made her voice crisp and took a step back to let her daughter say goodbye to Stephen.

For the first time ever, she'd stood up to her ex and it hadn't been as hard as she'd feared. Instead, and like her new feelings for Cole, being assertive with Stephen was good. Because of Skylar, she'd have to deal with Stephen for the rest of her life. Even when Skylar was an adult, if she had children of her own, Mel and Stephen would have to co-grandparent too. It had taken her a while, but from now on she was setting boundaries with him—as well as expectations.

She and Skylar stood inside the screen door as Stephen went out to his rental car parked at the curb, got into it and drove away.

"I'm sorry you didn't get to go to the water park, honey." Mel wrapped her daughter in a hug, breathing in the familiar scent of fruity shampoo and sunscreen. "It's not too late. If you want, it will only take me a few minutes to get ready and we can go together." Since it was Sunday, Mel had planned to go riding with Cole this afternoon but he'd understand. Maybe he'd even want to go to the water park with them.

"I'm still going to the water park. You are too." A big smile spread across Skylar's face. "After Dad canceled, I called Cole."

"You're not supposed to use my phone without asking, remember?" But Mel made the reprimand gentle. Her daughter had already been through enough today.

"You said I could if it was an emergency. That's why you gave me the password. And you left your phone in my room." Skylar's blue eyes were pleading. "Cole said I could call him anytime I wanted. I told him what happened and he said if I still wanted to go to the water park, him and Mrs. Joy and

Beth and Ellie and Paisley and Cam will all come with me. What do you say?"

"I say that's a great idea." Mel blinked back the burn of tears.

"I talked to Mrs. Joy too. She said she misses Molly and she'd love to spend the day with us doing something fun." Skylar stepped out of Mel's hug and her smile slid away. "We don't need Daddy at all."

Mel gave Skylar another hug and murmured something about going to get ready. Almost thirty years after his passing, Mel still missed her own dad every day. Skylar needed a dad, but she also needed something it might not ever be in Stephen to give.

As Mel rummaged in her bureau drawers for her swimsuit and beach towel, she caught sight of the daisy tattoo on her wrist.

Since moving to High Valley, and thanks to her job and Joy, Rosa and the rest of the Sunflower Sisterhood, she'd grown in both confidence and self-belief. Not only had she found the new beginning she'd wanted, but hope, fun and new friendships. Cole had been part of that. Working together on the cowboy challenge, going to the rodeo and the rest of the time they'd spent together had all helped Mel become the woman she was meant to be.

A woman who was open to love and being loved. A woman who, with him, had found a love both special and worth taking a risk for. With everyone around, she couldn't tell Cole about her feelings for him today. However, before the week was out, she'd find a time to talk to him alone.

He was a good, kind and caring man. A loving one too. If he loved her like she loved him, together, they could face anything.

CHAPTER EIGHTEEN

COLE EASED BANDIT to a walk and drew in a lungful of cool and fresh morning air. The sun had peeped over the eastern horizon fifteen minutes earlier and apart from the gentle lowing of cattle in the summer pasture, the air was still and held the promise of another beautiful August day.

After her work shift finished, he and Mel were going riding later. Since their trip to the water park eight days before, he and Mel had spent as much time together as they could but Skylar or one or more members of Cole's family had always joined in. Mel had said she wanted to talk to him, and he wanted to chat more about his ideas for stock contracting with her too.

His phone shrilled and he grabbed it from his jacket pocket. After checking the number, from an area code he didn't recognize, he hit Answer. "Yes?" He didn't recognize the man's voice either but he sure knew the name.

Roy Davis was a talent agent who handled a lot of rodeo stars and negotiated lucrative product sponsorship deals. Cole listened to what Roy said for several seconds before, when the man paused for breath, interjecting, "I'm retired." That was why Cole had parted ways with his own agent a few months back.

"Permanently?" Roy's voice held disbelief. "I never thought a guy like you would leave rodeo. I've watched you for years but since you had other representation I didn't want to overstep. But now... You're in good shape again, aren't you?"

"Yes." Cole was fit enough for ranch work but would he still be okay riding a bull or wrestling a several thousand pound steer?

"Hang on." Voices echoed in the background. Roy must start work early or maybe he never truly stopped. Ranching never stopped either, which was why Cole was out here checking cattle and fixing a fence. He liked early mornings, though, when dew clung to the grasses and the world was washed clean. "Sorry about that." Roy was back. "You know Jace Rodriguez?"

"Of course." In the rodeo world, everybody

knew Jace. Barely out of his teens, the guy had burst onto the professional rodeo scene a few years earlier and was already a legend.

"Jace broke his leg. He'll be fine but he'll be out of action for months for sure."

"I'm sorry to hear—"

"It was his own fault." Roy brushed away Cole's concern. "What was he thinking fooling around on a skateboard? Kids these days. Reckless! See, the thing is, Jace was booked solid, starting with headlining a rodeo in Wyoming this Saturday."

"And?" Cole's breathing sped up. This was Monday. Saturday was five days away.

"You're a crowd pleaser. I already talked to the local promoter. We want you to take Jace's place. If you agree, I'll sign you as a client too. I'd be able to get you new product endorsement deals now and for next season, assuming you're still riding. What do you say?"

Cole pulled Bandit to a halt and the horse turned to look at him as if wondering what they were doing stopping in the middle of a field. "I… It's a great offer." One, irrespective of his doctor's dire warnings, Cole would have jumped at only a few weeks ago.

Now he wasn't so sure. "How long can you give me to think about it?"

"A few hours?" Roy's voice was brusque.

"Twenty-four hours." Cole patted Bandit's neck. "It's a busy season on the ranch, and I can't leave my family in the lurch."

"Twelve hours. That's my last offer but I'm expecting a yes." On the other end of the phone, Roy's voice held grudging respect. "I never took you for a fool, but you'll be a bigger one than Jace if you turn me down. Don't you want a chance to make a comeback? If I pitch it right, you'll have all the top Western brands knocking on your door. Everybody likes a good story and here you'd be the hero who saves the day. You can't hide out in the back of beyond forever. Apart from ranching, rodeo and scenery, what else is there in Montana?"

"I appreciate the opportunity but—"

"I expect to hear from you in twelve hours. Hopefully less." Roy ended the call, cutting Cole off while he was still trying to thank him.

Cole stuffed his phone back in his pocket and leaned forward to rub Bandit's ears.

"What do you think, boy? Do you want to go back to the circuit?"

Bandit nickered and tossed his head.

"You'll go where I do." The horse's hair was warm beneath Cole's hand and his breathing reassuringly steady. "You're my best friend." Although in only a few months, Mel had become Cole's true best friend. The rodeo in Wyoming would only be the start. If he went back to the circuit, it would mean leaving behind Mel, Skylar and the new life he'd begun to build.

He nudged Bandit into a walk again. Even without talking to him, Cole knew what his doctor would say. His physical therapist too. If he went back to rodeo, he'd be risking another injury. Maybe he'd never get back in a saddle again, not even for ranch work.

He turned Bandit in a circle to ride around the edge of the field, tall pasture grass brushing the toes of his boots. Roy was wrong. There was a lot more in Montana than ranching, rodeo and scenery. There was home, family, community and roots.

As he and Bandit rounded the last corner of the field, heading toward the main part of the ranch, his phone rang again so he stopped by a fence line to answer it. There wasn't always cell service out here but this morning he'd had more calls than he usually got in a few days. In High Valley, he was more likely to bump into folks to chat than call or text them.

"This is Cole." It wasn't Roy but maybe the guy had gotten someone else to endorse his idea.

"I hear I'll be seeing you in Wyoming this weekend." Phil's mocking voice reverberated in Cole's ears.

"Who'd you hear that from?" Even before they'd had a run-in after that rodeo Cole had gone to with Mel, he and Phil had never been close friends, so this was a surprise.

"Roy's *my* agent. He thought you needed a nudge." Phil laughed and then sobered. "You might not believe it, but I've missed you. It'll be good to have you back."

"I haven't made any decisions yet." Cole patted Bandit's neck.

"What's holding you back? Rodeo's your life, isn't it? Like me. Neither of us knows anything else."

"Sure, but we'll both have to retire one day. You don't see many cowboys in their forties." His mentor, Mel, had remained on the circuit into his fifties but doing other jobs instead of riding competitively. He hadn't gone back permanently to his family's ranch in Texas, either, where Mel said he always felt like a guest who'd overstayed his welcome.

"That don't mean nothing. Besides, when the time comes there's senior rodeo." Phil's voice turned cajoling. "Cowboys are tough. So you get hurt? You get up and keep going no matter what."

But what if you wanted to go and do something else? Cole started Bandit walking. It was getting late and he had barn chores. "I told Roy I'd think about it and let him know later today."

"I always took you for an action guy." Phil chuckled. "What do you all of a sudden have to think about?"

"Lots of things." Along with leaving his family in the lurch with ranch work, Melissa and Skylar were a big part of the reason he'd asked Roy for time to consider but Cole wasn't going to give Phil any more information than he had to.

"Roy doesn't have time for people who

waste *his* time. You don't want to lose this chance, do you?"

"No, but… It's complicated."

Phil paused as if he was choosing his words with care. "After you brought Mel to that rodeo, Emmy—you know, the barrel racer?"

"Yes." The competitive rodeo community was small and Emmy had been friends with Ashley too.

"Emmy looked Mel up online. Before she got married, her name was Melissa Kearns. When it comes to the horse world, she's a huge deal. From what Emmy said, before Mel got hurt she was on a fast track to becoming a national or international champion. Her stepdad's a big equine breeder in California, and her ex-husband, Stephen McNeil, is a coach on the national equestrian team."

Although Mel had mentioned her stepdad, Pete, had a horse farm, Cole hadn't known he was a breeder too. Why hadn't she asked him for a horse instead of getting Shane to look for her? "That doesn't matter. Mel's still an ordinary person." At least Cole thought she was.

"Really?" Phil let out a long breath. "Makes you wonder, though, what she's doing in small-town Montana and hanging around a guy like you."

"She seems happy here." Cole made himself sound more certain than he felt. If he and Mel made a life together, would she truly be happy, forever happy, with someone like him? And could he be the kind of stepfather she wanted for Skylar? Cole couldn't provide financially for Skylar like Stephen did. And even though the ranch was doing well, ranching wouldn't give Mel the kind of stability she'd said she wanted.

"Good for her. And you too, of course." In the background, truck doors slammed and an engine revved. "I gotta hit the road. I'm in Texas and it's a long drive to Wyoming with a stop in Colorado along the way. You take care, you hear?"

"You too." Cole's stomach lurched. He and Phil had lived the same life for over fifteen years. The only life Cole knew and one he missed. "Tell Roy I'll let him know what I decide by tonight if not before."

"Will do." Phil ended the call.

As Cole rode Bandit back to the ranch,

his thoughts swirled. At his age, he'd never again get an opportunity like the one Roy was offering. Although Mel was happy in High Valley now, she hadn't lived in town long. Odds were sooner or later she and Skylar would go back to California. That's where their real family was and Mel had mentioned how much she missed her mom, Pete and her sisters. As for Cole's family, they'd made him welcome but would he one day end up like his mentor, Mel? A guest who'd overstayed his welcome? Zach and Bryce had their own plans for the ranch and although they'd tried to include him, would he ever truly fit in here?

Nearing the horse barn, Cole took out his phone again and typed a text to Melissa, canceling their afternoon riding date.

He needed time to think about his choice. And he needed time away from her, Skylar, his mom and others to do it. Despite what Roy or anyone else might think, Cole wasn't a fool. So maybe he didn't have a real choice to make at all.

"THANKS FOR WATCHING Skylar for me." Mel paused at the kitchen door of the ranch house and smiled at Joy. "I shouldn't be too long."

"Take as long as you need." Joy smiled back. She wore a yellow ruffled bib apron over her shorts and T-shirt and stood behind an island kneading bread dough. "Most of the time, Paisley and Skylar entertain themselves. They love that horse show play set Stephen sent Skylar. It's sure nice of Skylar to keep it here instead of at home."

Another extravagant gift, this one sent by courier two days after Stephen had left, when all Skylar truly wanted was her dad's time and attention. "Skylar says it's no fun playing horse show on her own and since she and Paisley are here so much, it makes sense to keep it with your toys."

"My home is yours. I hope you know that." Joy put the bread into the warming drawer and studied Mel. "I also hope you can talk to Cole. Goodness knows I've tried but he's been avoiding me since early this morning. Except for chores, as far as I can tell he's spent the entire day in the fields. Zach and Bryce haven't seen him either."

"He seems to have been avoiding me too." Mel's stomach clenched tight. "He's never canceled going riding with me and... Well, I'm sure it's nothing." But Cole hadn't replied to Mel's texts either.

"He should be out in the barn now because he didn't ask his brothers or any of the ranch hands to look after settling the horses." Joy shook her head. "You won't tell him I called you? I'm worried about Cole and you're the only one who might be able to help him."

"Of course not. If I find him, I'll say I'm here to see Christabel." Which wasn't a lie either. The saddle Stephen had bought for Skylar's pony didn't fit so Mel needed to measure Christabel again. She stepped out of the house onto the back porch and closed the screen door behind her.

As she walked down the porch steps and along the gravel lane to the horse barn, she shrugged into the hoodie she'd wrapped around her waist and tucked the flashlight Joy had given her into a pocket. After a hot day, the evening was cool and the first stars pricked out of a purple-gray sky. As she passed Joy's sunflower field, the carpet of yellow blooms towered above her head. The seasons were more defined here than in California. And as summer began to give way to fall, for the first time in years Mel was excited about what the new months would bring. She'd signed Skylar up for ice-skating lessons at the local arena, and after Halloween and Thanksgiving, there was Christmas to look forward to.

Mel glanced inside the open barn door where Princess and Cindy nickered to her from neighboring stalls. "Cole?"

No answer, only a soft coo of pigeons from the loft.

He had to be around somewhere. The barn, as always, was in perfect order, so he'd done chores. She walked around the barn, still calling his name, and along a grassy path to the creek.

Bandit whinnied, and it was a sound Mel would have recognized anywhere.

"Here you are." Mel stopped at the edge of the creek. "When I couldn't find you in the barn, I... What's wrong?"

"Nothing." Cole's face was shadowed by the brim of his hat and as he spoke he tucked his phone into the pocket of his jeans. "What are you doing here?"

"I came to measure Christabel. The saddle Stephen got for her..." She stopped. "The truth is, I'm here because I'm worried about you."

"I'm fine." Cole still avoided her gaze and stared instead at the creek. Water trickled over the scattered rocks, and in the trees beyond an owl made a series of hollow hoot sounds.

"You don't seem fine." Mel took a breath. "When you broke our date to go riding, it wasn't a big deal. On a ranch, things come up unexpectedly. But you didn't answer my texts, nobody has seen you the whole day and now you're out here on your own with Bandit." She rubbed the loyal horse's neck, and he snuffled and nosed her arm.

"It's not late." Cole's smile was tight. "If you're worried about me running into cattle rustlers, I can see the barn from here and I'm a big man." His laugh rang out but it was forced.

"That's not funny. Stealing livestock is a crime and people who…" She stopped as Cole turned away from her. "It's not like you to hide out."

"I'm not hiding out but even if I was maybe it *is* like me. I needed to be alone today because…" Cole stopped and stuck his hands in the pockets of his denim jacket. "I'm going back to riding rodeo. It's last-minute, but I'm replacing a cowboy at an event in Wyoming this weekend."

"What?" Mel's voice went up.

Bandit pawed the ground and snorted.

"Sorry, boy." She reassured the horse. "What do you mean you're going back to riding rodeo? You're still having physical therapy. Have you talked to your doctor?"

"I don't need to." Cole's expression was one Mel had never seen before. Although reckless and impulsive, it was fearful too. "I've got a new agent and… Well, we haven't signed the paperwork yet, but I can't pass up this opportunity."

"What if you get hurt again?" Mel crossed her arms over her chest. Even wearing her fleece-lined hoodie, she was chilled.

"I won't." Cole fiddled with Bandit's bridle.

"You can't promise me or anyone else that." Mel tried to steady her breathing. "From everything you've said and I've seen, you're not fully recovered from your last injury. You also haven't had time to practice or get back to the level of fitness you need."

"I'll manage." His mouth tightened as if he was angry, in pain or both. "I'm taking Bandit with me and he won't let anything bad happen."

"Bandit's a great horse but you're a team. It's you I'm most worried about."

"Thanks for caring but I just called Roy, that's the agent. I'm packing up and leaving for Wyoming early Friday morning."

"That's in four days. What about the Sunflower Festival? It starts on Friday afternoon and you promised you'd help with setup."

"I'll find someone else to help. I have the money to hire another ranch hand too." Cole scrubbed a hand across his face.

"Why would you need to hire another ranch hand? You talked about one rodeo in Wyoming. If you're determined to go, surely everyone can pitch in to cover for you for a few days. Are there other events after Wyoming?"

"Roy says so." Cole hesitated. "Don't you see this is my big chance? All I know is riding rodeo. I'll have to retire eventually but now I can have a few more good years." His voice was pleading, as if he was trying to convince himself as well as Mel.

"All I see is you're risking your life again." Mel hugged herself tighter. Maybe now wasn't the right time to tell Cole how she felt about him, but if it would show him he was making a bad mistake, she had to try. "I care about you. Skylar does too. I thought we were building something special together here. A future." Maybe even a family one day.

"I care about you and Skylar, no question." Cole's voice quavered and he cleared his throat. "But I've never been the kind of guy to settle down. You know that."

"But you were talking about stock contracting and plans for the ranch and you asked for my advice. From everything you said, I thought your retirement was permanent. Was it all a lie?"

"No, of course not." Cole raised his hands and dropped them again.

After finding out Stephen had cheated on her, Mel had resolved she'd never again be in a situation where a man or anyone else she cared about lied to her. Cole seemed sincere but how could she trust he was telling her the truth?

"Look." Cole exhaled. "My retirement was supposed to be permanent but I guess, inside, I never truly let myself come to terms with it. When I got hurt, at first I was angry and then sad. Now I have a chance to go back to rodeo so I have to grab it. You and Skylar need a guy who's settled. Someone like Zach or Bryce."

"Apart from the fact Zach is already married, and neither he nor Bryce are my type, don't tell me what kind of man I need." Anger of her own curled in the pit of Mel's stomach and circled up through her chest to lodge in her throat. "I *thought* I needed you. I also thought you needed me. That's why I'm hurt and disappointed you decided to go back to rodeo without talking to me. Even if you never thought of me in any way other than friendship, that's not how friends treat friends."

Mel still had her pride. She wasn't going to tell Cole she loved him and now she'd have to explain things to Skylar too.

"I'm sorry." Cole's voice was thick and choked. "It's better we break things off between us now before they go any farther. Professional rodeo life is hard on families and relationships. I don't want to put you or Skylar through all that."

"So once again you're deciding something without asking me what *I* think or feel?" Mel stared at him. "I thought we could talk honestly to each other but…" She pressed a hand to her throat.

"You and Skylar are better off without me. Besides, despite my time with Skylar, I wasn't meant to be any kind of dad. That's what Ashley said."

"Ashley? You mentioned her before. It sounded like she was important to you."

"At the time I thought she was." Cole rubbed a hand across his face. "But when we talked about settling down, she ended things. She wanted a family and she said I wasn't the kind of guy to have one with. She was right."

"Maybe a few years ago you weren't that guy. However, the man I've gotten to know would make a great dad. And…" Mel bit her lip. There was so much she wanted to say, but now she second-guessed herself.

Cole half turned from her. "You're a wonderful woman and you'll meet someone else."

What if Mel didn't want to? "Even if that's true, and setting aside the relationship I thought we had, I can't believe you're going to risk your life going back to rodeo. That's plain foolish. Your body hasn't had time to heal and maybe your mind hasn't either."

"Are you saying there's something wrong with me?" Cole's eyes narrowed.

"No, of course not. What I'm saying is that as a health care professional, I understand more than most how the mind and body are interconnected. To compete at a high level in any sport, including professional rodeo, you have to be in top physical and mental condition. It's not like a quiet Sunday afternoon horseback ride here on the ranch. I want you to be safe." She choked back tears.

"I'll be fine." Cole walked around Bandit as if to put as much distance from her as he could. "You'll be fine too. Some things aren't meant to work out."

"But…"

"Bandit and I will walk you back to the house. Don't want you tripping over a tree root or falling into a gopher or prairie dog hole." He pulled a flashlight from his jacket pocket.

"I can manage." In her hoodie, Mel found the flashlight Joy had given her. "You're right about one thing. I will be fine. I love your mom and Beth and I are getting to be good friends. Skylar loves your mom, Beth and Ellie too. I'm not losing their friendship because of you." She clicked on the flashlight and in the small circle of light, Cole's face was pale, his expression grim. "I guess this is goodbye."

Cole gave her a jerky nod.

Mel studied him for a long moment in case he changed his mind, but he bent his head and patted the horse.

Mel turned and walked across the pasture, leaving Cole and Bandit behind. Even though her heart was broken, she had to keep moving forward. For Skylar's sake as well as her own.

At least with Cole back riding rodeo for most of the year, she wouldn't have to see him around town. Except, she'd miss seeing him. Losing his friendship would leave an ache inside her that might never heal.

Since Mel couldn't change his mind, from now on she wouldn't try. Any change was about a lot more than her and Skylar and what Cole did or didn't feel for them. First, Cole had to want to change his life and how he saw himself. As Mel understood too well, that was a whole lot harder.

CHAPTER NINETEEN

"IF YOU'D SEEN Mel's face when she came back to the house last night to pick up Skylar, perhaps you wouldn't be so quick to rush out of here." On the bottom porch step in front of the ranch house, Joy stared Cole down. "She tried to pretend everything was okay but I know it wasn't. She was putting on a brave face for Skylar, that's all."

As a mom that's what you had to do. Right now, Joy was putting on a brave face for Cole too. As a teenager, Cole had done a lot of reckless and impulsive things, but returning to rodeo when he wasn't more than half-healed from his last injury was the most impulsive and reckless thing yet.

"Mel and Skylar will be okay." Cole tossed a duffel bag behind the driver's seat of his truck and moved toward Joy to take Bandit's lead rope from her.

"Eventually, but that depends on how you

define *okay.* Mel's a strong woman and she's raising Skylar to be strong too, but what you had with them was special. Why are you throwing it all away?"

Cole shrugged as he led Bandit to the trailer already hitched to the back of his pickup truck. "What did Mel tell you?"

"Nothing but she was on the verge of tears when she left me, and after you spoke to Skylar, that little girl was crying her eyes out. I saw her from the kitchen window. I had to assume you had something to do with upsetting both of them. When you came into the house and told me you were going back to rodeo and heading to Wyoming without hardly a word to anyone, I knew what the problem was."

"I have to do this, Mom. Don't you understand?"

"No, I don't." Joy walked to the back of the horse trailer, which also held living quarters, and tugged on Cole's arm. "Your dad and I brought you kids up to talk to us and share our feelings as a family. You're an adult so I don't expect you to talk to me about everything going on in your life, but you've been working on the ranch like the rest of us. Temporary ranch hands have given more notice they're leaving than you did."

"I hired someone to cover for me, didn't I? At the ranch and Sunflower Festival setup too." Cole busied himself with Bandit and avoided Joy's gaze. "Heidi's a hard worker and reliable."

"I'm not talking about Heidi. I'm talking about you." Heidi had gone to school with Molly and since she lived in town and wanted casual work, Joy often hired her to help out at busy times. "Why are you going back to rodeo when you might get hurt again? That last injury could have killed you."

"It didn't." Cole patted Bandit's rump to encourage the horse to go into the trailer. "You worry too much."

"I'm your mother. It comes with the job." Joy exhaled. "See?" She pointed to Bandit, who'd backed off the trailer's ramp and eyed Princess, Daisy-May and Cindy grazing in the nearby pasture. "Even your horse doesn't want to go. Doesn't that tell you something?"

"I haven't loaded Bandit into this trailer in a while. He's not used to it." Cole encouraged the horse to move forward again.

"Like you aren't used to riding rodeo." Joy joined Cole inside the horse trailer as Bandit backed out of it again. "I've already lost one son. I can't face losing another."

"You won't have to." As he continued to encourage Bandit, Cole gave Joy a sad smile. "I'm all right."

"Are you, truly?"

"Sure." Cole finally settled Bandit in the trailer.

"Why didn't you tell me your doctor had given you the all-clear?" Joy had raised her kids to tell the truth, but if Cole wasn't lying to her, he was stretching that truth.

"Mom, drop it, okay?" He patted Bandit and came out of the horse trailer to close the door and ramp. "I know what I'm doing."

"Then why did you hurt Mel? You made mistakes and bad choices as a teenager but as far as I know, you never set out to deliberately hurt someone." If only Dennis was here. Her husband had always been better at getting through to Cole than Joy. "In this case, you hurt Skylar too. With her dad not being around much, she looks up to you. I can't condone you hurting either of them, or your rashness in choosing to ride in another rodeo event right now."

"I told Mel I was sorry." Cole took out his truck keys and went around to the driver's side door as Joy followed him. "Like I said to her, some things aren't meant to work out."

"If something is worthwhile, you have to put in the effort to make it work." Joy glanced away as Beth and Bryce came around the side of the house, followed by Zach and Ellie. "Life hasn't been easy for any of us, but Zach and Bryce found a place for themselves here at the ranch and we all hoped you'd do the same."

"I'm not perfect like them." Cole flung the words at her.

"*Nobody* is perfect." Joy tried to keep her tone even. She couldn't let Cole go off mad. "Not me nor your brothers. All your dad and I ever expected of any of you was to do your best and use your gifts for doing good. Each of us, in our own small way, can leave the world a better place than we found it."

"I know." Cole's smile was stiff as he glanced over his shoulder at Joy before exchanging backslaps with his brothers and hugging Beth and Ellie.

He returned to where Joy still stood by the driver's side of the truck and she held out her arms and hugged Cole tight. As a little boy, and although Joy and Dennis had tried their best, he'd never seemed to fit in their family. Now a grown man who towered over her, in some ways he was still as vulnerable as he'd been as a child. "You take care of yourself. Promise me?"

"I promise." Cole's voice was gruff.

When he was with Mel and Skylar, Joy had glimpsed the man Cole could be, happy in himself, confident and more settled by loving and being loved in return. It broke her heart to see him chasing after a few more years in rodeo when he might have had a lifetime with a family of his own.

"Text me as soon as you get to that place in Wyoming." Joy swallowed a sob. She'd tried to change Cole's mind but, and like his dad, once her son set his mind on something, nobody could make him budge.

"Of course." He got into the truck, and inside the ranch house, Blue gave a mournful hound dog howl. "Look after him for me, okay?"

"Yes." Joy choked out the word. The dog

would miss Cole too. She leaned through the open window to give her son a last hug. "Good luck. Don't be a stranger. Home and family are always here when you need us."

"Yeah." Cole started the truck's engine, which drowned out anything else he might have said.

"It's okay, Mom." Zach took her arm and led her back to the group by the porch steps. "Cole has to do what he has to do."

He did, all her kids did, but why did it have to hurt so much? Nobody had told Joy about this part of motherhood. Back in the day, she'd thought teething, toddler tantrums, teenage attitude and Paul's illness were the hardest things she'd have to face. Instead, as her kids got older, the problems got harder and that didn't stop even once they were grown.

Joy made herself smile as Cole waved and turned the truck and trailer in a semicircle before pulling into the long drive that led to the main road.

From inside the house, Blue howled again and Joy's Gus and Ellie's Clementine joined in. Part of Joy wished she could howl too.

She wouldn't, though. Along with final

preparations for the town's Sunflower Festival, she had a heap of ranch work and family and friends counting on her.

Still, Joy leaned into Zach's shoulder as they went up the steps and into the house. Cole and Mel were meant to be together. Even though it seemed as if all was lost, Joy had to help both of them, and Skylar too, to try to make that happen.

ON FRIDAY MORNING, Mel handed Skylar the sunflower wreath her mom had made and sent from California. Then she balanced her purse on one shoulder and heaved a box of other festival decorations out of the trunk of her car and locked the vehicle. "Can you manage okay with Nana's wreath?" She glanced at Skylar and, with her free hand, patted her daughter's shoulder.

"Yeah." Skylar's voice was small. "I wish Nana and Grandpa Pete could have come for the festival."

"Me too, sweetie. But they'll be here for your birthday instead." Mel tried to make her voice as cheerful as the sunny sunflowers. "Watch for cars." Along with Skylar, she looked to the right and left and they headed across the street to Meadowlark Park on the outskirts of High Valley's small downtown.

She wouldn't let herself think about Cole. From the ever-efficient town grapevine, and when she'd picked up a coffee to go from the Bluebunch Café, the word was he'd been spotted on his way out of town, his pickup truck pulling a trailer holding Bandit.

That was it, then. Although Mel hadn't quite lost hope he'd change his mind, he'd returned to rodeo, and she had to put the pieces of her shattered heart back together again. She had to console Skylar too.

"Why did Cole have to go away? I didn't even get to say goodbye, not really." As if Skylar had read Mel's mind, her daughter's plaintive voice broke into Mel's own swirling thoughts.

"He had to leave town for work, honey." Like with Stephen, Mel wouldn't talk badly about Cole to Skylar. "But you did get to say goodbye. He was right there the other night when we were at the ranch house and you were playing with Paisley." That horrible night was something else Mel didn't want to think about.

"It wasn't a proper goodbye. We should

have had a party for him with cake, balloons and presents." As they walked under the sign that marked the park's entrance, Skylar's voice wobbled.

"Cole had to leave suddenly." The other members of the Sunflower Sisterhood were already gathered by the log-framed picnic shelter. Like Mel, they were here to set up for the festival, which opened later this afternoon and ran through Saturday. Anything that couldn't be left out overnight would be stored and locked in a shed the park's groundskeeper had given them access to. "Maybe you and Paisley and Mrs. Joy can plan a 'welcome home' party for him the next time he's back in town." A day Mel would make sure she'd have work or other plans and couldn't attend.

"That's not the same." Skylar stopped by one of the pine trees that lined the park's central asphalt path. "I love Cole. Did I do something wrong? Is that why he left? Daddy left too. Will everybody I love leave?" Skylar's face held confusion and sorrow.

"No, honey." Mel tugged Skylar to a wooden bench beneath a tall tree. "Come sit with me." As Mel set aside the box of decorations and she and Skylar sat side by side, Mel shook her head at Joy and Rosa, who'd begun to walk toward them.

The two women nodded they'd understood and returned to the picnic shelter.

Mel took the wreath from Skylar and put it on top of the box before holding her daughter close. "I'll never leave you. Neither will Nana and Grandpa Pete or your aunties. Even though they can't be around all the time, they're still close in our hearts. Cole and your dad are too." She spoke with confidence, knowing the words were true. "Cole's a rodeo cowboy and that means he has to go to rodeos in a lot of different places all across the United States and Canada. And your dad…" Mel's stomach knotted. "Well, he has to travel for his job too. Your dad and I both love you but we couldn't live together anymore. I explained all that to you a long time ago."

"Yeah." Skylar sniffed and Mel dug in her purse for a tissue. "But I thought Cole was different. He was supposed to be tired."

"*Re*tired." But Cole was *tired*. Mel had seen the fatigue on his face and in his eyes. A weariness that wasn't so much physical as emotional. "I thought he'd left rodeo too, but his plans changed. If you ask Mrs. Joy, I bet she'll send him pictures of Christabel for you."

"I guess. It won't be the same, though." Skylar's voice was muffled in the front of Mel's T-shirt. "Cole was gonna give Paisley barrel racing lessons, and he promised I could watch. I bet even Christabel will miss him."

"Maybe but she'll get used to Heidi taking care of her." Mel blinked away her own tears. "Paisley and Mrs. Joy aren't going anywhere. We'll still spend lots of time at the ranch."

Except without Cole there, the place wouldn't be the same. It was also filled with memories of him and how they'd ridden horses together and kissed from the tree house platform beneath a starlit sky.

"If Cole rides in a rodeo near here, Paisley's dad said he'd take her and Cam to see him. Can we go too?" Despite the thickness of tears, Skylar's voice held tentative hope.

"It depends on what else is going on at the time. We don't even know if he'll be in a rodeo close by." If Cole was, it would hurt too much for Mel to go and see him. Maybe Bryce could take Skylar with his kids.

"Okay." Skylar wiped her face with the tissue Mel had given her and tossed it in a nearby trash can. "But what if—"

"Right now, we have to lend Mrs. Joy and everyone else a hand to get ready for the Sunflower Festival. They're all waiting for us. See?" Mel gestured to try to distract Skylar. Although Mel hadn't told Joy what had happened with Cole, his mom was smart enough to guess. "Mrs. Carla from work said she'd bring her baby by today. Won't that be fun?"

Carla and her husband had welcomed a girl a week after the Fourth of July and when she'd brought little Ivy to meet everyone at Healing Paws, Mel's heart had squeezed. Ivy was so small, and Carla looked so happy as she held the baby and leaned against her husband, their two older boys clustered around them. That was the kind of family Mel wanted but had never found.

"Babies are boring." Skylar made a funny face. "Maybe Ivy will be fun when she's old enough to play with or ride a pony, but right now? Paisley said all babies do is sleep, eat and make yucky smells. That's what Cam did."

"Well, that happens sometimes, but babies are actually wonderful. You were." Mel gave Skylar a last hug. "Almost seven-year-old girls like you are wonderful too." Skylar was the best thing in Mel's life. She'd love her with everything she had and protect her too until she took her last breath. "You ready to come and help us out?"

"Yeah." Skylar picked up the wreath. "Can I go show Mrs. Joy and Mrs. Rosa what Nana made?"

"Of course. I'll be right behind you." Mel picked up the decoration box again and swallowed the tears that still threatened.

As Skylar ran toward the picnic shelter, Joy came to meet her, this time with Shane. The older man crouched to Skylar's level and listened intently to whatever Skylar was saying.

There *were* good and steadfast men out there. There were also second chances. Joy loved and grieved for her Dennis but she still was taking small and positive steps toward a new relationship with Shane.

No matter what they faced in life or love,

all the women of the Sunflower Sisterhood were trying to make the best of things. Despite what had happened with Cole, that's what Mel needed to do too.

CHAPTER TWENTY

As LONG AS Cole kept driving, he'd be fine. The Tall Grass Ranch, High Valley, his family and Melissa and Skylar were all now in his rearview mirror. He was looking ahead and looking southeast too. The rodeo in Wyoming was the start of a whole new life. It was his second chance and he wouldn't mess it up.

The narrow ribbon of highway wound through the rolling foothills toward the state border. Cole glanced at the gas gauge of his truck. He hadn't wanted to fill up in town or check the air in his tires. Knowing High Valley, he'd have had more questions than he wanted to answer, but out here, two hours from town, he wasn't likely to run into anyone he knew.

Spotting a sign for a gas station ahead, he slowed the truck and signaled to make the turn, waiting for oncoming traffic to pass. A transport truck followed by a pickup and an

SUV with a roof rack holding what looked like a box of camping gear. The back of the vehicle was also loaded and Cole spotted a kid's folding chair patterned with orange, yellow and blue cartoon animals. The vehicle turned into the gas station and stopped at the pump. Cole followed.

He got out of his truck and unlocked the gas cap, glancing at Bandit through the screen in the horse trailer's window. "How are you doing back there, boy?"

Bandit tossed his head and nickered.

"I can't let you out but you've had longer trips than this one. There'll be lots of time once we get to Wyoming to stretch those long legs of yours. Run too." He chuckled, abashed. Working alone in the barn, he'd gotten used to talking to the horses but out in public, other folks might not understand and think he was talking to himself.

"Can I go swimming when we get to the campground?"

Cole startled at the young girl's high-pitched voice. It wasn't Skylar but she sure sounded like her. As he prepaid for fuel, he took a step back and looked between the pumps to the one opposite. A girl about Skylar's age, with similar blond hair in two pigtails, sat in the rear seat of that SUV with the camping gear. With the window rolled down, she talked to her mom, he guessed, who was filling the vehicle's tank.

"It depends on how late we get there. Your dad doesn't finish work for another thirty minutes and it's a few hours to High Valley. The campground is twenty miles the other side of town. If you can't go swimming tonight, we can all go tomorrow morning." The mom was half-hidden by the bank of gas pumps. "No schedule, remember? We're on vacation."

Cole took another step to get a better view and drew in a sharp breath. It wasn't Mel either but with the woman's curly brown hair with reddish tones, glasses and curvy figure, the two of them could have been sisters or cousins.

The girl bounced in her seat. "I wish Daddy hadn't been called into work today."

"Me too, but let's be grateful he's got a new job *and* a week's vacation." The woman smiled at her daughter. "What do you like most about our family camping trips? Do you remember from last year?"

"Roasting marshmallows. Swimming without my water wings. Seeing that frog jump so high." The girl giggled. "Daddy outside the tent pretending to be a bear to scare me except I knew it was him all the time."

"You sure did. Those are great memories. We'll have to get firewood from the camp store and pick up marshmallows before—"

"Look, Mommy. There's a horse."

"Wow, there sure is." The woman poked her head around the gas pumps and grinned at Cole. "Although she's never ridden one, my daughter loves horses. What's yours called?"

"Bandit." Cole spoke around the lump in his throat. Mel had called him "plain foolish" and he was. Except he'd been foolish about a lot more than going back to rodeo.

"Are you a cowboy in a rodeo?" The girl leaned out the SUV's window to wave at Bandit. Her face was bright, interested and excited. Like a little girl's face should be. Not like Skylar's face the last time Cole had seen her with tears welling in her big blue eyes, and her mouth trying to make a sad smile as she said goodbye.

"You bet I am." So why, for the first time in Cole's adult life, didn't he feel the pride and excitement of being that rodeo cowboy?

"I'm seven. How old's Bandit?"

"He's seven too." Almost the same age as Skylar would be in a few weeks. A birthday he'd miss.

"What does Bandit eat?" The girl fired questions one after the other at Cole.

"Hay, mostly, but grass too. Apples and carrots for a treat."

The girl giggled. "I have cake and ice cream for treats. Chocolate's my favorite. Do you like cake and ice cream?"

"I sure do." Cole's stomach rolled. "Chocolate's my favorite too." Like the cake Mel and Skylar had made for him.

"Do you have any kids?"

"No, I, uh—"

"Why not?"

"Well, I don't have a wife, you see."

He glanced toward the mom talking to a station employee who'd come out to fix a problem with a fuel pump.

"Why not?"

"Why not what?" Cole pressed a hand to his head.

"Why don't you have a wife?"

"I haven't met the right woman, I guess, but—"

"Why?"

"Why what?" Cole felt sick and dizzy and it wasn't from gasoline fumes.

"Why haven't you met the right woman? Have you been looking for her? Maybe she's lost and you hafta find her."

I, well—" Maybe *he* was the lost one.

The mom thanked the employee and then turned back to them. "Remember what I said about not asking personal questions, Harper?" She made an apologetic face at Cole. "Sorry. My daughter's curious."

"Curiosity is good." Skylar was curious too. He liked her asking him questions about horses and everything else.

What had he done? As he put the nozzle back in the gas pump, his breath came out in a rush. He could have had a life with Mel and Skylar. A life of horseback riding, camping trips, birthday parties and making wonderful family memories. Compared with that, winning a few more rodeo buckles didn't matter. Signing sponsorship deals that might never come to anything didn't matter either. He had a second chance all right, but it wasn't a second chance at rodeo.

"You know, Harper, I used to be a rodeo cowboy. What I should have said is I've given it up. These days, I'm an ordinary cowboy working with horses on my family's ranch." If his mom, Zach and Bryce would have him back. "We have a big spread near High Valley. The Tall Grass Ranch. It's been in my family for over a hundred years."

"You're lucky to have roots like that." The woman glanced at her daughter. "Family too. My husband and I moved to Montana only two years ago. All our family is back in Iowa."

Cole had taken having his family nearby for granted. "I couldn't help overhearing you're going camping at the state park the other side of High Valley. If you want, Harper could come for a pony ride at my family's ranch sometime next week. We're halfway between High Valley and that campground. Here." He dug in his wallet for a business card for Camp Crocus Hill. Like the rest of his family, he always carried the cards but this was the first time he'd given one out. "My family also runs a summer camp. It's for children and teens with disabilities but this year we're offering introductory riding lessons to any kid under ten who's interested. If you call the office number, tell them Cole Carter sent you. That's me. No charge."

"Thank you, that's really kind." The woman took the card. "I'm Christine Larson. You've already met Harper, and her dad, my husband, is Jeff. He works at the county hospital nearby. We've had a couple of rough years and...well... This camping trip is a new start." Christine's mouth trembled as she tucked the card in her purse.

"When I come to ride a pony, can I see Bandit?" Harper bounced in her seat again.

"You bet. He's not going anywhere." Neither was Cole. "You two take care. If you visit High Valley later today or tomorrow, you might be interested in the Sunflower Festival they're holding there. My mom's one of the organizers. Joy Carter. I'll ask her to look out for you."

You always have choices in life and I hope one of yours is to be kind. His mom's words echoed in Cole's head. He'd tried to follow that advice but now it was as if he was hearing it for the first time. By rushing out the way he'd done, he hadn't been kind to his family or Mel and Skylar, the people he cared about most. He hadn't been kind to himself either.

He waved at Christine and Harper as they drove off, and then pulled over to a space in the small parking area by the air pump. Before he checked the air in his tires, he had to do something even more important. He took his phone from the console, scrolled to a number and listened to it ring.

"Hi, Wade, it's Cole Carter." As his buddy answered, Cole took a deep breath. "It's last-minute but I hope you can help me out." He'd made the biggest mistake of his life but this was the first step to try to fix it. "Great. If he's interested, I'll ask Roy to call you." He disconnected and then hit the other man's number.

"Cole." Roy's gravelly voice boomed in Cole's ear.

"I'm sorry but I can't replace Jace at the rodeo in Wyoming or anywhere else. I'm not coming back. I've lined up Wade Davis to take my place if you want him. He's waiting for your call."

Cole held the phone away from his ear as if he could physically distance himself from Roy's recriminations.

"Wade Davis? I want *you*, not *him*. Come on." Roy's voice was demanding. "I never thought you were the kind of guy to let us down."

"I'm not, but this time I let myself down." Along with a bunch of other people he still had to apologize to. "I'm sorry but my retirement is permanent."

"You won't ever get this kind of chance again."

"I know." And Cole was okay with that. This time he wanted another chance, one that had to do with the rest of his life instead of rodeo.

"If you're sure…"

"I am." He'd never been more certain of anything. For the first time, Cole had made a major decision based on what was good for him, not anyone else, and it felt right.

Roy grunted. "Wade can get there in time?"

"Yep. He's forty minutes west of Cheyenne. As soon as you give the word, he can be on his way." Cole held his breath.

"I guess Wade's the best we've got. Good luck to you then." Along with irritation, there was something in Roy's voice that sounded like reluctant admiration.

"I appreciate what you wanted to do for me but it's time for me to do something else with my life."

Cole didn't want to be like his mentor, Mel, hanging around the rodeo circuit years after other guys his age had left, still hoping for one last ride. Manuel Garcia had taught him a lot of lessons but he'd also taught Cole one he'd never intended. And maybe Melissa was finishing the job the other Mel had started.

After checking the air in his tires and talking to Bandit again, Cole got back in his truck and pulled out of the gas station back the way he'd come. To follow Christine and Harper's SUV and head north to High Valley instead of south to Wyoming.

He wasn't running away from rodeo life. Instead, he was making a choice to return to Melissa, Skylar and his family and to build a better future than rodeo could give him. The hole in his life didn't have anything to do with his siblings or anyone else in High Valley. The only person who'd thought he wasn't as good as his brothers and sister was Cole himself. And underneath his joking and troublemaking, he'd spent his life not believing in himself or being true to who he was. He hadn't fully appreciated High Valley either, taking the community for granted and, when it came to him, resenting and mistaking its caring for nosiness or judgment.

That was going to change. He'd start by apologizing to his mom and asking her and the Sunflower Sisterhood to help him apologize to Melissa too. Taking that kind of emotional risk would be harder than anything Cole had ever faced in a rodeo arena, but if it gave him a future with Mel and Skylar, it would be worth it.

"THE WEATHER IS PERFECT, and folks are having fun." Late Friday afternoon, Joy let out a relieved breath as she glanced around the park. The first annual Sunflower Festival was in full swing and booths selling the wares of local farmers and crafters were dotted around the tree-lined space. Over by the playground and splash pad, counselors from Camp Crocus Hill had set up games and other activities for children, and a group of young teenagers played basketball on the nearby court.

"We did good." To one side of the busy information booth, staffed by high school students, Rosa stood next to Joy in a small circle with the other members of the Sunflower Sisterhood. "What was only a vague idea a few months ago came together in an event the whole town can be proud of."

"Not only this event. But also the support we've given local people and organizations."

Mel's smile was forced and her eyes were shadowed with tiredness.

"It's only the start," Kate said, clapping her hands.

"All that's good but there's something even more special, at least to me." Joy looked around the circle again. "Rosa and I have been friends for years but now, with all of you, we've become a true sisterhood."

"We have." Beth looped an arm through Joy's. "And I for one will never stop being grateful for this community."

"Hear, hear." Kristi banged a wooden spoon on a metal bowl. "Now if you'll excuse me, I have to get back to my kitchen. The Bluebunch is busy. The whole town is buzzing and after some lean years, that's a gift."

"It sure is." Joy squeezed Beth's arm. Beth was more than a daughter-in-law. She was a daughter of Joy's heart, one she'd chosen. Like she'd hoped to happen with Mel. Cole should be in Wyoming by now but she'd only had one text from him saying he was safe and where he needed to be. If he'd just recognize that where he *truly* needed to be was right here.

As the other women, including Beth and

Mel, dispersed, Rosa said, "There's a man over there who looks like he wants to spend time with you." She tilted her head to indicate Shane, who waved from where he was helping a small band get set up on a portable stage.

"I want to spend time with him too, but I have to send a text first." Joy took her phone out of her shoulder bag.

"To Cole?" Rosa's dark eyes softened in understanding.

"You know me well." Joy found her son's number.

"True." Rosa laughed. "But Cole is a grown-up. If he can't figure out what's in front of him by now, it's not your job to tell him."

"No, but of all my kids, he's always been the lost one." And Joy needed to make one last try to bring him home.

"Mom?" Joy jerked and clutched her phone before dropping it back in her bag.

"Rosa's right. I *am* a grown-up." Cole nodded at the other woman. "And…" He stopped as Rosa stepped away and murmured she had to go to the craft center's tent. "I'm not lost any longer."

"You aren't?"

"Nope."

Joy made an apologetic face at Shane and tugged Cole around the corner of the information booth to the break area. Folding chairs and several picnic tables were set up under a shaded awning. Her legs shook and she sat on a chair. "Talk to me."

Cole sat on another chair beside Joy. "I'm sorry. I wouldn't listen to you or anyone else. I thought I had to go back to rodeo but I didn't. I was stuck in a way of thinking that no longer fits. I couldn't see how and why I was going wrong so I was afraid. But my being lost wasn't yours or anybody's fault but mine. Can you forgive me?"

"Of course. Always." Joy's voice shook as she touched Cole's cheek. "Oh, my son. You're back?"

"Back to stay if you'll have me." He caught Joy's hand in his.

"I'll have you. We all will." Joy choked back a sob as she hugged him. "The Tall Grass Ranch and High Valley are your home."

"Thank you." Cole's voice was husky. "See, the thing is, I want to be a real part of the ranch. I need my own job. I wanted to go back to rodeo because it was all I thought I knew. I had a role there and a place where I belonged. At the ranch, Zach, Bryce and you run things fine. I didn't think there was room for me."

"But the horses..." Joy brushed a hand across her eyes. "What do you want to do?"

"I love working with horses, but I want to become a stock contractor for rodeo too. Most of the time I'd be at the ranch, but I could still be part of the rodeo world." His expression was hesitant as if he expected Joy to tell him it was a bad idea.

"That sounds fine." She paused. "But what about start-up funds? We're only now, thanks to Beth's business smarts, getting the ranch and camp back on a solid financial footing."

"I have enough." Cole cleared his throat. "I saved most of the prize money I won riding rodeo and you remember my mentor, Mel?"

Joy nodded.

"He left me money too. A lot. At first I didn't want to touch it. He had brothers as well as nieces and nephews so it didn't seem right. But his attorney said Mel knew what he was doing when he made his will and the money is mine free and clear."

"And?"

"I took advice, invested it and got lucky. There's more than enough to start a stock contracting business and build a house of my own as well. I was thinking of that spot over by the creek where Grandpa Joe and Grandma Laura built their first house way back when they came from Vermont. If you didn't have something else in mind for it, I mean."

"That would be wonderful." Joy's heart swelled. "Are you thinking of sharing that house with anyone?"

"I'd like to, but the last time I saw Melissa, things ended pretty badly." Beneath the brim of his white cowboy hat, Cole's face was pink. "I messed up and I want to fix things with her and Skylar but I don't know how."

"You could start by saying sorry like you did with me." She kept her voice gentle. She and Cole talked, sure, but they'd never talked with quite the same honesty and openness as now.

"What if she won't listen?"

Joy took Cole's hand and twined his fingers with hers. As a little boy, he'd held her hand whenever they came to town and chattered beside her. Then, before she knew it, those days were gone and he'd retreated into himself. "You won't know unless you try."

"I love her, Mom. I love Skylar too. I only got two hours out of town before I realized I'd made the biggest mistake of my life. I can't mess up again. Would you talk to her first, find out if she's willing to see me?" Joy patted his hand. No matter how old your kids were, there were still times they needed you. She wasn't interfering because Cole had asked for her help, but now she had a chance to make things right.

"You leave Mel to me and the others. We'll talk to her. I bet we can convince her to listen to what you have to say." Exactly how, Joy wasn't sure but she'd figure it out. "In the meantime, go around the back way to Rosa's booth." She pointed. "If you stay in behind where she's got extra stock and packing material, you'll be out of sight. I'll come find you once we've spoken to Mel."

"Thanks, Mom. You're the best." Cole hugged her again and his hat slid off his head.

"You're the best too, and I'm glad you finally realize it." Joy straightened his hat and patted his cheek. "Now skedaddle."

"Yes, ma'am." Cole grinned before he darted away.

Joy took out her phone and tapped the Sunflower Sisterhood group chat. By working together, they could find a happy ending for Mel, Cole and Skylar too. She was sure of it.

CHAPTER TWENTY-ONE

"WHY SHOULD I talk to Cole?" Mel stared at her friends from the Sunflower Sisterhood. Except for Kristi, who couldn't leave the café, the women had gathered in the picnic shelter where Mel was unpacking cartons of soda and bottled water. All the food had been donated by a local grocery store for the free barbecue a service club was hosting as part of the festival.

"He wants to apologize. Won't you give him another chance?" Joy took Mel's hand and squeezed it.

Mel had already been with a man to whom she'd given too many chances. Only in hindsight had she recognized how Stephen had taken advantage of her, promising he'd changed when he hadn't and hurting her all over again. Now Stephen hurt Skylar too by making commitments and breaking them.

She took a shaky breath. "It's hard for

me. And Skylar…" She glanced toward her daughter, whom Ellie and Lily had taken to play on the slide in the nearby playground.

"You're looking out for your girl like all of us do our kids." Rosa's voice was kind. "None of us, not even Joy, expect you to fall into Cole's arms." Laughter rippled around the circle. "But wouldn't you always regret it if you didn't hear him out?"

Mel would but even if Cole apologized, he still had to show her he meant what he said and it would take time to rebuild the trust between them.

"I've always been one to hold a grudge." Angela Moretti gave Nina Shevchenko a wry smile. As of today, the two women were the newest members of the Sunflower Sisterhood and had joined at Mel's invitation. "For years, I thought Cole Carter was bad through and through, but I was wrong and I'll be the first to admit it." Angela glanced around the circle. "Mel helped me see another side of him. Even as a boy he was impulsive rather than bad and now? Well, he's become a fine man. He called me before he left town to tell me he'd arranged with a high school student to clear my snow this winter.

When I asked how much that would cost, Cole said not to worry, he'd taken care of it."

"He did the same for me," Nina added. "Somehow he knew neither of us were well-fixed as far as money goes and he wanted to help. He told us not to say anything because he didn't want any fuss, but now... Well, I want to give credit where credit is due."

Mel's chest squeezed. That was the Cole she knew and loved.

"I gave Zach another chance and I've never regretted it." Beth's smile was soft and filled with love. "We all make mistakes but, as I tell Ellie, you can't stay stuck in the past. You have to forgive and move on."

Lauren nodded. "By choosing forgiveness, you also choose to heal yourself."

Diana, the quietest member of the group, agreed. "That was me with my marriage. I let what happened with my ex poison my life too long. It poisoned my kids' lives too but now?" She laughed. "He said I'd never make a go of a ranch on my own but I sure have."

"You have indeed." Kate's voice was brisk. "Once I stopped letting what my ex thought or did influence my life, Lily and I moved here and built a whole new one. This summer, when Lily was in Seattle visiting her dad, I even went on a few dates. Nothing serious but they were what I needed. I also signed up to play volleyball with an adult women's team. I haven't played since high school but that doesn't matter. I am who I am and so is my middle-aged body. I'm going to get out on that court and have fun."

Murmurs of approval echoed around the group.

"Okay. Tell Cole I'll see him but I'm not promising anything." Mel had learned her lesson with Stephen.

Tears glistened in Joy's blue eyes, a mirror image of her son's. "I appreciate you giving him a chance."

"I'll ask Ellie to keep an eye on Skylar a while longer." Beth gave Mel a gentle hug. "The rest is up to you but no matter what happens, we all have your back."

"Thanks." Mel's voice hitched.

"Kristi just texted me." Lauren grinned. "She set aside one of her sunflower pies for us. Let's meet at the café later and put our feet up."

"After today, we'll have earned it." Rosa's ready laugh rang out.

With laughter, hugs and words of encouragement, the women dispersed until only Mel and Joy remained.

"I have your back too, as well as Cole's." Joy's voice faltered. "I'll find him and ask him to meet you on the other side of the park near the bridge by the willows and duck pond. You'll be away from the main festival and have privacy."

"Okay." Mel hugged Joy too, a woman she'd loved like a second mom long before she'd fallen in love with her son.

Fifteen minutes later, Mel sat on a shaded wooden bench by the white-painted bridge that spanned the small duck pond. In winter, she'd heard this part of Meadowlark Park was popular for cross-country skiing and skating on the frozen pond. Now, in late summer, it was deserted apart from several ducks gliding on the still water and orange and black butterflies darting among a patch of wildflowers. The Sunflower Festival was a faint burble in the distance, and a gray squirrel perched on a branch of a nearby tree studied Mel with beady dark eyes.

"Melissa?"

She turned at Cole's voice as he walked toward her from a grove of trees. "Yes?" She tried to work moisture into her mouth.

The squirrel darted higher up the tree and somewhere a bird squawked.

"Thanks for agreeing to see me." He sat on the bench beside her, keeping some distance between them.

"You have ten minutes to explain yourself." If she gave him more time, she might lose her nerve and fall into his arms like Rosa and the other women had joked about.

"Right." Cole traced the wood grain on the bench with an index finger. "I figured this would be my last chance with you."

"It is." *Stay firm.* Mel was a strong, confident woman and she needed and deserved a man in her life who valued and respected those qualities. She also needed to be a good role model for Skylar. If a man joined their family, he needed to be a good role model for her daughter too.

"I was wrong and I'm sorry." He raised his head and stared at her. Although his eyes were filled with pain, there was sincerity there as well as honesty, respect and what looked a lot like love. The kind she could count on.

"Wrong about what?" Mel tried to make her voice cool to hide the hope that surged in her heart.

"Wrong about almost everything." Cole's gaze never wavered from hers and there was not a hint of joking. "I was wrong to leave town the way I did. I was wrong to end our relationship. And I was wrong to think I could go back to rodeo as if nothing had changed."

"Yes." Mel's heart pounded.

"Losing rodeo never hurt as much as losing you. I wasn't even to the Wyoming border before I realized the life I want, my forever life, isn't rodeo at all. It's a life with you and Skylar. If both of you will forgive me?"

Mel put a hand to her face as a love she'd never felt before rolled over her. One that was good, right and true.

"The mess I made is my own fault," Cole said. "I got caught up in the lure of what I thought was the only life I knew. That's why when I had that chance to go back to rodeo, I grabbed it. Instead, with you, I have a chance of a life that's much better in every way."

"Are you sure you won't return to rodeo? What if another opportunity comes along?" For Skylar's sake, as well as her own, Mel had to be certain Cole meant what he said.

"If it does, which I doubt, I'll still say no.

Except this time…" Cole's expression turned sheepish. "I'd talk to you about it first. I want us to be a team." Cole inched closer until his arm was almost touching Mel's. "I love you and Skylar. I promise I'll wait as long as it takes for both of you to trust me again. For now, all I want is for us to go back to the way we were and work toward building a life together. What do you say?"

COLE DREW IN a shaky breath. He hadn't timed himself but if that had been ten minutes, it was the longest of his life. He'd opened himself to Mel heart and soul and now it was up to her. He'd never let himself be so vulnerable, but from now on, he wasn't hiding who he was or what he wanted. He'd still make mistakes but he'd own up to them like a man—and ask forgiveness like one too.

"I love you too but…" Mel hesitated and a range of expressions flitted across her face. Love, caring but also wariness. "I think you're telling me the truth. I want to believe you are, but I'm not good at trust and you didn't only hurt me, you also hurt Skylar."

"I know." There was a leaden weight in Cole's stomach. "You have every reason to doubt me." From what he knew about Stephen, it wasn't surprising Mel felt the way she did. "In addition to being sorry, I give you my word, and all the love I have in my heart, that from now on I'll show you how much I care for you and Skylar. I don't want to let either of you down ever again."

Mel's voice cracked. "I accept your apology and —"

"You do?" The old Cole would have pulled her into a hug and kissed her until they were both breathless. This new Cole, though, was more restrained. He had to let himself be guided by her.

"I do." Her voice held a smile.

"So you'll give me another chance?" He stared into her eyes and thought he saw the same feelings that he had for her.

"Yes." This time the smile spread across her face. "But you need to talk to Skylar too. She's afraid everyone she loves will leave her and I can't let her be hurt again."

Pain stabbed Cole's chest. "I'm sorry about that too and want to make it up to her. What does she want?"

"You'll have to ask her." Mel reached for Cole's hand and held it. Her touch was warm and confiding, and although they were only holding hands, Cole had never felt closer to anyone. "What I do know is Skylar doesn't want 'things.' Stephen gives her more than enough of those. She'll be happy with your time and attention."

"She's got it. You do too. Always." He moved closer until he was almost holding her in his arms. "After I talk to Skylar, I hope you'll both do me the honor of joining me for the barbecue?" He held his breath. It was only a small-town gathering with people he'd known since he was a kid, but it was also the first step in the rest of his new life.

"I'd love to, and I'm sure Skylar would too." Mel's expression was tender. "I'd also like your opinion on a horse. Shane found one for me and you're the best judge of horses I know."

"I'd be happy to give it." Still holding her hand, Cole took another shaky breath. "I'd like your opinion on my ideas for rodeo stock contracting and horse training. I have the money to finance several new ventures and help the ranch at the same time. I don't want you to ever worry about losing another ranch you love."

"What I've finally realized is life doesn't have guarantees. Whether it's ranching or another job, the only thing you have to hold to is doing your best. But you and me together, I like what you said about us working as a team."

"I mean it." Emotion tumbled through Cole. With this woman by his side, he'd never be afraid or lonely again.

Mel leaned in close and her expression turned teasing. "I also want to talk to you about snow clearing." Her beautiful hazel eyes twinkled behind her glasses.

"Snow clearing? In August?" Cole stopped, unsure.

"Since you helped Nina Shevchenko and Angela Moretti, I figured I needed to get my request in early."

His face warmed. "I asked them not to say anything."

"You're a good man, Cole Carter, and I love you with all my heart. Because of Skylar, we need to take things slowly but never doubt I want us to be a family."

"I do too." He traced the curve of her soft cheek. Having Mel and Skylar's love was a gift, as well as an honor and privilege, and he'd spend the rest of his life trying to be worthy of it and them. "I also love you with all my heart, Melissa."

She nestled closer. "I'll never get tired of hearing you tell me you love me. The way you say my name makes it special too. It feels right."

"Everything feels right." From now on, Cole wouldn't take any of it for granted. Not Melissa and Skylar, not his family and not the life he planned to build at the ranch and in High Valley.

"Since I'm on the organizing committee, I need to get back to the festival but before I do…" Mel tilted her head and gave him a loving smile. "I think we should seal our fresh start with a kiss."

"That's the best idea I've ever heard." He dipped his head and found her lips with his.

Kissing her was the best too. Always and forever together—sharing love, a family and home.

Epilogue

Three months later

ALMOST AS FAR back as Mel could remember, she'd celebrated two Thanksgiving holidays. The Canadian one in October and, after her mom married her stepdad, the American one in November. However, she'd never celebrated any Thanksgiving like this one.

She glanced around the long table in the ranch house's dining room and through to another table in the adjoining family room. Both were filled with family, her own as well as Cole's, and friends like Nina Shevchenko and Angela Moretti who'd otherwise have spent the holiday alone.

"The more the merrier is what Joy says." At Mel's right, Beth spoke under the buzz of conversation. "I grew up in a small family so at first these big gatherings felt strange but I've grown to love them. It's special having everyone here to celebrate."

"It is." This kind of gathering felt strange to Mel too but Joy had welcomed Mel's mom, stepdad and two sisters, who'd arrived yesterday, with the same warmth she'd showed Mel and Skylar six months ago.

Only six months. Mel glanced around the table again. November sunshine streamed through the windows and outside a scarecrow Cole and Skylar had made nodded at her from what had been Joy's summer vegetable patch. The table was decked with gold-colored place mats and a garland of fall leaves, and the cornucopia crafted by Skylar and the other children took center stage. The wicker basket brimmed with autumn fruits and vegetables, along with a turkey made from brown, red and yellow construction paper.

"The food will be ready soon but before we give thanks, Cole wants to say a few words." From her place at the head of the dining room table, Joy smiled and gestured to Cole, who sat at Mel's left.

"Thanks, Mom." Cole pushed back his chair and stood as conversation at both tables ceased. He wore a new pair of navy dress pants along with a white shirt and an uncharacteristically serious expression. "Skylar, would you please come here for a minute?" He waved to her where she sat at the family room table with the other children and teenagers.

As Skylar came into the dining room to stand by Cole, she gave Mel a quick hug and giggled.

"What—" Mel stopped as Skylar shook her head and pressed a finger to Mel's lips.

"Today is a time to give thanks." Cole's voice was strong, sure and confident. "And this year, I have a lot of reasons to be grateful." He rested one hand on the back of Mel's chair. "Twelve months ago, I was in a different place and I don't only mean Texas."

Muffled laughter echoed from both tables.

"I didn't even come home for Thanksgiving because it would have taken time out of rodeo. I missed too many Thanksgivings and other holidays for that reason." Cole cleared his throat. "But this year, I changed my life and a lot more besides. It wasn't easy but with the help of many of you, I did it. I'm still a work in progress, but I'm grateful where I've gotten to. My mom, Zach and Beth, Bryce and Molly." He looked at each of them in turn. "Shane." He nodded at the older man. "You've all been there for me and I appreciate it."

"That's what family does." From across the table, Zach's voice was decisive. "With the new stock contracting venture and horse training, you're more than pulling your weight."

"And thanks to all of you, the Tall Grass Ranch is in good hands for the next generation." Joy's voice trembled as her gaze landed on the sideboard and the framed photograph of Cole's dad.

"Zach's right," Cole said. "I didn't realize it until a few months ago but that's what family *is* all about. Not only our family by birth but also the family we choose. When Beth and Zach asked me to work on the cowboy challenge, at first I resented it and them." Cole's expression was rueful. "But it was the cowboy challenge that brought Melissa and Skylar into my life. Come stand here beside us, Melissa." Mel stood and joined them. "Melissa and Skylar are the best things to have ever happened to me. Not only did they help me in so many ways but they made my life a whole lot better."

"You did the same for us." Mel's voice quavered.

"I already talked to your mom and Pete." Cole's voice grew soft. "I talked to Skylar too." She smiled at him and Mel. "So…" He got down on one knee in front of Mel.

Around the table there was a collective indrawn breath.

"Yes?" Mel's legs trembled and she grabbed the back of her chair to steady herself.

"Most everyone here knows I never planned to settle down. I used to joke about it. But I'm not that man anymore. That's why I wanted to ask you here, with everyone we love gathered together. Would you do me the honor of marrying me and letting me be part of a family with you and Skylar?"

"Say yes, Mommy. I already said it's okay." Skylar took Mel's hand and put it in Cole's, her voice threaded with excitement.

"Yes." Mel's throat tightened as Cole dug in one of his pants pockets for a small white-velvet box. "I'd be honored to marry you." This time, she'd be marrying the right man for all the right reasons. "Oh." She gasped as Cole opened the box and took out a ring.

"Isn't it pretty? I helped Cole pick it out." Skylar looked between them.

"It's beautiful." A ruby in a platinum setting flanked by two diamonds, the ring was both stunning and timeless, as well as exactly what Mel would have chosen for herself.

His gaze never leaving hers, Cole slid the ring on the fourth finger of Mel's left hand. "You helped me learn how to trust in love and myself and you also made me a better man. I never believed I deserved someone like you but now I can't wait to get started on the rest of forever."

"Me too." Happiness filled Mel as she looked from the new ring on her finger to Cole.

Laughter, clapping and congratulations broke out but still Mel stared at Cole. "I love you," she whispered.

"I love you too." Cole rose and took Mel in his arms and Skylar joined the hug as everyone crowded around.

Dogs barked as Blue, Gus, Clementine and Jess skidded into the dining room to join the celebration. As Joy took a step back to shoo them away, she wiped away happy tears. "I never thought I'd see this day but…" She stopped and sniffed. "Oh my goodness, the turkey and the rest of our Thanksgiving dinner. Molly, Beth, Zach, Bryce." Joy gave instructions Mel barely heard, still caught up in the moment with Cole.

This Thanksgiving was the best ever but it was only the start. As the seasons and years slid into each other, she'd never stop being grateful for this moment, this man and this love—hard-won but all the more meaningful.

* * * * *

For more charming romances from author Jen Gilroy and Harlequin Heartwarming, visit www.Harlequin.com today!

Get 4 FREE REWARDS!

We'll send you 2 FREE Books plus 2 FREE Mystery Gifts.

FREE Value Over **$20**

Both the **Love Inspired®** and **Love Inspired®** Suspense series feature compelling novels filled with inspirational romance, faith, forgiveness and hope.

YES! Please send me 2 FREE novels from the Love Inspired or Love Inspired Suspense series and my 2 FREE gifts (gifts are worth about $10 retail). After receiving them, if I don't wish to receive any more books, I can return the shipping statement marked "cancel." If I don't cancel, I will receive 6 brand-new Love Inspired Larger-Print books or Love Inspired Suspense Larger-Print books every month and be billed just $6.49 each in the U.S. or $6.74 each in Canada. That is a savings of at least 16% off the cover price. It's quite a bargain! Shipping and handling is just 50¢ per book in the U.S. and $1.25 per book in Canada.* I understand that accepting the 2 free books and gifts places me under no obligation to buy anything. I can always return a shipment and cancel at any time by calling the number below. The free books and gifts are mine to keep no matter what I decide.

Choose one: ☐ **Love Inspired**
Larger-Print
(122/322 IDN GRHK)

☐ **Love Inspired Suspense**
Larger-Print
(107/307 IDN GRHK)

Name (please print)

Address   Apt. #

City   State/Province   Zip/Postal Code

Email: Please check this box ☐ if you would like to receive newsletters and promotional emails from Harlequin Enterprises ULC and its affiliates. You can unsubscribe anytime.

Mail to the **Harlequin Reader Service:**
IN U.S.A.: P.O. Box 1341, Buffalo, NY 14240-8531
IN CANADA: P.O. Box 603, Fort Erie, Ontario L2A 5X3

Want to try 2 free books from another series? Call 1-800-873-8635 or visit www.ReaderService.com.

COUNTRY LEGACY COLLECTION

19 FREE BOOKS IN ALL!

Cowboys, adventure and romance await you in this new collection! Enjoy superb reading all year long with books by bestselling authors like Diana Palmer, Sasha Summers and Marie Ferrarella!

YES! Please send me the **Country Legacy Collection**! This collection begins with 3 FREE books and 2 FREE gifts in the first shipment. Along with my 3 free books, I'll also get 3 more books from the **Country Legacy Collection**, which I may either return and owe nothing or keep for the low price of $24.60 U.S./$28.12 CDN each plus $2.99 U.S./$7.49 CDN for shipping and handling per shipment*. If I decide to continue, about once a month for 8 months, I will get 6 or 7 more books but will only pay for 4. That means 2 or 3 books in every shipment will be FREE! If I decide to keep the entire collection, I'll have paid for only 32 books because 19 are FREE! I understand that accepting the 3 free books and gifts places me under no obligation to buy anything. I can always return a shipment and cancel at any time. My free books and gifts are mine to keep no matter what I decide.

☐ 275 HCK 1939   ☐ 475 HCK 1939

Name (please print)

Address   Apt. #

City   State/Province   Zip/Postal Code

Mail to the Harlequin Reader Service:
IN U.S.A.: P.O. Box 1341, Buffalo, NY 14240-8571
IN CANADA: P.O. Box 603, Fort Erie, Ontario L2A 5X3

Get 4 FREE REWARDS!

We'll send you 2 FREE Books plus 2 FREE Mystery Gifts.

FREE Value Over **$20**

Both the **Romance** and **Suspense** collections feature compelling novels written by many of today's bestselling authors.

YES! Please send me 2 FREE novels from the Essential Romance or Essential Suspense Collection and my 2 FREE gifts (gifts are worth about $10 retail). After receiving them, if I don't wish to receive any more books, I can return the shipping statement marked "cancel." If I don't cancel, I will receive 4 brand-new novels every month and be billed just $7.49 each in the U.S. or $7.74 each in Canada. That's a savings of at least 17% off the cover price. It's quite a bargain! Shipping and handling is just 50¢ per book in the U.S. and $1.25 per book in Canada.* I understand that accepting the 2 free books and gifts places me under no obligation to buy anything. I can always return a shipment and cancel at any time by calling the number below. The free books and gifts are mine to keep no matter what I decide.

Choose one: ☐ **Essential Romance** (194/394 MDN GRHV) ☐ **Essential Suspense** (191/391 MDN GRHV)

Name (please print)

Address   Apt. #

City   State/Province   Zip/Postal Code

Email: Please check this box ☐ if you would like to receive newsletters and promotional emails from Harlequin Enterprises ULC and its affiliates. You can unsubscribe anytime.

Mail to the **Harlequin Reader Service:**
IN U.S.A.: P.O. Box 1341, Buffalo, NY 14240-8531
IN CANADA: P.O. Box 603, Fort Erie, Ontario L2A 5X3

Want to try 2 free books from another series? Call 1-800-873-8635 or visit www.ReaderService.com.

STRS22R3

COMING NEXT MONTH FROM

HARLEQUIN
HEARTWARMING

#471 HER ISLAND HOMECOMING
Hawaiian Reunions • by Anna J. Stewart
When by-the-numbers accountant Theo Fairfax arrives in Nalani, Hawai'i, to evaluate free-spirited pilot Sydney Calvert's inherited tour business, he just wants this assignment behind him. Until he begins to see Hawai'i's true beauty. And Sydney's, too...

#472 THE LAWMAN'S PROMISE
Heroes of Dunbar Mountain • by Alexis Morgan
Shelby Michaels wears several hats in her professional life, including museum curator in Dunbar, Washington, and acting as protector of the town's most prized possession. But after clashing with police chief Cade Peters, she'll have to guard her heart, too!

#473 HER KIND OF COWBOY
Destiny Springs, Wyoming • by Susan Breeden
Hailey Goodwin needs a cowboy to help her run trail rides at Sunrise Stables, not the big-city businessman who volunteers for the role. Opposites may attract—and Parker Donnelly is *certainly* attractive!—but can they find a happily-ever-after?

#474 HIS MONTANA STAR
by Shirley Hailstock
Cal Masters can't stand to see his temporary neighbor and former Hollywood stuntwoman Piper Logan feeling sorry for herself after a stunt gone wrong. He hopes re-creating it with her will help—but now he's falling for her...

HWCNM0423